# Praise for
# LIA RILEY

"*Upside Down* gave me all the feels. Romantic and poignant, the journey of love and acceptance lingers long after the book is closed."
—Jennifer L. Armentrout/J. Lynn, #1 *New York Times* bestselling author

"*Upside Down* is a sizzling and heartfelt addition to the new adult genre. Talia makes for a quirky and incredibly believable heroine, and her OCD adds unique depth to her character. She and Bran light up the pages with their intense chemistry."
—RT Book Reviews

"Riley writes a captivating story from beginning to breathtaking end."
—*Publishers Weekly*

"Lia Riley turned my emotions Upside Down with this book! Fast paced, electric, and sweetly emotional—I couldn't put it down!"
—Tracy Wolff, *New York Times* and *USA Today* bestselling author

# WITH EVERY BREATH

## ALSO BY LIA RILEY

*The Off the Map series:*

*Upside Down*

*Sideswiped*

*Inside Out*

*Carry Me Home*

*Into My Arms*

# WITH EVERY BREATH

## LIA RILEY

FOREVER

NEW YORK    BOSTON

Copyright © 2015 by Lia Riley
Excerpt from *Upside Down* © 2014 by Lia Riley

Forever
Hachette Book Group
1290 Avenue of the Americas
New York, NY 10104

www.HachetteBookGroup.com

Printed in the United States of America

RRD-C

First Edition: December 2015
10  9  8  7  6  5  4  3  2  1

Forever is an imprint of Grand Central Publishing.
The Forever name and logo are trademarks of Hachette Book Group, Inc.

The Hachette Speakers Bureau provides a wide range of authors for speaking events. To find out more, go to www.hachettespeakersbureau.com or call (866) 376-6591.

The publisher is not responsible for websites (or their content) that are not owned by the publisher.

Library of Congress Cataloging-in-Publication Data

Riley, Lia, author.
    With every breath / Lia Riley. — First edition.
        pages cm. — (Wanderlust)
    ISBN 978-1-4555-3557-6 (paperback) — ISBN 978-1-4789-0668-1 (audio download) — ISBN 978-1-4555-3558-3 (ebook)
    I. Title.
    PS3618.I53279W58 2015
    813'.6—dc23
                                                                    2015028834

*To PB & J, I love you*

*But remember that forgiveness too is a power.*

—Margaret Atwood

# I

## *AUDEN*

*A*ll the online "how to land your dream job" advice stresses the same point—expect the unexpected during an interview. But come on. How can one expect what's unexpected? Then again, my imagination is vivid. Surely I can expect anything, right? And if I expect the unexpected, maybe the unexpected will cease to exist. Or what if it never existed?

My brain fights not to implode while I fidget on the beanbag, the only available seating in the lobby. No, I didn't just smoke up outside in the parking lot—my messed-up lungs would never tolerate that sort of activity. For better or for worse, this is the usual functioning of my sober mind.

The *Outsider* magazine headquarters have evolved beyond sad little cubicles, beige carpet, and soul-sapping artificial light. I anticipated capital *C* cool, but this is a whole other alphabet of awesome. Platinum LEED-certified building? Check. Koi ponds? Check. Floor-to-ceiling windows with panoramic views of Bear Peak and the surrounding Flatiron rock formations? Check. And let's not forget about the team-building zip lines near the main entrance, the electric-car charging stations, or the indoor climbing wall.

It's office nirvana.

My heart does a pretty damn good imitation of Thor's hammer striking against my rib cage.

What's the name of that hammer again? Muehler? No, wait. Mjölnir.

*Stop! Focus. Random factoids won't save you. Get your head in the game.*

I valiantly try to look like the poster child for calm and collected. Pursuing a job with the country's oldest and most prestigious outdoor lifestyle magazine is the last thing anyone would expect me to do. I'm a play-it-safe girl suited for an entry-level role in the state capitol press corps, a reliable and responsible career path. Not this—guns blazing into the land of adventure junkies. But being here, pushing my limits, feels damn good, like I'm stepping from black and white into a world of color.

I shift position to scratch my knee, and the resulting bean crunch is noisy enough to cause the receptionist to glance over the plant-filled stack of timber beams that passes for her desk. Her gaze is cool, slightly annoyed, no doubt thinking that I don't have a prayer of fitting in here if I can't even manage to sit without making it an awkward production. I drop my eyes, diligently studying the ankle zip of my slim-fitting gray dress pants.

Everyone strolling past is the epitome of laid-back and earthy while simultaneously projecting this indefinable aura of capability. They are also really, really, ridiculously good-looking. Even the receptionist must moonlight as a Pilates instructor or a fitness model. The large yellow VISITOR sticker on my shirtfront makes it clear that I don't belong, especially with my poor attempt at a sophisticated French-twist hairstyle and awestruck stare.

My lips are dry so I lick them, resisting the urge to hum the "One of These Things (Is Not Like the Other)" song from *Sesame Street*. I've gone on hikes—it's hard to grow up in the Colorado Rockies and never spend time outdoors. But while I might be considered adventurous to someone in Manhattan or LA, the fact that I don't ice climb, whitewater raft, backcountry ski, or mountain bike makes me pretty darn boring around here.

An unaccompanied golden retriever pauses for me to give it a quick behind-the-ear scratch. In yet another unconventional nod, dogs are welcome around the office. The DIY espresso cart across the lobby offers complimentary organic, fair-trade coffee while understated indie folk music plays from the surround sound.

Holy Mother of God, I long to be part of this cool club.

*Except you're nothing compared to these people. Why are you even bothering? They'll laugh you out the front door.*

My cheeks burn as my breathing gets shakier. It's funny the way all my internal negative self-talk whispers in my twin sister's voice. Not funny ha-ha, either—funny, weird. But now isn't a time for dredging up self-worth issues. I need to pull it together. I *can* do this.

I have to.

My only firm job offer to date is a reporting gig with a community paper based in Bakersfield, California, recently rated America's most polluted city. Beggars can't be choosers in this struggling economy.

My phone buzzes. It's a text from Brett, my on-again, off-again boyfriend. Heard back from Rapid City. Looks like South Dakota is rejecting me, too.

That's it. No tacked-on "good luck today" message or anything. He wants to break into broadcast journalism but hasn't gotten a single callback in the seven months since he graduated. We're both from Aspen, attended the same high school and college, and shared a major—plenty in common to keep us going the last four years. He's not "the one" or anything, but our relationship feels familiar, comfortable, like an old pair of sweats that always comes in handy on the weekend.

The fact that I've gotten a few callbacks and even the Bakersfield offer is a current sore point. He's jealous and I hate it. I know the market is tough and that I should be grateful for any opportunity, but the California option isn't remotely tempting. Even though my asthma improved after my teens, I can't afford to play with fire, or more specifically, shitty air quality.

I need this *Outsider* position.

The city paper is on the floor next to me and the headline boasts, BOULDER VOTED THE PERFECT PLACE. Apparently the town hit some national list for both happiest and brainiest city. In addition to topping community well-being indexes, it's also been my de facto home for the last four years, and even with the freedom that comes from having a shiny new University of Colorado degree under my belt, I don't want to live anywhere else. I skim the article and the facts don't lie. Three hundred days of sun a year, fabulous food, hundreds of local hiking trails, amazing street performances on Pearl Street, and a small-town feel with a big arts scene—where could be better?

"Miss Woods? They're ready for you." The receptionist gestures to the three-sided glass cube meeting room behind her, the one where four strangers lounge around the *Outsider* version of a conference table, an orange picnic table on rollers.

*Go time.*

Asthmatics can be mouth breathers. Not a great first impression. Lip check. Ensure mine are politely closed. Yes, good. Now inhale through the nose, shallow breathing at a controlled rate. The trick is to remain calm and keep the self-doubt under lock and key.

Four people are on the panel: Tortoiseshell Glasses Lady, Bushy Sideburns Guy, Red Turban Girl, and Man-Who-Has-Seen-So-Much-Sun-He-Resembles-Beef-Jerky. They introduce themselves as Amber (editor in chief), Capp (assistant editor), Briar (associate editor), and Reed (editor). There's a phrase scrawled over the table in stenciled words: "To live is the rarest thing in the world. Most people exist, that is all." There isn't an attribution to the quote, but I have a smug private moment of recognition: Oscar Wilde.

Tortoiseshell Glasses sits in the center and lobs an easy, "So, Auden, can you tell us a little bit about yourself?"

Why, yes, indeed. In fact, I'm so rehearsed, it's almost as if I'm reciting bullet points.

"Where to start? Let me see. I'm a twenty-one-year-old journalism grad from Aspen." (Omit the whole depressing childhood asthma part, when I spent winters nose pressed to the ski lodge windows while snow fell on the slopes).

"I also held several different positions on the university paper with progressive responsibility." (Don't leave out the 3.94 GPA. That's all in my résumé, but worth reiterating.)

"My grandfather was Dale Woods, one of the twentieth century's most revered explorers." (Ignore the pesky detail that I'm more enamored of Booker Prize–winning author Hilary Mantel than Edmund Hillary, the first person to summit Everest.)

Tortoiseshell Glasses Lady actually gasps. "Dale Woods? Oh

my. I had the wildest crush on him during the seventies. His poster hung on my wall next to David Cassidy and John Travolta."

Beef Jerky Face snorts.

"Oh, shut up." She shoots him a mock glare. "He climbed El Capitan in nothing but a pair of cutoff denim shorts. And oh good Lord, that Burt Reynolds mustache."

"He was pretty famous for that 'stache, huh?" I say. Apparently it was his trademark.

"What was he like?" Tortoiseshell leans forward. "In real life?"

"Um, I'm not sure." I fidget with the corner of my résumé. "His accident happened when I was still a kid."

"Yes." She nods slowly, drawing back. "The Alaska Affair."

Grandpa disappeared down a crevasse with three other climbers. Their bodies were never recovered, but our family erected a tombstone for him at the Aspen Grove Cemetery. Bushy Sideburns coughs into his fist. Red Turban fiddles with a pen cap. No one on the panel speaks or makes eye contact.

Death is a buzzkill.

Time to switch gears—fast. I mention that my identical twin, Harper, is heading to the Olympics (and conveniently overlook the not-so-fun-fact that our relationship sucks. When people hear the word *twins*, they often imagine besties who finish each other's sentences. Yes, some twins behave that way. I've encountered a few, and they're mystifying. Harper and I never shared a mirror-image relationship, unless it was one from a fun house).

My instincts are right. Their posture relaxes. Grandpa might be a hero to these people, but they want to celebrate his achievements, not his untimely demise in a blizzard or that his ambition may or may not have contributed to the loss of three other lives.

I dry my sweaty hands on my knees and on we go.

Beef Jerky Face: "Tell us about your experience with social media."

Bushy Sideburns: "Are you OK working evenings and weekends?"

Red Turban: "Share an example of a time you've worked as part of a team to get something accomplished."

Back over to Tortoiseshell: "What cartoon character best describes you?"

That last one's random, but the by-the-seat-of-my-pants answer, "Scrappy from *Scooby-Doo*," earns a few chuckles.

I'm on fire and they're taking notes, smiling and giving one another subtle nods. My guard drops and I start mentally decorating my desk in the rustic but chic open-plan office space when it happens.

The unexpected turns up when—wait for it—I least expect it.

Guess it exists after all.

Red Turban (who would be my boss): "Tell us about a unique, personal adventure you've undertaken that would be of interest to *Outsider* readers."

From the way the panel leans in, making direct eye contact—this is it, the money question. The proof in the pudding that I'm their people: rugged, exciting, interesting. The reality is this elite crowd isn't going to be impressed with the fact that I'm a fair-weather day hiker, decent croquet player, and rock the house in darts, especially after a few pitchers of PBR.

*Blow this moment and kiss Boulder good-bye. You'll be living in the nation's worst place to breathe, clutching your inhaler. Childhood asthma will seem like a time of rainbows and unicorns after a smog-filled year in Bakersfield.*

A framed woodcut poster hangs on the mud-brick wall behind

their heads. The image is of a massive stone tower, below which are printed the words "La Aguja, Torres del Paine, Patagonia."

*Wait ... What if?*

My tongue forms the next words before my brain can slam on the brakes. "You know ... traveling to South America is a personal aspiration." There are a few faint frowns. "One I'm about to make a reality," I amend hastily. "To see the dream-maker mountain." Seriously, if I had a firstborn child handy, I'd offer it up to get this opportunity.

My quick thinking works—the four frowns turn upside down.

I start rattling off upcoming plans to visit South America's most famous mountain even though the idea never crossed my mind until sixty seconds ago. Many cultures around the world revere high places as possessing supernatural aspects. I took a special topics seminar on sacred landscapes during my final semester, including Mount Olympus in Greece, Mount Taranaki in New Zealand, Tibet's Mount Kailash, and Chile's La Aguja—also known as "the Needle."

The Kaweskar, or indigenous people of that region in Patagonia, believed that if a person stood alone on top of La Aguja, they'd find their heart's desire. A pretty good deal except for the fact the summit is perpetually shrouded in impenetrable clouds and no one in living memory has made it there and lived to tell the tale. According to my professor, meteorological predictions suggested that this enigmatic peak might experience a once-in-a-generation clear-weather window around the New Year, and hotshot climbers from all over the world were expected to come flocking for a chance at glory.

Maybe this mountain could be a dream maker for me, too.

"I want to do a story on La Aguja, profiling climbers attempting the summit," I blurt. Who knows where these words come from? It's like I've been plotting the trip for years. I'm even getting excited about the outrageous prospect. My Spanish is better than decent, and this internship isn't set to begin for another month. This could be a perfect way to get out in the world, live a little, and land the perfect story to build my street cred.

Plus, there are huge bonus points to being on another continent during the lead-up to Harper's Olympic bid. A Patagonian trip is an acceptable way to avoid Sister Dearest's mounting stress and her inevitable wire-hanger-esque meltdowns. Imagine not having to be her human punching bag for once?

I hike on weekends (fine, like once or twice a month), but I am in pretty good shape, so getting to climbing base camp isn't out of the question. It only requires some stamina, not actual technical ability. Damn it. I want this internship: the freaking koi ponds with Japanese-style footbridges, the environmentally responsible toilets and cappuccino on tap.

Tortoiseshell Glasses sits back and crosses her arms, studies me with an assessing expression.

Have I done it? Have I convinced them? I cross and recross my legs. *Come on, come on, come on.* At this point, I've almost half convinced myself.

"I must say, I'm impressed, Miss Woods," she says. The others nod in unison.

"Thank you," I answer quickly, nerves exploding like miniature bottle rockets.

"La Aguja has the potential to be of great interest to our audience," she continues. "There is another vacant position here at *Outsider*, one we are vetting during the internship interviews. It's for an online content writer, putting out one to two items a day on our website with a guaranteed byline."

"Um…yes, I'd be very interested in that," I manage to murmur even though my mouth rivals the Saharan Desert. A paid position building clips for my portfolio?

*Glory, glory hallelujah.*

Tortoiseshells gives me a tight smile. "I'm sure you are. So are the other thirty-five applicants we've interviewed. We are hiring three interns, and the one who electrifies us the most will secure the position."

It takes a massive effort, but somehow I keep my nod more casual and less desperate. An internship would be a dream come true. An actual job here would be akin to discovering a pot of gold.

It's a tight fit inside my pointy flats, but I cross my toes with a quiet plea to the universe. *Please.*

Fate must have taken pity on my sorry butt, because the next day I get the call from human resources. "Miss Woods, congratulations. We are pleased to inform you that you've been selected for an internship with *Outsider* magazine." She keeps talking, but it is hard to register anything else over my silent screams and fist-pumping booty-shaking victory dance.

"Miss Woods? Are you still there? I asked if you are happy to accept the position."

"What? Oh, oops, sorry! Yes, yes, a hundred, no, wait, a million times yes," I blurt as the woman laughs.

I'm starting the position after New Year's. My grandfather left me a small inheritance, and I think he'd be more than happy to see his money fund my adventure. I'm going to do it. I'm going to book my ticket and live life a new way, without a list of rules and regulations. My story doesn't have to be ho-hum, safe, and predictable anymore.

OK, I stretched the truth—fine, outright lied—to get here. Perhaps I should feel guilty, but I don't. For once I'm going to be the one who takes a risk, reaches out to grab opportunity with both hands. Growing up, I never picked the more daring path while reading Choose Your Own Adventure books. High time to take a different direction.

It's now or never.

# 2

## *AUDEN*

*H*ip-hop shakes my town house walls, and everyone—except me—is wasted or well on their way. My roommate is holding a "Chranukkah party," a mash-up celebration of her Christian and Jewish heritage, plus a play on the term *chronic*, making this an excuse to smoke way too much weed. Brett's lifting people's legs as they do keg stands.

He nicknamed me "Nana," because going to bed before eleven and getting up at dawn is how I roll. I'm ducking out from the festivities to avoid the smoke and because Dad's picking me up at six a.m. to get to Denver Airport on time.

I'm almost at the stairs when the front door bursts open. It's Harper. My twin is flanked by four handsome ski bums and channels her inner snow bunny with hot-pink fingerless gloves, a quilted down vest, and badass knee-high boots. Two braids poke beneath her pom-pom beanie. The white wool renders her bright eyes an even deeper shade of blue. If I sported that style, I'd look ready to skip off to Sunday school. On my sister, however, the effect is nothing short of alluring.

"Sis." She does that ironic eyebrow raise and head-tilt gesture that drives me nuts. To the casual listener, perhaps her nickname sounds affectionate but I know better. Sis really stands for Shit-Ingesting-Sister. During our birth, I aspirated meconium and my lung collapsed. When Mom told us the story during middle school, Harper repeated it to everyone in our class and started calling me SIS as if it were the most hysterical joke ever.

"Hey," I say flatly, biting back my next question. What is she doing here?

"I didn't want to miss the big send-off." Her nose wrinkles as her gaze rakes my outfit. "No offense, but why are you wearing those jeans? They make your ass look huge."

"What?" I glance over my shoulder as if my butt cheeks somehow tripled in size.

"Kidding!" Her smirk belies the word.

I shove my hands into my back pockets; it's either that or strangle her and I don't want to star in a real-life *Orange Is the New Black*. "I thought you were training in Telluride."

"Plans changed. Where's Brett?" She makes a show of glancing around. "He texted me to come, you know."

He did? Then again, that's no big surprise. Brett's brainwashed by Harper. He always grills her about the famous skiers she rubs shoulders with and then brags to his buddies, basking in her glory. I barely even notice it. Everyone who gets within my sister's orbit turns into a starfucker.

A cheer erupts from the living room. "Drink! Drink! Drink!" the crowd chants, and Brett's trademark whoop is loudest of all.

"So are you coming to the airport tomorrow?" I ask.

"Why?" Her brows smash together like I've just asked her to mentally compute the square root of 43,650.

*Because you must have some shred of sisterly affection within you?*
"I'm leaving the country for almost a whole month."

"Eh, I give you a week," she says, turning away.

"A week?" My voice rises and I have to take a breath, count to three. "Care to translate?"

"One week before you're flying home with your tail tucked between your legs. You know this trip is a joke, right?" She rolls her eyes. "I mean, you? Backpacking in South America? Please. People are taking bets on how long you'll last."

I huddle against the banister, cheeks burning. "What people?" Harper and I don't even have the same friends.

"Everyone," she says in a singsong voice, rocking on her heels. "I know you want attention and all, but let's face it, you're out of your league."

Baiting me is her favorite pastime, and I'm getting tired as hell of it. "That's the pot calling the kettle black. The sky won't fall if you support me for once—"

"Support you?" Her voice drops to a hiss. "You mean like I did my entire fucking childhood?"

"You want to hash this out again? Mom and Dad really wasted their cash on all our sibling therapy sessions. Shoot me, I was a sickly kid—my life revolved around breathing treatments." She never lets me forget how many birthday parties and vacations I ruined.

"At least I did something cooler to get in the spotlight than wheeze." She beckons to her groupies. "Come on. This party looks lame. Let's see if we can liven it up." She slings her arms around the shoulders of the two guys closest to her, squealing as they whisk her off her feet and carry her down the hall without a backward look.

I bite the inside of my cheek, trying not to cry as I march up the stairs to my bedroom. I can do this. It's the perfect chance to prove my own capability. A trip alone to South America won't be easy, but the world is my oyster, right?

*Right.*

*I think.*

I enter the bathroom and reach for my toothbrush, catching my reflection in the mirror. My eyes shimmer with unshed tears.

"Stop it." I shake the toothbrush at my crushed expression. "She's wrong. You can kick butt."

There's no doubt the next few weeks will bring unexpected hardships and occasional discomfort, but that's part of the experience.

After all, a little grit makes pearls.

———

I wake an hour before my alarm clock is set to go off. Anticipation makes it hard to stay asleep. The spot next to me in bed is empty. Brett must have crashed on the couch. He's been drinking more and more since having nothing to show for all his job hunting, but I don't want to leave without saying good-bye, or worse, stick my roommate with cleaning up his puke.

I creep down the stairs and pick through the comatose bodies scattered through the living room. No boyfriend. Unease slithers up my spine. He wouldn't have driven anywhere in his condition, right? The basement door is open, so I descend, flicking on the light. The couch bed is unfolded, and a body is tangled in the sheets. Wait. Make that two bodies.

"Brett?"

He stares back with wide, bloodshot eyes. "Fuck."

"What are you doing?" My stomach muscles cramp as my brain struggles to process the scene.

Harper half sits and snakes her hand over his waist with a sleepy giggle. "Me."

I open my mouth, but no actual sound is forthcoming. "You... slept with my twin sister?" Ah, there's my voice, barely a whisper.

He scrubs his face before turning to lace his fingers with hers. "I—shit. Look, Auden, don't freak out. I think I'm in love with her."

"Jesus Christ, you have got to be kidding." My vocal cords kick into gear. Borrowing shoes without asking is one thing. Snide comments another. But screwing my boyfriend is a declaration of war. Looks like my previous opossum survival strategy, aka "roll over and play dead," was a dismal failure.

I turn away because what Harper wants is to watch me lose my shit. Like hell will I give her the satisfaction. No way does she return Brett's feelings. Not with how she always mocks his beer gut behind his back. This was a calculated attack designed to strip away the sheen from my trip. When I get to my room, I don't even slam the door. Instead, I sit and fold my trembling hands in my lap. I'm at the end of my rope with my sister. Maybe she's won this battle, but there's no way she'll win the war.

# 3

## RHYS

*T*he wind wails through the beech trees, Patagonia's wild version of a cradlesong. The banshee lullaby means it's time to brew another cup of Earl Grey, skim *Heart of Darkness*, and ignore the falling barometer. Lying low for a good-weather window is almost peaceful, except for one looming fact. Beyond this dark valley, La Aguja, The Needle, the whole reason for my last-ditch Chilean trip, waits. I trace my thumb over the letter folded between the final pages.

No. Not true. I slam the book with a thump. The granite buttress isn't waiting. It doesn't give a flying fuck about my goal to make the first solo, unsupported climb to its summit. Stone exists in a state of indifference, rising beyond rage, shame, judgment, those of us unable to be satisfied with a flat life. *Do or die trying*—the words have a certain dramatic flair, a nicer ring than *Do or bash your skull against a rock slab*.

The cost of my attempt may come at the ultimate price, but even such an exacting toll is worth the chance.

Probably nothing to the old legend, but that's all I've got left to lose.

Desperate men do desperate deeds.

The tent shakes as I crawl from my sleeping bag and kneel in the vestibule, grinding open the rainfly's zipper. Cold air whips my face. The wind has a hell of a bite tonight. The Andes are known for sudden, violent weather patterns, and it looks like they plan on living up to their reputation. Mine is the only tent here. I have Campamento Britanico to myself, a backcountry campground in Valle del Frances, an out-of-the-way section of Torres del Paine National Park, named for a British team who climbed here in the late sixties.

These gusts must clock in close to seventy kilometers an hour. Rain is imminent. *Good.* Shite conditions will keep the hikers along the popular main route at bay. Southern hemisphere summer means the trekking season is in full swing. Tonight they'll cower in one of the trail-side *refugios* with warm beds and hot meals. No one will bother coming up here, and that suits me better than fine. I need a fucking break from people.

I've had more than my fill of bloody journalists camped on my doorstep, or ringing and e-mailing at all hours, saying the same words a million different ways. "We're giving you an opportunity, Rhys. Share your side of the story. The whole world wants to know what happened with your brother on that mountain."

I crawl outside and push down my woolen beanie before it's snatched away. My bare feet sting against the earth, but I need to keep my body tough, my instincts honed.

A snout pokes from the bracken.

"*Halò, Zorro.*" My shout is piss weak against this bloody howl. "*Ciamar a tha thu?*"

Mum's a member of the Scottish National Party, speaks fluent Gaelic, but to her great annoyance, I only ever picked up the most rudimentary phrases. "Hello, how are you?" tests the outer reaches of my ability.

The gray fox has been checking on me since my arrival yesterday morning. Black fur bands his eyes, hence the nickname. Zorro's not much past a pup, curious, albeit wary.

"Looks like we're in for a bit of it, eh?"

He opens his mouth, hard to say in a yawn or silent laugh.

"Got any big plans this evening?" Good thing no one can see me chatting up a fox like a lonely dobber. "Me?" I jerk a thumb to my chest. "Suspect I'll be getting rat-arsed to ride out the storm." There's a flask inside my backpack. Whiskey is a sure way to annihilate bad dreams.

Zorro's ears twitch, and he huffs once before slinking into the shadows.

I grab an overhead branch, gnarled from the brutal elements, and haul into a series of pull-ups, striving for a slow, steady rhythm. "One. Two. Three." Soon it's "Sixteen. Seventeen. Eighteen." As my heart rate increases, my shoulders burn, and my triceps scream, I focus my attention through the clearing to Cerro Aleta del Tiburón. The prominent rock shears the overcast sky like its namesake, a shark's fin, a blatant reminder of the danger associated with my objective.

I need to yank my head out of my arse and get back in the game, because it's almost time to put the last thing I've got on the line—myself. No one's ever successfully survived a solo climb on La Aguja, but that doesn't mean this trip is a death wish. Far from it. My mission is to survive, conquer, and yeah, risk it all, because I'd rather nail my nuts to my knees than continue living like a ghost.

Everyone wants what they don't have. I used to fancy myself set apart from the rat race, believed mountaineering kept me humble, pure even, but it turns out I'm just another greedy bastard. In my case, instead of a sports car, money, or a beautiful woman, I crave forgiveness, but I haven't earned the right to ask for it.

Cold rain splatters my face, an introductory drizzle, coming harder by the second, and I stride back to the tent. The world calls me a monster, a murderer, and for once "they," whoever the fuck those tedious opinion makers are, have it right. I spent the last few months before South America sequestered at Da's place in the Colorado Rockies, where he's one of those evangelical ministers. My own religious views fall in the gray area between atheist and agnostic, but the many Bibles on his guest room bookshelf provided reading material when late-night cable or bourbon refused to numb me.

I read and reread one particular passage until my eyes lost the ability to focus. "If your right hand makes you stumble, cut it off and throw it, for better to lose a part of your body than the whole of your body to go to hell."

I flex my right hand, the knuckles scarred and fingertips callused. I hate this part of me more than anything else. Here's the hand that cut my brother loose, my best friend tied to my body for protection on the mountain, sentenced to the worst kind of death.

I duck into my tent to escape from the bitter wind. Let the weather rage. Anything is better than to have people hound me for my story.

There's nothing to tell. I traveled to hell and haven't found a way back.

If atonement doesn't wait atop La Aguja, I'm out of options.

# 4

## *AUDEN*

*I*t's a truth universally acknowledged that a single girl alone in dark woods with a complete stranger does not wish to be asked, "What did I tell you my name was again?" I'm only a handful of hours into the South American backpacking expedition designed to ring in a new year and kick-start my big La Aguja story. Nowhere does the plan include an untimely end in a temperate Patagonian rain forest. Looks like the random hiker who's dogged me since starting at the trailhead has finally succeeded in killing our struggling conversation.

Hopefully that's the only thing he's going to kill today.

"Excuse me?" Trepidation slams my belly like a hard-flung stone. Why would he give me a fake name? Maybe I heard the guy wrong, a caffeine-deprived auditory hallucination. Knotty trees line the trail, forming a dense wall that blocks any possible escape route.

The stranger repeats the strange question before resuming his off-key humming of Journey's "Don't Stop Believin'." Yep, looks like my ears are in fine working order. I'm alone in a foreign continent with a potential nutcase, just my luck. My heart pumps harder, eager to offer its two cents. *Yo, I'd sure love to remain in this cozy chest cavity.*

This guy has been driving me crazy for miles, and I'd done my best to tune out his warbling and direct my attention to the beautiful forest, seemingly lifted from the pages of Tolkien. Right now I'd swap the emergency chocolate stashed in my backpack for a hot elf to the rescue.

Norman Bates Jr. zeroes in with an uncomfortably intense gaze. "Sometimes I tell people different names!"

"But…why?" I'd mistaken Diedrick—or whoever the hell he is—for a typical run-of-the-mill Annoyasurus. There are plenty of his species roaming about, overeager guys looking for love in all the wrong hostels.

"I'm Dutch!" He gives a maniacal giggle. Why does he slap an exclamation mark to the end of every sentence?

"So was van Gogh." Not exactly a poster boy for mental health.

He claps and bounces as if I answered a game show's prize-winning question. "You're so funny! Ah, I love American girls!"

I'm pretty sure that I'm not in actual danger, but this is definitely one strange fellow. We're on one of the most classic treks in the continent. Another hiker will happen upon us momentarily, and anyway, I'm booked into a refugio for the night. My name is on a list. I'll be expected. Parque Nacional Torres del Paine staff maintain four huts along the trail, marketed to folks who want to experience the great outdoors without the more hard-core "roughing it" aspects. For a reasonable price, one can spend the night in a cozy bunk, eat a hot meal, and get a cold beer. I'm hardly giving Lewis and Clark a run for their explorer money, but hey, not bad for an asthmatic with a fondness for memory foam. I'll sleep in comfort all the way to the La Aguja climbers' camp.

*Please let this hike be a good idea instead of a situation where my parents will eventually have to alert Interpol, who'll discover my dismembered body stuffed inside a tree hollow.*

Sometimes having an overactive imagination is more of a curse than a blessing.

Besides, I could be missing for weeks before my folks even noticed. All their attention is currently focused on their golden daughter and her gold-medal dreams. Their last e-mail made that point exceedingly clear: "Merry Christmas, honey! Glad you arrived safe and sound. Good timing to be away. Your sister is in a mood, and it's better that we help her focus for the Olympics alone."

In other words, don't come back and set Veruca Salt off.

Harper didn't send a single word of apology. No earth-shattering surprise there. It could be that she was too busy training. Or it could be her heart is three sizes too small. Whatever the reason, Someecards is her preferred method of communication. Guess they don't make one for "Hey, twin, sorry I got busy with your boyfriend the night before your trip. My bad."

*OK, concentrate, Woods. Get that head back in the game.* This Dutchman doesn't know who he's dealing with. I'm not taking shit from anyone.

Not anymore.

The new tune Diedrick is humming sounds vaguely familiar. It's not…Oh, God, it is…"Eye of the Tiger." Please, Sweet Little Non-Colicky and Well-Rested Baby Jesus, I'd offer up my eardrums to be magically teleported from this torture.

"True or false?" I level my best "don't bullshit me" expression at him. The one perfected while conducting interviews for the university paper on topics like the Board of Regents tuition hike proposals or the spike in sexual assaults in the dorms. "Is your name really Diedrick?"

"Ding! Ding! Ding! Ladies and gentlemen, we have a winner." He gyrates his hips in a manner truly unpleasant to witness. I'd get stabbed by his beef bayonet if those khaki shorts were any smaller. He pulls out a roll-your-own cigarette from his shirt pocket, lighting it before I can stop him.

"No, wait. Don't…" His exhalation wreathes my head. "Please put that out." I wave my hands in front of my face with a grimace. Smoke is one of my worst asthma triggers.

"Hold on…Yes…Good. That's it. Freeze." Diedrick thoughtfully chews his cigarette, framing my face with his hands, ignoring my plea. "With the mountains behind you, and that pose? Oh, wow, what a great shot!" He claims to be a freelance photojournalist, and the expensive gear slung around his neck suggests he's told the truth, at least on that front.

"Cigarette. Out." I'm enveloped in yet another horrid stinky cloud before he catches the point of my frantic miming and grinds the stub with his boot.

A slash appears across his forehead. "Forgot most Americans don't like smoking."

I downgrade my internal terror ranking from "Alarmed" to "Aggravated." This guy doesn't appear to be a threat except to my sanity and lungs. "Can't speak for my entire nation, but it makes *me* sick."

I readjust my backpack straps—the weight is giving me neck pain—and eye the low-slung clouds spreading across the sky like a deep-set bruise. "The weather looks like it might turn bad. We should probably—"

"We need a selfie. Capture the moment!" Diedrick wraps a wiry arm around my shoulders and his skullet tickles the side of my cheek. No judgment on the male-pattern baldness, but what is the point of growing out all that scraggly hair in back? And why does his breath reek of old sausage? I hold my own while he procures a small digital camera from his neon fanny pack.

"One, two, three, Gouda!"

I force a good-natured "cheese," because for all my tough talk, my default setting is still to grin and bear whatever comes my way. All I need to do is keep that act up for a few more miles. There will be unsuspecting hikers at the next refugio to foist this guy on. No doubt Diedrick would glom on to another group if given the right opportunity.

*Yes. Perfect.*

I might be well mannered, but inside I'm a passively evil genius.

Out of nowhere, Diedrick rams his tongue at my face. I duck, and he ends up violating my nostrils.

"Jesus, what are you—"

"Gotcha!" he crows while I lurch back, wiping my face with undisguised disgust. He frowns at the viewfinder. "Oh no. The setting was on video. I demand a redo!"

I glance around, desperate for a suitable threat, before zeroing in on his tiny man shorts. "Stop. Hold it right there." My hiking boots are heavy-duty. I could scro-tack, cause his testicles real and painful harm. "Listen good and hard, buddy." *Buddy? Seriously? That's the best I've got?* "Forget this. I'm hiking ahead on my own. You have a watch? Yes, good. Stay put and don't you dare budge for the next ten minutes if you ever want to reproduce."

There we go. That's how it's done.

He steps away uncertainly, and an unfamiliar power surge

heats my chest. Who knew speaking your mind could feel so damn good? I need to do this more often. I spin on my heel and resist the urge to throw my arms in a victory *V*. Brett said I never shared my opinions, kept too much to myself, and hid behind asking other people questions.

Maybe that's how wimpy old-school Auden rolled. Well, I've found my voice, and it's loud, proud, and—ouch! I trip on a boulder and kick a rock to my shin. A weathered sign to the left of the trail reads VALLE DEL FRANCES in faded white paint.

A carved arrow points to a faint footpath, and scratched beneath it is 2.8 MILES/4.5KM. Hmm, not too far. Deviating from my route wasn't even a question until ten minutes ago. But following the guidebook-recommended itineraries word for word is how I've always lived—doing the expected, obeying the rules.

That's not how this trip came about. That's not what my big adventure in South America is supposed to be.

I reach out and trace the arrow. How many thousands of miles did I fly to find a big story, something that would make my future boss at *Outsider* magazine sit up and take notice, think, *Wow, here's a girl with potential*? Plus, I have to prove Harper wrong, that I have what it takes to be bold. I pull out the guidebook from my backpack's side pocket and reread the brief description. There's not much written about Valle del Frances, only that it's a popular side route with a backcountry campground. Maybe there's some bonus material here to pad out my profile piece.

But backcountry campground? That means drop toilets. Ew. Not even sinks.

Saying I want to be more adventurous is a whole other kettle of fish to actually choosing adventure. A detour represents an unknown. There's no warm bed. There's no hut full stop. But if I'm going to spend time at La Aguja's rustic climbing camp, I might as well get comfortable with tent living sooner rather than later.

I tip my weight forward, then waffle back. Forward, then back.

Aw, hell, I have hand sanitizer. What can go wrong?

Sucking in a deep breath, I step off the main path.

# 5

## *AUDEN*

*T*he trail rises steadily uphill. Granite walls tower impos-
ingly as wind whips loose hair into my eyes. My lungs
burn, emitting a high-pitched whistle on the exhalations. Only a
matter of time before the wheezing spreads to my inhalations. A
cloudy gloom conceals the mountaintops, and the temperature is
dropping, bad news for someone whose asthma can be exacerbated
by cold. Every book or article on Patagonia stresses the weather can
be notoriously wild and unpredictable.

*Breathe, just breathe. Stupid Diedrick and his stupid-ass cancer
sticks.*

I unsling my pack to grab Albuterol from the top pouch. A wall
of water unleashes from the heavens, soaking through my fleece and
Capilene long underwear. I shake the inhaler, suck in a few puffs,
unable to savor the relief in my urgency to dig out my balled-up rain
gear before I am soaked to the bone.

"Shitballs," I mutter, thrusting my arms into my Gore-Tex
jacket. If I put my head down and don't dawdle, I'll reach the campground within the hour. Too bad boot-deep mud, or falling, three

separate times, each more miserable than the last, didn't factor into my calculations.

At last I stumble into the campground's clearing. Who am I kidding, setting out on my own like this? *Stupid and irresponsible.* I shiver so hard my teeth sound like miniature maracas. The place is deserted except for a yellow tent up the hill, nestled beside a large boulder sheltering it from the storm's brunt.

Inside are probably dry, contented hikers, sipping hot cocoa and congratulating themselves that they aren't in my sodden boots.

*OK, OK. Focus. Everything is going to be OK.*

*No, it's not. I'm big-time screwed.*

Looks like wanting to be a badass future employee for *Outsider* magazine is better in theory than in practice. It's all fun and games until someone has an asthma attack next to a glacier during a torrential downpour.

Why didn't I apply to work for *Better Homes and Gardens* instead? Articles like "Ten Tips for Growing Perfect Roses" or "How to Brew the Perfect Cup of Sun Tea" have a certain appeal right about now.

I heave my backpack square into a puddle; there is nowhere dry to set it down. Frozen fingers make opening the buckles a trick, same with digging through my tight-packed belongings. There it is. The tent I borrowed from Dad. I haven't set it up yet, but how hard can it be? I mop rain from my eyes, crouch, untie the bag, and peer inside. Fear scuttles around my stomach like a tarantula. Something doesn't look right.

*Where's the main pole?*

There's a strange sound. It takes a second before I realize it's coming from my own throat, a low keen, just this side of panic. It's hard to know where the rain stops and my tears begin. I scrub a

hand over my face and blink a few times before turning the backpack upside down. Out tumbles a clothing stuff sack, a travel-sized
bottle of shampoo and body wash combo, a food bag, a thirty-two-
ounce stainless-steel water bottle, a moleskin notebook, an orange
nylon first aid kit, a quick-dry pack towel, matches in a ziplock
bag, a flashlight, and a down sleeping bag. The tent's two smaller
poles are there and that's it. There's nothing else. I stand, pace back
and forth, giving dread ample amounts of time to settle in, get
comfortable.

"Son of a bitch," I gasp, punching my fist into my upper thigh.
It doesn't hurt, barely feels like anything. I'm either weak or cold, or
weak *and* cold. Neither is an optimum situation.

I'm the naïve idiot who didn't open up the tent bag and check
that all the pieces were present before leaving. I wiggle my toes.
Numb. As soon as I ceased hiking, the cold started to leach into my
bones. A thunderclap ricochets off the mountains, and a few seconds later, lightning spears a cliff face, illuminating the gear strewn
at my feet.

I muffle a shriek and paw through the contents three times
before accepting the obvious. The main pole is definitely missing,
and with this wheeze, there's no way in hell I'll manage a three-
hour hike back to the refugio. My only viable option is to go to the
yellow tent and ask for help from a total stranger.

Relentless rain runs down the back of my neck, between my
shoulder blades, to pool in my bra strap.

I cram my wet gear back into my pack, grab my high-powered
lithium flashlight, and trudge up the escarpment, chewing the
inside of my cheek.

I pause two feet from the entrance—whoever's inside might not
take kindly to a scared, winded American barging into their per-

sonal space—and cup my hands to my mouth. "Hello, um, excuse me? *Hola? Discúlpeme?*" If they don't speak English or Spanish, things are going to get lost in translation pretty quick.

No answer. The dull pain in my chest intensifies. I pinch the bridge of my nose, taking the deepest breath allowable by my defective airways. Are they sleeping? All this shivering can't be a good sign. I need to get warm, pronto. No other viable option but to yell. I clear my throat and project my voice into a shouty rasp. "Sorry. I don't mean to bother you, but—"

"What do you want?" A guy—not a very happy one by the sound of it—growls from inside.

"Sorry?" I bend closer to the nylon to hear above the deluge.

"What. Do. You. Want?"

My unwilling savior has a testy accent and a worse attitude. British maybe? No one does disdain like the English. Under normal circumstances, I'd swoon. I'm such a sucker for Mr. Darcy fantasies, but this isn't Pemberley. It's the Patagonian wilderness.

I lurch backward and trip over a tent peg. The flashlight slips from my grasp and hits the ground, shining on a coiled rope topped by a helmet. A mountaineer. Wonderful. He's not exactly going to roll out the welcome mat for my inept ass, and I'm the type of girl who hates asking for help carrying groceries to the car. But what's the alternative? Hypothermic death in a bog?

The tent unzips. My thoughts are jumbled, but there's enough common sense left remaining to not fall to my knees and praise Jesus, Mary, and all the angels.

The diffuse light reveals the guy inside rising to his knees. Too dark to make out a face, especially when his headlamp burns my retinas. He seems very big, very shirtless, and very alone.

My nails cut into my palms, but no feeling remains in my

hands. This damsel-in-distress business sucks. "My tent, see. It's short a pole, and I can't set it up. Can I...? Can I...?" *Out with it, like ripping off a bandage.* Strange my mouth can be so dry when the rest of me is drenched. I have to get inside that tent. "May I come in? Please. I don't know what else to do." I have nothing left to say. My social skills toolbox is empty.

A few seconds tick by. "Can't leave you out there." He sounds disappointed by the fact. "Come in, then, but those muddy boots need to stay in the vestibule."

I step forward unsteadily, half wishing I could see him better, get a good look at the situation, and half not caring. At least I'm going to have shelter, and surviving is worth dealing with the uncomfortable situation. As I bend to unlace my boots, the glow from his headlamp reveals carved abs and low-slung pants barely hanging on to narrow hips. My throat constricts. Looks like tonight will be spent between a rock and a hard place.

# 6

## RHYS

*T*he girl hovers outside the tent, her cheeks and lips bleached bloodless. I blink groggily, stomach knotted, the aftereffects of my restless nap. A gust of wind whooshes through the entrance, and my skin prickles to gooseflesh. Is this lost ghost hallucinatory proof I've finally gone and cracked it? Unthinkable anyone would venture this far into the valley alone, under such wild conditions, but as she crawls inside, her kneecap crushes my little finger.

Aye, fuck, she's real enough.

"Oh, sorry. I'm so sorry. Did I hurt you?" She slurs a little, sounds as if she can't draw enough air into her lungs. The last thing I need is the distraction of a sick stranger. Unbreakable concentration doesn't simply happen on the mountain. It's honed through a long-term commitment to reducing disruptions and narrowing focus.

I shift to one side, trying to maintain a semblance of personal space. She does the same, and our bodies collide, shoulder to shoulder, nose to nose. A wet tendril escapes her braid and skims my neck. Rainwater perfumes her hair. Deep inside my chest, something breaks free, a loose rock clattering to the pit of my stomach. I spring back, thigh muscles taut.

*What the hell?* The physical response catches me unawares. I'm not used to feeling much these days, and the sensation prickles in the pins-and-needles way a limb has after falling asleep for too long.

The girl tugs off her beanie and peers from under bold slashing brows. Despite the fact that her features are drawn, her eyes shine in my torchlight, echoing the bottomless blue of a deep crevasse. I hold her gaze for the briefest of instants before zipping the entrance shut, sealing us both inside.

It's been pouring for a fair few hours, and the girl's demonstrating a lack of coordination, one of the first symptoms of hypothermia. "You have a problem," I say flatly, drawing my brows together.

She tucks her chin to her chest, struggling to close her fingers around her rain jacket's zipper. As she works herself free of the Gore-Tex, it becomes apparent she's soaked to the bone.

I inwardly curse while setting my jaw. No easy way to say this. If she doesn't raise her core body temperature, things could go downhill fast. Clumsiness will give way to lethargy, confusion, loss of consciousness, and even death. "You need to strip."

Her gaze narrows to suspicious slits. She's not going to take this well.

Too bad. We're not at a tea party. It's cold and damp outside, and hypothermia is nothing to fuck around with.

"Get your kit off." I sit back on my heels.

She scuttles with surprising speed, crab-like, to the entrance, leaving damp sock imprints across my mat, knocking about my gear. "Stay back." She lifts a bare foot, as if warding me off. "If you come closer—" A cough rattles away the rest of her sentence.

I don't move a muscle. Mum drilled sexual harassment threats into me and Cameron when our voices broke.

*If I ever catch so much as a whisper on the wind that my sons did anything untoward to a lass, I'll be having your beebaws for breakfast.* Her warning came without a trace of humor. Mum isn't the joking sort.

Anyway, it didn't matter. We never found getting consent a particular challenge.

"Am no' trying to..." For one fucking second wouldn't it be grand to be viewed as a good guy? "Staying in those saturated clothes is bloody dangerous."

She doubles over with a great wet cough, her lungs crackling audibly over the lashing rain.

*Sod it.* "Are you traveling with anyone? Someone who might be looking for you?"

"No." She braces her head in her hands. "If you're a serial killer, consider me a belated Christmas surprise." She glances up, pupils nearly eclipsing her irises. "You're not, though, are you?"

"What's today? Tuesday, is it?"

She frowns. "Um, I think so?"

"Monday is my preferred murder day," I answer dryly.

Her strangled choke might be a dry laugh under better conditions.

"Lucky me." She squeezes her eyes tight.

Poor lass doesn't know I'm the antithesis of a lucky charm. I move closer, tug her jacket free from her arms. She tries to assist and makes everything twice as difficult. My fingers graze the flat plane of her lower abdomen. "Please. Stop wiggling," I say through clenched teeth as a jolt of warmth spreads up my arm.

I fold her jacket in the corner, and a cursory check of her belongings confirms my suspicions. Her backpack is soaked through, all clothing varying degrees of damp.

"Off with your shirt."

She halts. Is it going to be like this with every article of clothing? Hell if I am going to waste time arguing about her modesty. I'd rather take a running fuck at a rolling doughnut.

"Go on, then," I say with impatience. "There is no' time for shyness, ken? Besides, you're not the first lass I've ever seen undressed." I reach into my dry bag and tug out a thermal shirt, resisting the urge to give it a self-conscious sniff. I make a point to only wear merino wool in the field—the natural fibers resist odor—but still, I've been away from a functioning washing machine for weeks. All my clothes are subjected to stream dunkings, dried on sun-warmed rocks, and will have to do. "Change to this." I fist it over.

"Fine." She rips off her top.

I square my gaze on my lap, but not before catching a glimpse of pink bra and a tattoo on her lower belly, a half-blown dandelion disappearing into her waistband. Not that I should be noticing any of that. Or have this frisson of awareness slam through my guts. This isn't the time or the place to start taking an interest in the opposite sex again.

"What's your name?" she whispers through chattering teeth, more hoarse than I'd like.

I'm not a celebrity. Still, my name circulated through most major news outlets and starred in more than a few magazine features. Outside the climbing world, I've been recognized, and never favorably. "Rhys," I mutter. "Rhys MacAskill." And brace.

She frowns slightly. "Really?"

Fine hairs bristle at the base of my neck. Here we go. "Aye, that's my name, true enough."

She shakes her head. "On the trail earlier today, I met this Dutch guy, and he..." Much can be said with a sigh. Hers is eloquent. A proper Scot's sigh. "Never mind all that. I'm Auden. Auden Woods."

"As in the poet?"

"Yes." She blinks, her gaze curious. "No one ever knows that."

I give a small shrug. "Good name."

"Thanks." Her smile is wry even as her breathing is a trifle labored. "Normally, I tell it to a guy before letting him strip me."

"You're Canadian?" I can't ever tell their accents apart from the Yanks, but it seems a safe inroad and talking keeps her calm. Canadians are invariably pleased at the courtesy, and Americans never mind correcting. Doesn't work half so well the other way around.

"No, American. From Colorado."

"Small world. So's my da," I say with a grunt. "Lots of mountains there." *Think she'd have better sense in them.*

She stops coughing long enough to ask, "Your father is from the US?"

"Aye. Gave me dual citizenship and all that."

"But you're English?"

Now here's a sure way to hurt my finer feelings. "English?"

She makes a face, knowing she's said something wrong even if she can't quite put a finger on it. "Um…British? Sorry. I don't really know the—"

"I'm Scottish."

"Oh, right. I should have recognized. Who doesn't love *Braveheart?*"

"The Mel Gibson movie?" Jesus. A headache gathers behind my eye sockets, the first twinge of a miserable throb. Next she'll be asking if I wear a kilt or play "Scotland the Brave" on the bagpipes.

"I didn't mean to make it sound like you guys run around yelling 'Freedom' or anything, but—"

"That we don't," I say curtly. Indulging in stereotypes about my country is one of my least favorite conversations. I shift and bump her outer thigh. Tension hums through me, an irrational slow burn. This is a real mess. No way can we avoid touching in such cramped quarters. I practically fill the tent on my own. "Your pants are wet."

Her cheeks go tomato red. "Let me guess. You want them off, too?"

"Like I said, it's no' a question of want. It's—"

"Fine." She wiggles from her pants. Her knickers are yellow, have an outline of two kittens romping over the words "Take These Off Right Meow."

"Here." I gesture at my mat, my gut clenching. "Crawl into my sleeping bag."

Her sigh becomes a gasp. "I hate being a nuisance."

"Then do us both a favor and don't go into a hypothermic coma."

"Trying my best," she mutters, sliding past.

*Stop staring at her arse.*

Instead I focus on her red-painted toes—one is encircled by a thin silver band. Pressure builds in my hips, radiates to my stomach, and then sinks lower, but her rattling exhalation refocuses me in an instant. Being single-minded has its uses. "What's wrong with your breathing?"

"I have asthma. Cold often exacerbates the symptoms." She coughs again. "Can you please go in my bag and get out my peak meter?"

"What's that?"

"It measures my lung function. You'll find it in the top pocket. There's lots of numbers on the front."

Good. A job. I'm always better with something useful to do. "Too easy." It's the first thing I see in her pack, and I pass it over.

"Thanks." She lifts the contraption to her mouth and blows. It doesn't sound like she's trying; or rather, it sounds like she's tried too hard and hardly any air remains. Somehow my hand finds its way to her shoulder.

Her face snaps to mine, defensive, confused, and something else, not coy, nothing like that, just... Bugger all. I wasn't making a move, just trying to give a little piss-poor human comfort. I yank my hand away, ignoring the fact my stomach muscles are twisting and not altogether unpleasantly or that the feel of her has tattooed itself on my palm. I mentally shake myself.

*Get it together, man.*

She stares through veiled lashes, giving a single wide-eyed blink, her gaze brighter than a moment ago. At least before she turns to check the reading. "Shit."

"Bad?"

"Not good." She circles her thumb around the pads of her pointer and middle finger.

I recognize that nervous habit. During our climbs, I'd often find myself aimlessly finger snapping in the tent, until Cameron would ask when I planned on auditioning for *West Side Story*. *The smart-arse.*

"Do you take medication?"

"Albuterol." She tries to keep worry from her expression, but I see it there, hovering on the edge of her fine features all the same. "I keep it in the same pocket."

I reopen her pack, rifling through chocolate bars and loose tampons. Jesus, someone put me out of my bloody misery. I fist the purple canister and shove it in her direction, dreading she'll graze my fingers and hoping she does. Jesus Christ.

"Sorry. That one's a steroid for mornings. Albuterol is the light blue one."

More digging, past birth control pills, and—I swallow hard— condoms. "OK. Here we go, light blue."

I pass her the inhaler and she shakes it, exhaling before setting the opening to her mouth, pressing and holding her breath. She does this for a few more puffs before lowering it with a sigh.

"Better?" I ask.

"It will help." She fidgets. "Makes me jittery though. Just need to focus on my breathing and—" A clap of thunder sounds, as if the sky wrenches in two. A strangled squeak escapes her. "Sorry. I don't like s-s-storms."

Even in my sleeping bag and dry shirt, her teeth chatter. If she balked at my request to undress, she's going to go ape over this. Fuck it. There isn't a choice.

"Auden."

A thin furrow appears between her brows. "Yeah?"

My stomach tightens. "I'm going to warm you."

"How?" Her eyes widen.

I can't hold her gaze and say what I must. "Body-to-body contact."

The world outside rips apart, but in the tent, a heavy silence reigns. She shifts to a half sit. "Oh, no, it's OK. Look, I'll be better in a few minutes."

"You said yourself the cold makes your asthma worse."

"Yes, but—"

"I know you don't have a reason to trust me. In fact, if this were normal circumstances, I'd no' recommend it. But here we are."

"Nothing about today is normal." She slowly reclines to the

mat, folding her arms across her chest like a mummy, eyes screwed shut.

"No harm's going to come to you." It sounds as if I'm making a solemn oath.

She opens one eye, gives me an unfathomable look, before closing it again. I'm not used to a woman regarding me like something to endure. Uncertainty weaves through me.

I ease beside her. "This'll go easier if you turn to the side." Away from me.

"Good idea." She rolls to face the tent wall. Her features are hidden, but I can hear each uneven breath, the slightly shuddering inhalation followed by a pause before giving way to a raspy exhalation.

She remains still when I reach, warily securing a handhold on her ribs, their sudden rise and fall the only sign of her silent gasp. "This all right?"

She utters no reply, only gives a brief nod, and grips the sleeping bag tighter.

"Everything will be fine, I promise you." I keep my voice cool, aloof. Give no sign that my chest aches, as if instead of a heart, a great wallowing drunk stumbles about. I never cuddle. Prior to my last girlfriend, Sadie, my dealings with the opposite sex were kept to simple and straightforward shags. Occasionally girls tried to compete with the mountains, but they never stood a chance.

Auden gives another tentative nod, and her scent invades my senses, simple and straightforward, a hint of sweat from exertion, combined with the fresh fragrance of rain. She begins to settle, her violent shiver attacks growing fewer and further between, same with her coughing fits. I keep my pose rigid, controlled, resisting the mad urge to relax into her body as blood pounds thickly in my ears. I can't do this, be with another person, be human. I need to be a machine. A robot with one goal and one goal alone. To conquer a mountain like La Aguja there can be no room left inside me for any other desire.

When my mind quiets and other wants are eliminated, my attention naturally focuses on visualizing the climb. Once on the rock, this single-minded concentration will translate effortlessly into correct hand- and footholds or gear placements. In order to climb like you are the only person in the world, you can't care about anything other than living in the moment. There can be no significant other in the mind's periphery wielding the power to distract.

Outside the wind shakes the nylon, redoubling its assault. Zipped tight, shut away from the world, we could be anywhere. I'd always appreciated that about tents, how once inside, you became the ruler of your own cramped kingdom of cast-off socks, sleeping bags, and carefully chosen gear. This time in Valle del Frances, away from the scene at the main climbing camp, is meant to be a chance to establish a cease-fire in the battle with myself. Being in a tent, in the wilderness, far from a world I don't understand and that sure as hell doesn't understand me, is calming.

Now Auden Woods has come along and triggered a whole new conflict with her icy blue eyes.

*Icy blue eyes?* Looks like prolonged abstinence brings out a lad's poetic side. If she looks back, she'll see my mouth twisted in a humorless smile.

She doesn't, though. She's too busy trembling, and so I gather her closer, an unfamiliar protective sensation welling inside me. "Better?" I whisper, more a hoarse croak than anything gallant.

"Yes," she says, turning, her full lips slightly parting to offer the word.

We're two strangers, haven't even shaken hands, and yet our bodies press flush. Despite every intention, mine starts to react, and Christ, quick, what are unsexy topics to ponder? When in doubt, go for geology. The Andes are the result of which type of plate boundary?

Conquering La Aguja is going to take all my mental resources. The next few days are needed for getting focused, concentrated, and prepared for the challenge ahead. Auden shifts, drawing closer, and my next breath is almost as ragged as hers.

Aye, this girl is just the sort of distraction that could ruin everything.

# 7

## *AUDEN*

*J* traveled to Torres del Paine as an aspiring journalist on the hunt for a career-making story, but getting what I wanted might be more than I can handle. Suddenly, I'm a half-naked girl snuggled against a stranger with the kind of face I'd pin to my "Sexy Men" Pinterest page. My next shiver isn't from the cold. I'm normally not a huge facial hair fan, but Rhys's dark scruff only serves to amplify those eyes. Seriously, who has irises like that? I can't even begin to describe the color, not a brown or even a green. Hazel is probably the correct definition, but there is lots of yellow, too, and the overall effect is nothing short of intense.

Theoretically, forced proximity with a hot guy should be an amazing stroke of luck worth throwing a mental ticker-tape parade over. Scratch that. Calling this guy hot is like describing Godzilla as a cute gecko. I've never encountered an actual six-pack in real life. How would those muscles feel under my fingertips? If given the opportunity, I'd take my sweet time, trace each one, and commit the entire experience to memory.

Wait? What am I doing?

*Stop mentally fondling the abs of the guy who's been forced to rescue you.*

I lick my lips, not that the gesture does much—my mouth is bone dry. The only reason we're together is because I'm an underprepared idiot who forced myself into his personal space. He's probably rolling his eyes behind my back, hoping I'll beat it at first light.

"Auden." The way he says my name, I can tell without looking that he's frowning. He seems to excel at that particular expression. His features are broody perfection. "You're tense. Why?"

The silent Scot is going to engage? Thank God because I can't bear lying here, surrounded by a howling storm, uncomfortably aware of his big body pressed hard against me. "Well…" I clear my throat, unable to dish up the truth. "Wandering into strange forests à la Little Red Riding Hood can have that effect on a girl."

"If you're Red Riding Hood, lass, then what does that make me?" Is it my imagination, or does his lilting accent take on growly edge? "The wolf or the woodcutter?"

"Guess that depends on how much you want to eat me?" My eyes widen in the dark. I didn't say that out loud, did I?

*Did I?*

He shakes behind me in silent laughter as another thunder boom reverberates through the mountains.

*Hello, Thor? It's me, Auden. Please end my blabbering misery with a merciful lightning bolt.*

"You're a funny one."

I turn to face him. "Funny ha, or funny weird?" The indent above his top lip is incredibly cute, as top lip indents go, but why? Hard to say, especially when further investigation means staring like a creeper.

"Both." The corner of his mouth jerks up, albeit a little unwillingly. "Tell me, how did you come to find yourself in Patagonia?"

"I wanted to see La Aguja, the dream-making mountain."

His retreat is subtle, only a few inches, but the sudden tension is obvious. "Why? You're no' a climber?"

"Nope. A journalist."

"Journalist?"

What's with that salty tone? Is he afraid I'm part of the grammar police or extra nosy? "Aspiring anyway," I confess. "I'm doing a story on the dream maker mountain." A thought occurs to me. "Wait, are you here for the rumored good-weather window on La Aguja?"

"Aye." His voice is cold and his gaze avoids mine, fixes into the corner of the tent, giving the merest hint of an indrawn breath.

I place my hand to the tent wall, and the force of the wind presses against my palm. An interesting stroke of luck. I wonder if he'd take part in my story. Landing the position at *Outsider* was a great first step, but the only way to land the paid job means writing a kick-ass feature. I need to do this, to make a name for myself. Otherwise I might live my whole life letting Harper make one for me. I don't want to be the butt of her jokes forever, and if I can't be remarkable, I can build a solid career writing about people who are.

Busting out and asking Rhys to star in my story probably isn't the wisest move. I need to play this just right, and he strikes me as the sort who requires some buttering up first. Better to ask in the morning, after he's had a good night's sleep. "Think the storm will let up tonight?"

"Nah. We're in for it."

"If I hadn't come, you'd have been up here all alone?"

"I like my own company." His tone is still tight.

"Do you really?" I dare another peek at his face. Rhys MacAskill, that name. Something about it niggles my subconscious, a weird déjà vu, like I've heard it before.

He freezes a moment before his low chuckle turns my bones to jelly. My cheeks warm. "No, wait, that didn't come out right." I play up the goofy, wanting to hear that infectious laugh again. "I get that you'd rather be alone, and my presence makes you a little grumpy—"

"Hold up. You're calling me grumpy now?" He rolls his *r*'s with emotion. The effect would be ten kinds of charming if my nerves weren't making me ramble.

"Sorry. I didn't mean it like that. Everything keeps coming out all wrong." I fall over my words in the rush to apologize. He's a grump but not a dick or anything. "You actually rescued me, which makes you kind of a hero—"

"That's enough, lass." His shoulders nearly slam into his ears, and boom, just like that, his playful mood vanishes. Shadows slant over his grim face as he waves a hand, a muscle twitching in his jaw even as he attempts a smile.

I press two fingers against his ever-present forehead furrow, smoothing it out. He jerks in surprise, and I drop my hand, clearing my throat. We might be stuck together, but that's no excuse to get handsy. "In all seriousness though, I should be thanking you. After all, I barged into your tent, got pretty much naked, hogged your sleeping bag, sat on—" There's a book spine gouging the side of my hip. "Hello, what's this?" I pull it out. "*Heart of Darkness.* Whoa, not exactly light campfire reading." I can't resist poking. "The horror! The horror! I had to read this at school and it was basically a slow death by metaphor."

No response, but he doesn't seem impressed by my literary assessment.

A letter falls out onto my stomach. "Give me that." He snatches it and the book, sliding the letter between the back pages and setting it to his side, protective as a dragon guarding his hoard.

"Careful," I mutter. "Keep making that face, it'll get stuck that way."

"I'll take that under advisement," he says with a snort.

*Smart-ass.* His forearm flexes, each muscle clearly defined. *Fine, smart-ass with beautiful arms.* Looks like climbing does a body good. Imagine what it would be like to cling to stone, knowing your survival relied solely upon your own strength and wits. "Do you ever get afraid? When you're up high?"

"Yes," he says simply, before crawling to his knees, literally giving me the shoulder. "I'm going to fix some tea. Want a cuppa?" He moves without waiting for a response. Pots bang and water pours, followed by the low hum of a stove. After a few minutes he's back, and so is his subtle spicy scent, bay rum, seductive and undeniably masculine.

There's some invisible weight settled over him, but why? All I know is that asking him personal questions is akin to tiptoeing over a river of thin ice.

The weight of his arm returns to settle heavily across my lower belly. He places a stainless-steel mug of tea beside me, and I breathe as deeply as my lungs allow. Peppermint vapors are nice, relaxing even. Maybe it's a placebo, but research has proven certain smells decrease stress and that helps reduce inflammation.

I take a tentative sip and almost moan as the warm liquid hits my stomach. "Oh, wow, that's good." I half sit and give him a small smile. "Thank you."

The headlamp leaves his face in shadow but shines directly on his broad bare chest. Dark hair dusts between his defined pecs, sharpening into an arrow that cuts across his abdomen, pointing lower. "Careful now." He frowns at my tremble. "It's hot."

*Yeah, it is.* Goose bumps break out over my arms. Why am I freezing and he's shirtless? "Shit." Tea splashes against my shirt, right on the boob. It burns and oh, God, my nipple peeks through the thin white fabric like someone's rubbed a foggy window to peer outside.

I burrow back into his sleeping bag, hiding the peep show. "I'm a klutz. I should get some rest." I'm not at all tired, and the hard ground has a subtle slant, makes getting comfortable a trick. But maybe I've had enough comfort. Life isn't a Snuggie.

"Do you mind if I keep the light on? I'd like to read for a while yet." He picks up his book and unfolds a bent page.

Yikes, my least favorite habit. "Not a fan of bookmarks?"

"Don't see the point," he mutters. His voice is low, could even be described as velvety. I get that now, hearing him, the whole idea of a velvety voice. Some forward-thinking entrepreneur could package it up as Chanel Number Give It to Me, Baby.

"I can't fold pages," I say. "It hurts my heart."

He arches a brow. "You're a delicate flower."

"I just love books."

His other brow joins its friend. "Me, too."

"I might love them a teeny-tiny bit more." I reach out and run my finger over the page. But it's too late. Once you bend a corner, you can't smooth the crease away.

He regards me curiously. "You speak your mind quite freely."

I peel my eyes from his direct gaze. "No, actually, I don't." It's strange that as much as he's the kind of guy who should intimidate the crap out of me, he doesn't. I don't have a clue what that means.

There's a long pause. I assume he's gone back to his book, but instead a quick glance confirms that he's still staring.

"You look warmer," he says.

"You're really hot." I cringe. "From purely a temperature standpoint."

He props his cheek in his hand. "What you're saying is you don't find me attractive?"

"No!" As if I hadn't feasted on his bare skin with my eyes for the past hour. As if he's not the perfect specimen of the male sex.

"Oh, so you do?" His tone is low, devastatingly gruff.

My lips work soundlessly. Flustered doesn't begin to describe what's happening inside me.

His full lips crook into an unexpected smile. "How's that, then?"

"Sorry?" My nerves, the second hit of Albuterol, and the proximity to a large male with a panty-melting accent is turning my brain to mashed potatoes.

"My attempt at humor," he says with a wink.

He winked? "Oh, right." I give a shaky laugh. "Yes. I'm going to give you a five out of ten there."

"That rated at least a seven point five." He reaches for his book. As he ducks his chin, a thick scar appears on the side of his neck, disappearing into his shaggy dark hair.

My stomach tightens as my smile fades. What happened there?

"Good night, Auden Woods." The cover blocks his face.

I've asked more than enough questions for one night. He's got me rattled, and it's probably better if I try to get some sleep.

"'Night, Rhys." I roll away and tuck my knees against my chest. The tent shakes and the rain falls hard, but here I'm dry, safe, and protected, finding unexpected comfort in the arms of a stranger.

Sleep is seconds from claiming me when strange tingles break out over my body. "Hey, do you feel—" Any other words are crushed as he hurls his large body over mine, sheltering me with his very flesh and bone.

"Don't move," he orders. There's a sharp crack, as if an ancient god flicked a whip across the heavens.

"What was—"

"Lightning, and bloody close, almost upon us." His breath is hot in my ear. "Must have struck right outside."

"Seriously?" No point pretending cool nonchalance. My voice is three octaves too high. Half from terror and half because he's squeezing out the little air left in my lungs. I'm slammed against him hip to hip, chest to chest, helpless as a rag doll. "Lightning? What are the chances?"

Looks like Thor heard my prayer after all, just a little too late, and decided to answer a little too enthusiastically.

# 8

## RHYS

*D*on't panic." I'm telling myself this more than her. Our limbs are tangled and I surround her like a strange cocoon. Her nails dig into my shoulders, deep and desperate. Better to concentrate on that than the feel of her lips, the barely there brush of her mouth at the base of my neck. I push away. "I'm going to investigate, see if it struck a tree. Last thing we need is a great bloody branch crashing down on us."

Auden rises to her knees. "I'm coming, too."

"No." The word comes out gruffer than needed. "You stay here." The tent's walls are whisper thin, but even a little protection is better than none at all.

She sets her jaw. "Look, I can't sit still and wait to transform into a human pancake. Let me try to—"

"Not make a bad situation worse," I snap. Shite, no point biting her head off. None of this is her fault. Not the storm or my own damn physical reactions. "There are no safe places outdoors right now. We're in a wee depression surrounded by taller trees. It's no' ideal, but it'll have to do in a pinch. If there's another bolt, the biggest danger could be from lethal shrapnel."

"Lightning doesn't ever strike the same place twice," she protests, but I'm already unzipping the door and stepping into the howling gale.

Can't see shite. The storm's noise fills me up, shrieking, mocking, groaning. It doesn't want me here and assaults my body accordingly. I swipe my eyes and angle the head torch, trying to see where the bolt hit. If it struck the closest tree, with this wind, it wouldn't take much to send a charred limb crashing down upon our heads. We were lucky, bloody lucky, to be missed, for there's no help out here. No one to call. No one for miles to come running to our aid.

My abdominal muscles tense as my heart kicks into the next gear. I hate bad weather. It's too easy for my thoughts to slip back to that night I lost Cameron on the mountain, far too easy. Invisible snow stings my eyes, ice needling my sockets. Gusts slam me like a punch to the face. Time has a way of passing strangely up at great heights. A second can be an hour or vice versa. The dull pain throbbing across the back of my head was nothing to the way my vocal cords burned as I screamed my brother's name again and again, hearing nothing answer but the mimicking gale.

Who knows? Maybe it's the same wind rushing past now, forever circling the Earth, taunting me.

A hand presses against the small of my back and sends me vaulting forward. "Fuck," I manage, turning. Auden is rugged up in her sodden rain jacket, hood pulled tight around her face, masking everything but those brilliant, haunting blue eyes. "Are you daft? Get back inside."

She hands over my Gore-Tex jacket. "You're shirtless," she shouts to be heard over the raging wind. "Don't you go freezing, OK?"

I sling it on. "Looks like we escaped." My hair is drenched from the rain, and yet small hairs prickle at the nape of my neck.

"Hey." She stares at the sky. "Do you feel that?"

Time slows down. The prickling spreads to the hairs on my arms. I step forward to do what? I have nothing to offer but the protection of my body.

"Oh, shit, shit, shit. Again? Don't we have to get down? Get small?" She grabs my hand and drops like a stone, curling into a ball. Her grasp yanks me off-balance, and I go down, too, seconds before a crash turns the storm to silence. For seconds nothing is audible but ringing in my ears.

Only two thoughts rattle around my brain.

Looks like lightning can strike the same place twice after all.

This girl might have saved my life.

What does this mean? And what debt do I now owe?

———

I open my eyes and it's dawn. I'm in a tent and another face stares into mine, close enough to distinguish each individual eyelash. The world returns in jagged pieces that I'm meant to fashion sense from. A storm. Rain, but not snow. The Andes. Not the Himalayas. Patagonia, not the Karakorum. Arms are wound around my neck. "Fuck." I jerk back, throat constricting.

"You had a nightmare." Auden peers at me with undisguised concern. "I'm not surprised after that crazy storm. Two lightning bolts? What are the chances?"

She held me? What did I do? Or say? I can't let down my guard in front of a stranger, especially not a bloody journalist, even if by some miracle she doesn't know my name or story. A diversion is needed, and fast.

"You a coffee drinker?" I sit and scrub my face, the coarse hair on my jaw rough against my palms. I'm close to sporting a full beard.

"Sure, but—"

"Good. Fair warning, I brew it strong." I slide to the far end of the tent but our legs are still touching.

"That's music to my ears." She stretches with a soft sigh, but holds my gaze. "Bring it." Her dubious expression lets me know she won't let this go easily. Who knows what I said in my sleep?

"Hmph. I doubt you can handle it," I mutter, turning my attention to the food bag. The last thing I need is anyone bearing witness to my tenuous grip on control.

She narrows her eyes with mock ferocity. "You'd be surprised what I can handle."

I bite back an unwilling smile at the fractious tone. She's got a wee bit of strop to her. A feisty lass is the best sort. And she just so happens to be named after the poet who penned some of my favorite verses. Mum's an English teacher who used to make Cameron and me recite poetry by heart, mostly Robert Burns, a bit of Byron, but I liked W. H. Auden best. Mostly because of his "Musée des Beaux Arts," where he writes about Brueghel's famous painting *Landscape with the Fall of Icarus*. How the image perfectly captures the human condition, the way the world continues on despite tragedy.

He describes how a farmer plows his field as a boy falls from the heavens, and it could very well be me and my mates sprawled on a couch, eating cereal while half-watching a refugee crisis unfold on the evening news. Or a stranger reading about me and Cameron on a news site before moving on to celebrity gossip or the day's Nasdaq trading.

"Hey." Auden brushes my shoulder. The touch is so light it's almost nothing at all. "What's up?"

I've been amiss thinking her irises ice-like. They are warm enough to melt the frozen sea inside me.

"What are you thinking about so seriously?"

"Life." My chest is tight, doesn't allow a full breath. "How we're alone in our individual troubles." I need to stay focused. Hard. Inside and out. No cracks. Climbers have a bad rap for being selfish, for walking past others dying on the mountain, to ensure their own success. But those people who talk shite have probably never been to the death zones, the places on Earth where it becomes impossible to breathe and your organs shut down. Death comes easily in those high places while people below continue on, pausing only to cast judgment on our actions above.

The rain is down to a gentle patter. The wind still comes in strong gusts, but less frequently. I clear my throat. "The storm is ending."

"You're not OK, are you?" she murmurs.

"I'm good. Fine." Not that I tell anyone anything, a journalist least of all.

In the soft dawn light, her features are more distinct, and a tremor quickens through me. Auden has the kind of face you need to look at twice, and then a third time. On their own, her features aren't particularly interesting, but combine them and the effect is extraordinary. A face I won't easily forget.

"Hey," she says. "I know we're not friends, or even really acquaintances, but I need to ask you something. And it's the kind of something that you could blow off."

"Go ahead." She's going to ask regardless of my answer.

"I don't think you're fine at all." Her fingers graze my knee, and I flinch. "In fact, you're really shaken up over something more than that crazy storm."

"Let it go."

"But I—"

"I said leave it." And there I am, raising my voice to a woman. Mum must be at home, sensing a disturbance in the force. I should apologize and—

"Knock it off." She says the words slowly, as if she's trying on a fierce tone. It works for her, as if she's channeled Mum, except that's a thought tugging me in two different directions. I love and respect that hard-nosed woman who raised me something fierce, but I've also apparently struck up a mad sort of fancy for this girl.

My pause is fuel to her fire. "I spent the last hour holding on while you thrashed about. It was like wrestling a crocodile."

There's a question in her eyes. One I can't begin to answer.

The silence is long. "I never asked you to do that."

"You wouldn't wake up. I tried. I shook you. I was—" Her voice cracks, and she sniffles. "I got a little scared."

I hate this, hate that she saw me as a broken, worthless thing. "I don't even know you." My voice is no better than a snarl. "You wandered up here off the main trail, out of your element, irresponsible, without a bloody clue what you were in for. So thanks for your opinions, but let's leave it there."

"Has anyone ever told you, that you…that you…that you can be a real asshole?" She says the word in a rush, eyes wide, as if she's surprised herself.

"Aye, that and much worse."

She gives another of her long and searching stares, a wee witch, rooting out my secrets.

"You know what I think?"

"No," I say. "And I don't care." I use my size to my advantage, taking up space in the tent. She doesn't quell though. In fact, she pushes me hard, right in the chest. I'm not expecting that, and I fall backward.

She doesn't anticipate my capitulation and goes with me, smacking against my chest with a thud. "Don't ever try that," she says, not missing a beat.

"What?"

She raises a warning finger. "Intimidating me. You're…you're not even that good at it."

Now it's my turn to stare. My temper is notorious. So why doesn't this girl budge, give an inch? It is like the wind carried her here. It won't stay to torment me, so it plonked her behind to do the dirty work.

My legs are splayed open, and since I get hot when I sleep, I'm shirtless. She's wrapped in my thermal top, too big for her petite frame. The neckline gapes, reveals the line of her clavicle, the dip of her shoulder.

I set my hands to her hips, to move her away. I get the first part of the job done, but the second proves trickier to execute. "Mind shoving off?" As if she can move free when I've locked her in this grip against me.

She purses her lips, her head tilting a fraction. "Here's what I think. You're all bark and no bite."

"Careful, lass. I bite." My fingers clasp her a little harder.

She takes hold of my hair as defiance flashes in her gaze. Closer, she comes. Her quickened breath warms my face. There's a strangled noise. Shit, that's me. A freckle punctuates the corner of her top lip. She bypasses my mouth and gives my jaw a sweetly sharp nip. "Bet I can bite harder."

I don't move for a long moment, even after she wiggles free. When I sit, she's unraveled her plait and is finger combing the wild snarls as if nothing has happened. And nothing *has* happened, even though my heart is doing a damn good job of bursting from my chest.

Strange the way nothing can feel like everything.

# 9

## *AUDEN*

ancy a wee dram?" Rhys unearths a battered silver flask from under a lightweight down jacket. "A sip," he says, noting my blank expression. "I don't know about you, but I need a drink."

"Somehow I don't think that's orange juice, is it?" It's amazing how my voice comes out light and natural. Not like a person who just bit him. Jesus Jones on toast. What was I thinking? There's no telltale mark through all that thick jaw scruff, but the taste of his skin lingers on my tongue.

*Simmer down, girlie. You can't go around gnawing hot men like cobs of corn, no matter how tasty.*

"Talisker whiskey, single malt." His Adam's apple rises with a swallow before he thrusts me the flask. "Go on; try it. This is one of the world's finest whiskeys, made in Skye."

"Sky?"

"Isle of Skye. Where I was born..." He trails off, his gaze faraway.

I take the flask and sniff the opening. Hard alcohol isn't my thing, but it seems rude to refuse when he's obviously having a moment. Besides, a stiff drink might steady my jacked-up nerves.

My sip is tentative, but no matter, my esophagus revolts. I half swallow, half cough the searing liquid, twitching with an inadvertent shiver. Pretty sure some of that poison water travels into my lungs. My whole chest burns. I clear my throat and need to do it twice more before speech is possible. "I'm sure your island is lovely and everything, but you might need a better method to take a trip down memory lane."

"Aye, Skye's lovely, all right. I haven't been back for a long time now." He closes his eyes, and my thumb itches to trace along the fringe of his dark lashes. They are a shade lighter than his hair, which is only a shade lighter than black. There's no trace of a differentiating highlight anywhere. The thick strands gleam like a rich, polished ebony.

He's still talking. "...a land of razor-sharp ridgelines and dark water. The air holds a certain strange magic, forces your awareness. In such a place you never forget you're alive." He breaks off, eyes snapping open, locking on my own. "What is it?"

"I've never met anyone like you," I whisper.

He makes a dismissive noise.

My mouth drops open for a second. "Did you just snort?"

He shrugs.

Indignation douses my lust. Good, probably better this way. "Wow. I tell you something nice and you snort. How about that?" I reach for the corner of his tent and do a clothes check. My shirt is still damp but wearable. Happily, my pants are quick drying. I haul those under the sleeping bag, wiggling into the legs, tugging them over my hips. "One second you are reciting poetry, and the next you're making that frowny face."

"Frowny face?"

"Yes, that one." I wag my finger. "There it comes again."

"I'm not good with people," he says, resigned. "They don't like me." His brow creases. "My disposition is…"

"Not awesome?" I shrug with exaggerated wide-eyed innocence.

He doesn't notice, or more likely ignores, my attempt at sarcasm. "Mum says I can be unbearable." Despite his sullenness, the loneliness in his eyes beckons me. I don't buy what he says, about preferring solitude, for a second. He hasn't run away from the world to be alone, but because he feels he has no other option. "My brother, Cameron, he…Well, some people bring light, you ken? And others…don't." He glances at the ceiling, growing still. "Hear that?"

"No. Nothing." Except for the uncertain judder of my heart, silence reigns supreme.

"Exactly. The storm's over," he says abruptly, and in a flash he's unzipped the tent and crawled outside.

My tongue still tingles from the whiskey, and the rest of me tingles from a confusing confluence, desire and annoyance fighting for supremacy. I take a deep breath, close my eyes and listen, assess my body—still a slight catch on the exhalation, but nothing to fret about. I take a few puffs off my inhaler and glance around. For the first time since climbing into Rhys's tent, I'm alone.

Is there a wayward clue lying about to help define the person with whom I've just spent the strangest night of my life? Not really. Hints are few and far between. There's his book, the ever-cheerful *Heart of Darkness*. A pair of black-framed, polarized sunglasses. A red toothbrush with half the handle sawn off. A GoPro camera thingy that can mount on helmets and record live-action footage.

Nothing that gives me the secret of him.

Rhys pops his head back in. "Hey."

"Hey."

"Hungry?"

My belly rumbles as soon as he asks the question. I forgot dinner last night, and after such a big day yesterday, my body is not-so-subtly reminding me of the fact. "Starving."

"Don't suppose you'd want a hot breakfast."

"Actually, that sounds amazing, thank you."

I exit the tent and wobble into my mud-caked boots, noticing the view for the first time. "Whoa." My arms drop to my sides, and I'm pretty sure my jaw ends up somewhere near my knees.

He gives me a knowing look. "Didn't have a chance to see much of the surrounds last night, eh?"

"Not a thing." We're standing in a large amphitheater. Clouds cling to the highest peaks in a thin, translucent veil. I grew up in the mountains—they are my de facto scenery—but never have I experienced such a raw landscape firsthand. There is a different rhythm here, a greater force at work. A twisted old tree on the rise above us is scorched with a thin black line. Danger came close last night. A little too close for comfort. This hike isn't a simple walk in the woods. Civilization is far away, and the surrounding country is undeniably wild. It's impossible to restrain a shiver at the idea of continuing alone.

"The place stirs the blood, aye?"

"Yeah," I say, becoming aware of his proximity. If I move my arm a centimeter—two max—I'll graze his wrist. Heat licks between my legs. I'm, ahem, stirred in more ways than one. "So." I clap my hands and step to a safer distance. "What's for breakfast?"

"Porridge." He saunters to a flat rock where the camp stove is lit, checks the pot, his wide stance allowing his pants to hug the firm outline of his ass.

"Porridge?" I wrinkle my nose even as I lick my lower lip. *Look away. That ass is not on the menu.* Neither is bacon, eggs, and toast, but hey, a girl can dream a little.

"Don't sound too excited."

"There's trail mix in my bag. I might just stick with that." Why did I think of eggs? Now Denver omelets dance through my head, hand in hand with banana bread French toast and Rhys doused in maple syrup. He's not the friendliest sort, but there is something about him that's making me hungrier for more than breakfast.

"Nuts and raisins won't warm you up." He idly scratches beneath his navel, revealing a tantalizing view of a sharply defined V-line muscle. Two veins run over the top, disappearing into the waistband of black boxer briefs.

I volunteer as tribute to discover their end point.

"Trust me," he says. "I make it good."

*Oh, I bet you do.* Time to dig my sunglasses from my vest pocket and shove them on before it's all too obvious that my mind is floating down the gutter. I never had thoughts like that about Brett, ever. In hindsight, maybe that was a big huge warning sign, or is horndogness a side effect of being on the rebound?

I clear my throat. "Is there a wrong way to cook porridge? I mean, how hard can it be to boil oats?"

He makes a derisive noise. "There are more wrong ways than right ones."

"OK." I screw up my nose.

"It's the backbone of many a sturdy Scot. Mum raised me on the stuff."

*Guess it does a body good.*

He grabs a bag and sniffs inside. "Ah, love that smell."

I cough into my fist. "Weirdo."

"You can eat 'em raw, too, but it's parching."

"Boil 'em up, Scotty."

He gives me a weird look.

*Awesome. Way to whip out the random sci-fi references.* "*Star Trek?*" I mumble. "Scotty is Scottish and, er, never mind. I've got to take a quick walk." I need to use the bathroom, but declaring an intention to pee seems too intimate. But I need to. Badly.

"Don't wander far," he says, shaking his head. "This will cook up quick."

I check to make sure my boots are laced up properly and to hide the fact I'm blushing yet again. He's going to think I have a blood pressure problem. "OK, I'll be back soon."

I meander through the trees, scouting for a well-hidden spot to relieve myself. A hollow behind a tree has decent privacy and a distinct lack of mud. I undo my pants and crouch.

I'm finishing when a furtive scuffle and low woof sends me leaping to my feet. "What the hell?"

A snout pokes through the bush, and I scream, turning and tearing in the direction I came. Branches scratch my face. There's a sting. I swipe, and a streak of blood spreads over my palm.

I stumble around a boulder and slam straight into another rock, this one of a warm, human variety.

"What happened?" Rhys braces my shoulders. "You screamed."

My hastily hiked pants drop to my ankles.

He glances down, eyes twinkling. "Last night didn't seem quite the time to mention it, but those are quite the knickers."

"A gentleman wouldn't have looked." I tug my pants back up, this time fastening the button.

"I'm no' a gentleman, love." A gleam highlights the yellow in his irises, giving him a wild, predatory edge. In another blink it's gone, back to business. "Now, what scared you so?"

"A wolf. There's a freaking wolf in the bushes."

He gives a dismissive shake of the head. "There aren't any wolves left in these mountains."

I thrust back my shoulders. Who made him a wildlife biology expert? "There's one back there in the bushes that disagrees with you."

"That was a fox," he says with a tone of finality. "One hunts in this area. Did it happen to have a black band of fur over its eyes?"

"Yeah." My shoulders deflate a little. Guess he does have the upper hand here.

"Zorro."

"You named him?" I didn't take Rhys as the kind of guy who befriends woodland animals, but the idea has a certain appeal.

"He's friendly enough." And then he traces my cheekbone.

*What the what?*

My stomach flip-flops as his finger travels the branch scratch from my frantic forest run. I lean in to him, not much, just a fraction, and he moves like I've burned him.

For a moment we stand here, both breathing a little too fast. Goose bumps pepper the base of my neck.

"If you've had enough excitement, are you prepared to experience the finest porridge this side of the Atlantic?" He abruptly turns away, walking briskly in the direction of camp, apparently assuming I'll follow, which I do, albeit with a sigh. My body aches for more of his touch, and face it, that's not going to happen.

He has a graceful, unconscious way of navigating loose rock and uneven terrain. I'm a water buffalo in comparison, tripping and stomping in the rear. With the sun out, I'm clear to leave after breakfast, but the whole point of this little expedition is to profile climbers and Mr. Scottish Congeniality Runner-Up here could be the perfect guinea pig.

"Hey," I say, dialing my brightest smile. "Do you mind if I ask you a question?"

He seems impervious to my charms. "Depends."

*Play it cool. Don't blow the shot.* "So...um, sticking my journalistic hat on for a second. I'm doing this story on La Aguja, a series of climber character profiles."

His gaze flies to my face. "Go on."

Whoa, what crawled up his butt? "I want to learn more about why people have come to face off with the mountain, whether it's to reach the summit or if there's more at stake." Great. I'm officially rambling.

His lids narrow to slits. "The legend, you mean?"

"Yes, uh, you know," I stammer, unsure where his hostility is originating from. "The whole part about attaining your heart's desire."

"No."

"That's not why you are doing it?"

"I don't talk to the press," he says firmly. Is it my imagination, or is he paler? "Ever."

"Oh." I keep my shoulders from slumping, just. "Why?"

"Because." Pain etches his features. We're dancing close to the mysterious edge of what he's able to bear.

I could ask a million more questions but bite my tongue. The less I speak, the more he seems to say. "OK, noted. My journalistic hat is coming off now. I'm packing it away. It's just that I know next to nothing about climbing, so I wanted to pick your brain."

He gives me another long look before dropping his shoulders. I'm not sure why, but I get the sense I passed some secret test. He keeps walking. "People dream of being the first to thread the needle, ken."

"Excuse me?" His pace is faster now and hard to match.

"The rock is called The Needle."

"Right, *La Aguja*. I speak Spanish."

"At the top there's a keyhole formation. It's supposed to be easier for a man to enter heaven than to pass through the eye of the needle." His smile is more than a little ghostly. "I'm no' getting into heaven, so…"

"It sounds like a death wish." Rhys is alive, strong, so vital. "I can't fathom you risking your life for what amounts to a fleeting moment on top of a rock."

His jaw tightens. "You don't understand. This climb is important."

"Why don't you go with a team at least? Safety in numbers and all that jazz."

"The legend's clear on that point." His gaze sweeps over my face, pausing not quite long enough to focus before turning to regard the empty sky. "It says if you stand on La Aguja's summit alone, you'll find the thing you most desire."

"What do you hope waits there?"

But we're back at camp, and he motions for me to take a seat on a sun-warmed rock. "My turn to ask the questions. What about you? What do you do?" He looks over, stirring the pot. "When not causing trouble, that is?"

I sit and rest my chin in my hand. "You're excellent at evading."

He focuses his attention on the spoon. Is it my imagination, or does his jaw set a little tighter? Hard to tell under the scruff.

"Fine. Never mind," he mutters. "Sorry I bothered."

"Hey, I was just kidding." I anticipated a smart-ass retort, but his sudden retreat gives me whiplash.

"Should I be laughing?" he asks. His merino wool top fits him like a second skin as he flexes his back. I don't have a clue what the muscles beneath his shoulder blades are called. I didn't even know those particular ones existed.

"You're confusing." I make my hand teeter-totter. "Hot. Cold. Nice. Not so nice. Talkative. Silent."

The muscles in his neck cord as if I'm tap-dancing across the last shred of his self-control. He's got this wounded hangdog posture going on, like he expects to be kicked, so snarls, but really he wants a good bed and a scratch behind the ears.

I also might be going a little insane.

"You don't scare me. I have a sister," I say.

"What's that supposed to mean?"

"In my case? It means I have experience fighting dirty."

"Do you, now?" He faces me head-on, raises an eyebrow, and his tongue skims the corner of his mouth, a gesture that's meant to look aggravating but is somehow appealing.

That's him really, in a nutshell.

His tawny gaze drills through me as he reclines against the cooking rock, and a prickling awareness radiates through my spine. God, look at the way his forearm flexes as he grips the small hold.

I'm testing him, teasing like a thirteen-year-old with her first crush. It would be far more advisable to return my gaze to the surrounding mountains, but I can't help ogling his obvious strength, or letting my thoughts explore what it would feel like to be gripped against all that hard male body.

He seems to sense the direction of my thoughts. "Get a good look?"

For once the burning in my lungs has nothing to do with asthma. He idly circles his thumb over a little nob of granite. The gesture is nothing in reality, but the inadvertently sexy motion is making me wet. What if I stand, step closer? There's a part of me wondering that as much as I'm driving him crazy, his covert stares indicate perhaps I can use his hermitage to my advantage.

He's clearly been alone for some time.

+

He's a guy.

= There's a decent chance he'll go for me just out of sheer physical desperation.

My body suggests this demeaning fantasy is the best idea I've had since hiking into the national park. When else will I get another chance at this kind of opportunity? *God, God, God.* I wrap my hands around my knees.

He comes closer and squats. Every movement he makes is purposeful, deliberate.

I tip back and almost lose my balance, reach for his arm to steady myself.

His grins as my fingers lock onto his biceps, teeth white against his dark scruff. "Am I making you swoon, lass?"

Bark from the tree behind me prickles against my back. Shit. Nowhere to retreat.

He leans forward until only inches separate us.

"I don't know what you're talking about," I rasp, gripping him tighter.

"Fine." He sounds smug, as if he's scored a point in whatever strange game we are playing. "Like a taste?"

His mouth is wide and expressive, encircled by rough beard. He'd feel soft against me, but also coarse. My breath comes faster, a little ragged. I release my grip and touch the side of my cheek. "Taste?"

He brings a spoon from behind his back. "Of porridge." He smirks at my obvious flustered state. "You've a filthy mind."

"You bring it out in me." I force myself to hold his gaze while opening my mouth. The porridge is hot, creamy. "Oh, wow. That's actually delicious."

"Told you." He pops the spoon in his mouth, runs his tongue over the concave metal, the same place I just licked.

My heart thumps hard enough he can probably hear it. "Are we fighting or flirting?"

"Maybe a bit of both." He stares at my mouth with scorching eyes. Holy shit. That's an "I'm going to kiss you" look.

My entire body flashes hot. *Do it.* The urge hits me with something approaching violence. My brain is a dizzy fog. *Do it. Do it. Do it.* A shaft of light breaks from the clouds, hits my face, and I sneeze.

Gah—and just like that, the moment's gone.

"You'll have good weather for your hike out," he says, standing, squinting at the sky.

So much for my powers of telepathy.

"Yes." The sun warms my face, even as a frustrated coldness settles in my belly. I'm being ridiculous. Fighting, flirting, it might be a bit of fun. He seems to need some lighthearted distraction, and I certainly wouldn't mind a little rebound action, but I'm first and foremost here to advance my career. And this thing sparking between us isn't going to lead any further.

It's certainly not foreplay.

# 10

# RHYS

*A*uden scrapes the inside of the pot. "Oh no." She peers down. "All gone!"

Watching this girl eat is a rare pleasure, not to mention a serious fucking turn-on. She takes each bite seriously, making these sexy, appreciative noises while her eyes are half-closed. It sounds like she's having an orgasm in her mouth.

I swallow. Hard. "For someone who claims to despise porridge, you cleaned up." It's a wonder I manage to think; rational thought is all but impossible. Something restless roams within me, hungry and merciless.

"What can I say?" She gives a quick grin. "You made it just right."

"Happy you enjoyed, Goldilocks." I take the pan to wash up. Of all the girls to finally get a hard-on for, it's a bloody novice journalist. Somewhere above the clouds, some snarky god is no doubt having a good laugh. "Sure you're not Scottish?"

She shakes her head, licking her lips. "English and German, a hint of Norwegian."

A muscle in my cheek tenses at that flash of pink tongue. "Maybe that's the link. The Vikings settled in Scotland."

"We could be long-lost relatives?"

"I hope not," I mutter, more to myself than her.

She puzzles that a moment, and a blush creeps up her rounded cheeks before she tosses her head. "How do you know 'Goldilocks and the Three Bears' anyway? Isn't that American?"

I chuckle hoarsely, and the unfamiliar sound surprises me. "You're joking, yes?"

Her features are gentle, no sign of sharp cheekbones, and her chin ends in a small heart-shape point that appears whittled to a softer edge. Only her eyes and brows belie the easy, cute, bordering-on-adorable topography of her face. Together they give an impression of boldness, having a keener edge, being quick to assess a situation or form an opinion.

"The 'Three Bears' is from Britain, written by the poet Robert Southey."

Her brow knits. "How do you know that?"

"Surprised you don't." I stretch, feigning relaxation. It's hard to resist a smile when smoke is practically visible coming out of her ears.

This back-and-forth teasing is uncharted territory. Girls normally approach me, and if I'm free enough, between trips, I take them up on an uncomplicated fuck. Physically, they get off. That's simple enough. Years of placing careful handholds has its advantages off the mountain. But I'm not made for the give-and-takes that relationships require. My moods trend darker. Laughter doesn't come to me easily.

Cameron was different, more jovial than the average climber. Mum says he's "a lover, not a fighter." He fell for half a dozen girls before Amelia snapped him up. I'm not sure why I've always held back. I've never been at ease with myself; I'm restless, hungry for the next adventure. I'm too bloody selfish, hoarding my passion, myself, keeping everything for climbing.

I don't have anything left over.

I don't *want* anything left over.

She arches a brow. "Don't mess with me, buster." My pulse increases because that's exactly what I do want. And that inclination will make everything messy. Chaos is treacherous and unpredictable.

What I need is a return to order, to routine. The sooner Auden is out of the valley, the better. I turn my attention to rinsing the porridge pot, and then go to the tent to help her pack, even as she protests, "Hey, I'm more than able to do that."

"Watch and learn." I set up her backpack. "It's about how you balance the weight inside, ken? Last night you had things placed all wrong. Don't make it harder to carry than it needs to be."

"Fine." She crouches beside me, unzipping her vest. She still hasn't put her bra back on, and her breasts are full, round, large enough that it would be a challenge to span them, even with splayed fingers, but I'd be willing to give it a good long try.

"Thank you," she says after I finish. "Seriously, I appreciate the quick lesson. I've never hiked on my own before."

"Got to say, Patagonia is one hell of a place to start." I bunch my hand into a fist, gouge the knuckle against the ground, but the grating pain does little to quell the tantalizing promise of a moment ago. I hate to see her leave, and that means she needs to disappear as soon as possible. Before the wall inside me begins to give way.

"Go big or go home, right?" She flips her long plait over her shoulder and fiddles with the end while avoiding my eyes.

If she doesn't want to talk, I don't have a right to press. She makes me curious, and curiosity distracts. *Remember the return to order.* Better I focus on the climb ahead, the one that's going to suck every last ounce of my reserve strength. "You have your inhalers?"

"Yes, Mom." She pats her pocket with a wry grin. "Go Go, Albuterol. But it's all downhill from here back to the main trail. Plus, the temperature is warming up."

"Yes." I cinch and then buckle her pack. "All set. Let me take it outside for you while you get changed."

I wait in front of the tent, eyes closed, all my attention directed to the noises inside the tent, the soft slide of fabric against flesh painting an image in my mind of how she looks: breast, ass, the slope of her inner thighs.

She climbs through the vestibule, and I hold her backpack as she threads her arms into the straps. I clip her chest buckle, a show of chivalry that in truth is the only way I can politely graze the tits that are driving me daft.

"Thanks." She rocks back and forth testing the feel. Jesus, even in her bra, they give a little bounce. "Hey, you're right. This does feel more comfortable."

"Good." I strangle on the word.

"Well . . . guess I should be going?" I don't understand the look she's giving. It's as if there's a promise there and all I need to do is meet her halfway.

Better to step back to safety. "Good-bye, then."

Her smile doesn't waver even as the invitation extinguishes in her eyes. "Thanks for, you know, saving my life. Guess I'll see you at the climbing camp?"

"Aye. More than likely. I'm going to train in the valley a few more days before heading over. It's quieter here, less of a scene." I swallow the impulse to ask her to stay with me. Odd, this feeling she conjures in me, a sort of protective rush. Odder still that I don't mind it.

She hovers a second, as if she's going to hug me. And terrifyingly, a part of me wants nothing more.

"It's weird, right?" She crinkles her nose. "Saying good-bye to someone you might never see again."

"Shaking hands is the usual way." I stick mine out.

"I can do that." She grips mine. Her hand is so small in comparison. "I'm not sure if it was nice to meet you, but it was something."

"Aye, something indeed. Stay safe, all right?" Should I be letting her go on her own? Suddenly I'm as nervous as a fretting nana.

"I really do hope to see you again…at the camp…" Her cheeks flush as her voice trails away. I don't mean to, but I end up watching her go, compelled to see her off. She stops, turns, and her smile hits me right in the guts.

I find myself responding with a great shite-eating smile.

Then she vanishes, swallowed by the forest.

I linger another moment, my smile fading. The wind rustles and birds call to one another. The great glacier at the base of the valley rumbles in an imitation of the thunder from last night as I trudge back to the tent. A trail run is in order. A good hard one. Maybe followed by a bouldering session. Get my body and mind back in control.

But first I need bloody relief.

I duck inside the tent, rip off my shirt, and settle on the sleeping bag. It smells like girl, of Auden, her rainy, wild scent. I free my cock, inhaling as the weight of my shaft settles heavily in my palm. When I brush my thumb over my head, my hips levitate. Fuck, it's been a while. I slide to my base and squeeze, sucking in a sharp breath as I thicken even more. For a moment I do nothing but grip, distill my world to the pulse against my palm, the keen shudder of expectancy.

I begin to stroke myself the regular way, hard and urgent. I like it a little rough, something most girls don't manage. For a wank, I'm better alone, can bring myself off quickly, without much fanfare, but as pressure builds, another inclination also rises, an urge to slow, linger on the sensations. My mind wanders to Auden's fucking knickers, the "Take Me Off Right Meow," and an unexpected groan rips from my chest.

I don't make noise during sex. Take my pleasure quietly. What the fuck is it about those absurd kitten knickers that nearly brings me off straightaway? I drag my free hand through my hair, seizing a handful, and force my head to the side, my neck muscles cording, abs flexed with anticipation of what's to come. Auden was sent as a cosmic joke, a test to my resolve, one I'm failing quickly.

As hard as I want to come, I continue to work myself in measured strokes, base to tip, let the pressure build in my sac. Strange how easy it is to recall her little details. The heavy weight of her breasts molded through my shirt, the way her nipples strained against the fabric. The glimpse of the dandelion on her stomach, the way the ink slipped from sight, teasing me. The few places I touched, those inches of precious real estate, were all soft and yielding. My fingers slid over her supple skin, foreign to my own hard ridges and planes. She had a body I could sink into, bury myself alive.

The sleeping bag crinkles against my face, her lingering fresh scent intensifies, and the orgasm slams me from nowhere, any remaining coherent thoughts obliterated in a rush that leaves me gasping, a vague headache pulsing in my temples.

"Rhys? You OK?"

Auden? *Fuck.* I glance at my sticky abdomen. "What're you doing here?" I grab an old wool sock to wipe myself clean, yank up my trousers. *She's back. She's back. She's back.* Even in my panic, my heart beats to the exultant shout in my brain.

There's a great stramash outside. Twigs crackle. Stones crunch.
How had I not heard a thing?

"The stream's too high." Her voice is strange. I have known her
for all of twelve hours, but I can tell this is her uncertain, nervous
tone.

*Shite.* Does she have any idea what I've been up to? No. No.
That's impossible.

I crawl outside, and her face is averted, body language all off.

*Shite. She knows.* Bloody hell, I wanked to her and she knows.

"I tried to cross the stream, but it was so high, the trail submerged." Her expression is frustratingly unreadable. "Couldn't
even hop across the rocks. There was one log, but it was mossy and
that seemed dangerous, so I—"

"You made a smart call." Here's to hoping my feigned indifference is believable. I'm happy she's back, and while I shouldn't be,
that's how it is. "The waters will retreat soon enough, but it's wise
you waited. We can hike to the camp together. It's better for you to
have someone to travel with. You've a rare knack for attracting trouble." Something we have in common, but I'm still stupidly happy
she won't be going at it alone.

"Asthma, malfunctioning tents, and lightning, oh my." She
worries a stone with the toe of her boot, unwilling to meet my gaze.
"You sure that would be OK? I don't want to be annoying or force
you into babysitting duties while you're stuck here."

I don't mention that I could get out of the valley without breaking a sweat. No big challenge to scale one of the walls, cross on the
glacier, or balance over the raging creek on a downed log. But better
to go the safer route while she's under my care. At least that's what
I tell myself. We'll wait for the trail to open up for her sake, and sod
it, because I want to spend more time with her.

*Idiot.*

"I want you...your company, I mean. Haven't had a good argument in the last five minutes."

She cocks her head. "Did you hurt yourself?"

"Sorry?"

"When I walked up," she mumbles. "Thought I heard you shout."

*While coming like a high-speed train.* "I was careless. Snapped my finger in a carabiner." I need to distract her, and I glance around for inspiration. Mountains, mountains, and more mountains. Good enough. "I'm thinking of going for a wee explore to pass the time."

"Really?" Again her voice. I can't read minds, but she's off. "You mean like a climb?" She stares at my equipment with the oddest expression.

I'm reading too much into everything. It's my own guilt. Cameron always said I'd make an excellent Catholic.

"I can't even tie knots," Auden rambles. "Can barely tie my shoes."

"Knots? Knots are good fun." I bend and grab rope, tying a figure-eight knot on one end. I'm being quite the show-off, as if this will impress her. "Surely you can manage that?"

"Um." She turns it over. "Yeah, probably not."

"Here. I'll help." I undo it quickly and settle my hands over hers. Her shoulders jerk, and I realize mine do, too, the same exact moment our skin presses against each other's. "First you do this, and then tuck it through here and pull tight."

"You're quite an expert." She lowers her sunglasses, hiding any clue to her thoughts. "Guess that's one of the perks of dating a mountaineer. Rope play."

Look at that blush. Yeah. There's no doubt she knows that I rubbed one out in my tent. If we're in this uncomfortable situation, fuck it. I allow my gaze to take its time running over her sweet body, lingering where I please. "You have a dirty mind."

"Maybe a little, but a clean criminal record." She gives me an uneasy smile and passes back the rope. "Trust me, I'm as vanilla as a cupcake."

No idea what she's talking about.

"Vanilla. You know." She smooths an invisible wisp of hair from her forehead. "Like not kinky. I mean, I've never even..." She ducks her head and lowers her voice into a deep, exaggerated voice-over. "No one wants to hear about your sex life, Auden."

"I—"

"No. Sorry. That was way too far. Told you my filter is non-existent."

I wouldn't mind hearing more about her sex life. Well, not the ins and outs; more what she likes. She's a perfect blend of cute and feisty, an ideal combination. My physical responses are simple biology at work. The stream rising could be a sign—the gods giving me a chance not to be a chump and blow my shot.

She's not part of my plan, but hearing her find pleasure, her blue eyes glazing while I bring her off, aye, might be worth the detour.

I drop the rope and kick it to the side. Auden and I have the day, alone, in a beautiful valley, cut off from the world at large, without any strings. This I can do, a short-term way to forget everything, if only for a few fiery seconds.

But that's it. That's as far as this can go.

Tempting as it seems, I can't be tied to anyone again.

# 11

## *AUDEN*

*R*hys hauls himself in pull-ups from a nearby tree branch, shirtless, very sans shirt. Every few seconds, he raises and lowers a body that looks like a slide from a human anatomy PowerPoint or a Renaissance sculpting class. If Leonardo da Vinci were here, he'd knuckle bite over this perfect male specimen. I'm tempted to do it anyway except my brain is about to explode.

*MacAskill. MacAskill. Holy shit. Rhys MacAskill. Brother of Cameron MacAskill.*

He'd even shouted Cameron's name in his sleep, but I was in such a messed-up headspace that I didn't connect the dots. His name had sounded familiar. All the plot points were there, but I was too shaken by the asthma attack and the overbearing presence of *him*. Once I calmed down and stood, hypnotized on the banks of the engorged stream, the trail submerged under rushing water, the déjà vu linked to his name washed away.

I knew it had sounded familiar.

*Rhys freaking MacAskill. What are the chances? Life has basically handed me a gift-wrapped present and I was almost too dumb to realize it.*

*Outsider* ran a cover story on the Cameron MacAskill saga this summer. The story had all the right components, one of those larger-than-life survival tales everyone reads, comments on, and expects to be made into a movie within a year or two, like that one about the trapped climber in Utah who sawed off his own arm with a pocketknife.

In this case, two brothers were involved in a horrific climbing accident in the Himalayas. One cut the other loose, dropping him to his supposed death.

That was Rhys. He's the guy who cut the rope, the villain who cast his brother into an abyss to save himself. At least that's what everyone says.

I roll my eyes to the sky and let loose a sound that sits between a huff and a groan. Time to stick my tongue back in my mouth, hike up my big-girl panties, and figure out what the hell I'm going to do.

"Want me to set up a slackline?"

I startle at the sound of his lilting accent. "Slackline?" It's hard to maintain eye contact. I've stumbled straight into a serious doozy, a game changer, a career-advancing situation. Imagine scoring an exclusive feature with one of the most notorious mountain climbers in history? With such a coup, there's no doubt *Outsider* would yank me straight from internship anonymity and fast-track me into their full-time position and I'd prove once and for all that I can exist outside of Harper's long shadow.

If my memory serves, no reporter has gained a single comment from Rhys. Granted, I hadn't followed the story super closely, but I do recall vague details, like the photograph of the two brothers.

Rhys was dark, his brother fair. Rhys didn't sport a beard then, and his hair was clipped much shorter.

I close my eyes, in part wishing to recall every last scant detail from the story, but at the same time, desperate to act natural, to not give a hint everything has changed. When I first barged into his tent, after we exchanged names, he visibly relaxed after I proved ignorant of his notoriety. If I mention anything that reveals I've strung two and two together, I'm not going to get four. Instead it will be a complete and total shutdown.

No wonder he was wary the second I mentioned I was a journalist.

So what's my next move going to be?

I don't know this guy well, but it doesn't take a psychology degree to know he isn't holed up in a remote South American valley because he's eager to share his side of the story. My heart thumps so loudly that he'll hear the dim pounding if I stand any closer.

"…like tightrope walking," he's saying.

I try to reassemble my features to make it appear I'm paying avid attention to his slacklining chitchat.

"Except the tension's not rigid, ken? More stretching and bouncing, like a trampoline except skinny, long, and drawn out. I could anchor some webbing between two trees. It's good fun." He's facing out over the valley, his profile rugged, but he doesn't resemble any sort of murderous monster. I've looked in his eyes, and while they can be distant, they aren't cold or calculating. Why did he cut the rope? I've devoted more than a few hours to concocting revenge schemes for Harper, but I wouldn't abandon her in a storm, leave her to freeze to death. Is it a good idea to have agreed to travel with him? Hard to say, hard to think anything except *a story.*

*A story. I have a story. He could be my story. If I get it out of him, my career is made.*

"Good fun doesn't sound like snapping a wrist or giving myself a concussion." I can do this, right? Keep up the banter we've established as our de facto conversation until I've figured out how to play the situation.

I'm reeling from shock, but there's a change within him, too. He's different from when I left half an hour ago. He prowls the campsite with restless energy, doing pull-ups, kicking around a Hacky Sack. I'm not sure if it's my unexpected return or if this is his normal state when not caged in a tent.

"Don't let me keep you from doing what you'd normally get up to." Jesus, I sound like a director. *Pretend I'm not here. Act natural for the camera. Let me observe you in your natural habitat.* It kind of makes me hate myself.

*Who are you, Rhys MacAskill? What happened to you on that mountain?*

"All right, then." He links his hands behind his back and stretches out his shoulders. "Let's go for a scramble."

"Scramble?" The word comes out clipped, sharp, like I'm guilty of something.

"You've a better offer?"

*How about star fishing on the ground and slowing my frenzied journalist heart?*

"There." He points to a steep scree slope. "We'll get a good view from that vantage." He glances back. "You up for that?"

I took my steroid inhaler this morning; everything seems under control except my nerves. "I'll bring the Albuterol just in case, but if I go slow, I should be OK." That's a much more even tone. Better.

"I'll grab us a snack."

"You think about food a lot."

"I'm always hungry," he answers dryly even as his lips lift in a smile.

How does he manage to do that? He makes simple things sound so dirty. I can't afford to be writhing. I need to figure out my next move. Jesus. Is this how Harper sees the world? Reducing people to stepping-stones, tools for her personal advancement?

"Do you think the stream will drop by tomorrow?" I call out as we set off. I'm trying to keep his pace and failing, my muscles stiff from yesterday's hike.

"I imagine so, but it's hard to say. You want to be rid of me, is that it?" He slows and waits for me to catch up on the rise ahead.

How much time do I have before it gets weird that I don't disclose knowing who he is? Jesus, it's already weird. I'm like an embedded reporter and can't help but look at him with new eyes. Yes, he's still as beautiful as before, but now he's a story, something that I am almost genetically designed to react to, assess, and record. This would slam-dunk me into the coveted *Outsider* position. I'd be able to be a functioning grown-up with a job in my chosen field.

"Your company isn't totally unlikable," I say when I reach his side, hoping my panting isn't massively obvious. The sweat sheening my forehead is no doubt a good look, not to mention my whole back is wet.

"Funny." He puts me on lockdown with his wolf eyes, or maybe they're hawk-like. There's a predatory gleam to them, a little wild, and I can't shake the feeling I'm in over my head. "I feel the same way about you."

"Well, then." My laugh is weak, a whistle like the last squeeze in a ketchup bottle. "We're in good company."

We continue up the slope. He's doing switchbacks, obviously

for my benefit, rather than heading straight up, but it's nice of him. He could no doubt rocket up this hill like the Flash. "So..."

"So..."

I hunt around for random chitchat and arrive at the most obvious. "Have any resolutions?"

He frowns. "Resolutions?"

"For the next year. It's New Year's Eve today." Normally this day doesn't hold much meaning to me. If anything, it's a depressing reminder how year in and year out, very little changes in my life. Today is just the opposite. It's as if the hard rain from last night washed the dust from my eyes. Everything around me seems to sparkle with possibility.

"New Year's Eve? Aye, I suppose it is. I've lost track of the days." He's quiet for a little while. "I'm glad, though. It will be good to see this year finish."

"Yeah." I'm dizzy but not from the thinner air. Rhys's lazy hooded gaze seems to be sucking away all the available oxygen from my immediate vicinity.

"You have a boyfriend?" he asks, taking things unexpectedly personal.

"A boyfriend? Now, just a, um, recent ex," I answer, flustered. "Brett, to be specific."

"What did he do to lose you?"

I love that he automatically assumes I'm the wronged party. "My twin sister."

"A twin?" He turns around slowly.

I nod my head. "Yeah, I meant that statement in the most literal sense."

"Your man shagged your twin sister?" He looks repulsed. Clearly, he has a moral code here. Uncertainty licks me. He can't be a bad guy despite the fact that the media crowned him as Cain to Cameron's Abel.

Maybe he had good reasons for his actions.

I could help him share his side of the story. Relief floods me. We could be on the same team. Work together. I just need to build his trust, let him see I could help. This relationship could be a win-win.

"The night before I left to come down here."

"Cold."

I allow a single nod. "Ice-cold."

"Is she identical?"

"Yeah." I bite the inside of my cheek. Is he going to turn out to be a creeper like everyone else with an identical-twin fantasy?

"I can't imagine there being two of you."

"We are nothing like each other."

"How so?"

"Well, OK, here's one example. Even though we are identical, her genes don't carry asthma. That's my special part of the deal."

"Really? I thought everything was split."

"No. She might possess the capability, but some unknown environmental trigger flipped my switch. I had attacks as a kid. Bad ones. We lived at altitude, in Aspen, where I spent winters inside while she hit the slopes. Mom and Dad saw my sister was good at skiing, a natural athlete, and spared no expense making sure she became great. And great she is, like going to the Olympics in a few months great."

He makes an impressed face. "Really?"

"Yep." I'm so used to the reaction it's not even a struggle to restrain my eye roll.

"She must be driven."

I resist the urge to shudder. "An understatement."

He scrutinizes me. "You aren't friendly."

"What tipped you off? The part where she screwed my boyfriend?" I'm getting testy, which is unfair. I want him to open up to me, so I need to share my own stuff. Fair's fair. But fair also kind of sucks.

"That…and, well, you say her name as if she's your worst enemy."

"She is." I force a laugh. "Imagine that. My worst enemy shares my face."

"So does mine." He turns and keeps advancing upward. "It's my reflection in the mirror."

I take three steps for his one, trying to focus on the brisk twinge to the air, that my lungs feel OK, anything other than the fact there was still more up to go. "You said you had a brother. What's your relationship like? Is he an enemy? Frenemy?"

He hesitates a fraction of a second. "Best friend."

"He's a climber, too?" I keep my voice light, my face relaxed. Just chatting about family, no biggie, certainly not fishing for information. Interviews may be casual, but they aren't conversations.

This act is getting dangerously close to being willfully disingenuous.

# 12

## *AUDEN*

*D*isingenuousness creates a sickening sensation, as if my insides host a colony of eels. The feeling doesn't improve when Rhys twists his sexy mouth into an even sexier lopsided smile. "Guess what?" he says. "I've sorted my resolution for the coming year."

"Care to share?" I'm pumping him for information, but I am also honestly interested. *Gah.* Second-guessing my own motives sucks. A few hours ago my reactions to him were pure, or at least based on a peculiar mixture of lust, fascination, and curiosity. Now all these different feelings tangle together with guilt and temptation and I'm not sure how to unknot this.

He squares his broad shoulders. "I want to stop looking backward."

The unexpected flash of vulnerability squeezes my heart. "Easier said than done."

He stares into the distance. "Is anything worth having ever easy?"

Farther up the slope a sudden *scitter-scatter* sound intensifies to a dull roar.

"Fuck." Rhys grabs me as if I weigh as much as air, slams my body against his, protecting me, as mere feet away the mountain's scree slope transforms into a loose river of rock. Some stones are as big as my fist, others larger than beach balls. The rockslide picks up speed, the sound reverberating through my skull, practically rattling my teeth. Is this how my end will come, death not by lightning but stoning? The notion would be ridiculous if it weren't absolutely terrifying. I bury my face in Rhys's chest as if he's an anchor able to hold me fast.

"I'm scared," I whimper. That's all I have air for. All I can think.

"Easy, lass." His breath is hot in my ear. "All will be well."

And it is easy, far too easy, to trust him. Not just for the confident words, but the way he shields my body with his own, like I'm something precious, worth protecting at all costs.

And as suddenly as it started, the rocks come to a stop and the mountain returns to silence. The only sign anything happened is my racing pulse and the fact I'm locked in his embrace.

"A wee landslip." He releases some pressure, not much.

"Wee? But...but...I mean, could the whole slope give way?" The idea of the earth slipping underfoot sends a panicked jolt down my spine.

"No. That was nothing more than a few rocks." His fierce grip belies the casual tone. The pounding against my back comes from his own heart, a clue he's not as relaxed as he pretends.

"You protected me."

"Nah, it was nothing."

"You're kidding, right? You almost took a bullet for me, or at least a rock to the head." The thick scar on his neck, the one that disappears into his hairline—was that caused by a similar sort of accident? "Look at your hands. They're shaking." I settle mine over the back of his, travel the ridgeline of his knuckles, trace my fingertips through the narrow valleys between, riveted by the rough, latent strength.

The way Rhys reacted a moment ago, there wasn't time to think. He protected me on instinct. This is the second time he's safeguarded me without a single thought to his well-being. I'm convinced there's more to his story. He's not a villain. No way. A bad guy wouldn't be so naturally self-sacrificing.

"Perhaps I shouldn't have brought you up here." A note of uncertainty punctuates his sentence. "I wanted to show you something beautiful, not scare you into an early grave."

"No, it's OK. I'm glad you did. The view's amazing." And I tell no tales. *Amazing* is a weak word for snow-capped peak after peak, bare rock breaking from the dark forest. Far below, a glacier cuts through the valley's heart, a frozen tongue of ice.

We stand quietly, and I wait to see if he'll say more. When he doesn't, I do. "I actually have my own resolution."

The intense way he watches me is intoxicating. Not a stare, it's active, as if he searches for something. I can't shake the feeling the landslide cracked whatever wall's been between us and I'm glimpsing him, the real Rhys, and he can see me a little better, too.

"I want to say yes more," I say softly. "I'm always playing it safe. By coming to South America, I took a risk, but I'm glad about how it's working out. And I'm glad I met you." And I am. I really am. The story notwithstanding, he is like no one I've ever met, and I can't get enough.

His gruff laugh is a trifle uncertain. The display of male bluster lodges in my throat like one of these stones. Even though he's physically strong, there's a deep fragility about him, as if on the inside he's unraveled to a gossamer-thin thread. *Who are you? What makes you tick?*

"Shall we go back down?" he asks.

"Good idea."

He walks beside me, palpable focus radiating off him. He pays attention to every foothold, guiding me down in a way that's as safe as possible. Even still, the idea of lurking danger lingers, making me hyperaware and nervous. When I trip over my own feet, he asks me to tell him more about my sister.

I don't know if he cares or wants to calm me down, but either way I start talking.

"Let me see. Harper's Olympic bid is part of why I came down here. She's always had this sibling rivalry thing with me. When we were kids, my asthma was bad, sometimes really bad. I had to do breathing treatments, spent lots of time going to the hospital. Harper figured out that skiing got her our parents' attention. So the long and short is I had the inhaler and the worry; my sister obtained the skis, praise, and success."

"How did such a rivalry last beyond your childhood?"

I throw up my hands. "That's the million-dollar question. I have no idea. All I know is my sickness seems to have been the seed, and those roots grew deep. Ever since, anything I did, she had to do better, and not just surpass me, but blow up the bridge behind her so I'd never catch up. But I don't want to compete with her. I don't want to jockey for any spotlight."

"You talk about what you don't want." Rhys pauses, leg braced on a boulder, brow quizzical. He's not particularly close, but it's like he's everywhere. All around. Every square inch of my body feels his presence. "What about what you want, Auden?"

*You.*

I could say it, such a simple word, but what if I am misreading the signals? It seems like he's interested in me, but that could be my wishful thinking. God, Rhys could tell whole stories with those expressive brows. What would it be like to kiss the space between, those deep-set twin lines that hint at worry and pain?

"How old are you?" I blurt. He doesn't appear much older than me, but get a good look in his ancient eyes and he could be over a hundred.

"Twenty-five. You're evading."

I press my lips together for a moment, weighing my words. "I want to know what to do with myself."

"Do you have a plan?"

"Just publish the profile on La Aguja climbers for now," I say with a shrug. If I spill the beans that I am considering writing his story, the chances are between very good and excellent that we won't return to this easy relationship. Not that this is easy. I don't even know what it is, or if it can be defined as a relationship or even a friendship. But I'm not sure I'm ready to risk it, have him retreat right at the point he's opening up.

Or I can do nothing. Ignore the story potential.

And if I don't tell him, nothing will happen.

No one will ever know how close I got to the story of the year or my dream job.

No one but me.

He waits for an answer, so I decide to tell him the next-best thing, the partial truth. "I don't know what I want. I assume eventually I'll land a job with two weeks' vacation, dental, and health insurance. I'll buy a new car with dual airbags and have to make monthly payments. I'll decorate my apartment in some mash-up of Anthropologie sales items and cute but kinda crappy stuff from Target. Eventually I'll probably meet someone who I can't think of a bad reason not to be with. We'll get married, a spring wedding.

Add a mortgage. Stir in a few kids and a yearly trip to Disney World. And suddenly I'd be old. And that will have been my life."

His features don't shift. "Lots of people would be content with that."

"But will I?" I shake my head. "I want more. I want to do big things, challenge myself."

He reaches out and traces the edge of my jaw in a gesture so quick it's over before I can register the action. "You can be anything you want."

"But I can't. Not really." I clear my throat and point at the granite spire looming above us. Hopefully, turning my head hides the sudden hectic warmth spreading across my face. "Can you climb that?"

"Sure, guess so," he says offhandedly.

"That makes me want to pee my pants a little. I'm jealous of hard-core people like you. I see pictures in magazines: scaling cliffs, base jumping, climbing frozen waterfalls, and it feels like you guys must know what it's like to be really alive. I wish I had the part inside me that could risk everything for a moment of glory, but I don't. I don't even have crumbs of it."

His eyes suck air from the atmosphere. "You don't strike me as someone who isn't living."

"Ignore me." I look away, and the deflective action helps my lungs return to normal function. "I'm being stupid. First-world white-girl problems."

"FWWGP?" He mashes the acronym together into an unexpectedly funny sound.

I laugh. "Yeah. If you hear me talking like that again, just make that noise, *fwwgp*." I reach out; my touch is barely a shoulder skim.

He stiffens but doesn't shake me off. I don't move. "You're a good listener. I don't talk to people like this in my real life."

"I'm interested in you."

I fake a laugh to cover the lurch in my chest. "Trust me, if I wrote an autobiography, you'd be asleep before chapter two. I'm the human equivalent of Nyquil."

*"Fwwgp."*

"Thank you. See, you save me from a rockslide and also my own capacity for emo."

He pulls me toward the boulder he's standing on.

My up-jump motion is ungainly, and I fall against him. He steadies me with an arm around my waist. Never, in the whole history of touches, have I felt as conscious of body contact as I am right now. I can't bring myself to look over. I don't want to break the spell. The valley is spread below, and it's only us. Stone. Ice. Wind. No sign of anyone. We could be the last two humans on Earth.

"This valley feels a bit like Eden," he murmurs, reaching out to smooth a piece of my flyaway hair.

"So, what, you're Adam?" I bump my hip at him. "Does that make me Eve?"

"Depends." He trails his fingers along the back of my head and leans closer. "You fancy apples, lass?"

"I fancy a lot of things." If I turn now, look at him, what will happen?

There's another sound, not of rock falling, but gravel crunching. He releases me and points downward, to the west. I hug myself, cooler without his touch.

"There's your wolf."

A small gray fox regards us with a stoic, unblinking gaze.

"He looks smaller when not poking his snout out of the bushes," I say.

"We fear what we can't see clearly." Rhys hooks his thumbs in his belt loops, no idea he's slaying me. "Zorro!" He cocks his chin in my direction. "Allow me to introduce my new friend, Auden Woods. She's come looking for the meaning of life. Perhaps you can help her."

Zorro stares as if we're a pair of idiots before retreating into the boulder field. His gray fur is a perfect camouflage against the stone.

"Guess he's not giving up any state secrets today," I say.

"Nope. We're on our own."

"I need to stop thinking about my future so much. Live more in the present."

"Maybe that's why I like you. You look ahead. I keep looking behind."

He likes me? I mean, he must like me, but the idea combined with my sudden realization that there's a sharp sixty-foot drop behind him makes me woozy.

"All I know is that I can't look down."

He points north to a thick cloud rise. "That way, beyond this valley, on the far side of the park, is where La Aguja is waiting."

For both of us. To make our dreams or crush them to dust.

I give an involuntary shiver even though the day has grown steadily warmer. I resist the urge to hug myself. "Can we go back down?" The impulse for flatter earth is overwhelming.

We walk in silence and end up in a clearing beside the stream. The water level has dropped enough that I could easily boulder hop across and return to the main route.

"Look, there's the trail." My feet don't budge toward camp,

where my backpack is sitting, ready to go. Despite his offer to hike with me to the climbing camp, this is an easy out for him.

"Aye."

We watch the water rush over the rocks, wash them clean. If he tells me to go, I won't be forced to decide on what to do with his story.

I rise on my toes, flex my calf muscles, unable to get rid of the tension that's gripping my body. "I know you said we could hike together, but now that I can, should I leave?"

He considers his words. "Only you can answer that."

"I'm serious. Do you want me to stay?" I'm not sure how I want him to answer.

"The answer should be no, and it's not." The dark note to his voice makes the warm space between my legs turn molten.

"Rhys."

He crosses the space between us in five long strides. His expression is furious and his eyes more than a little wild. Here he is, the guy crazy enough to want to climb a deadly mountain. The kind of guy who doesn't back down from a challenge.

We stand toe to toe, and he towers over me. "You asked if I want you to go. Aye, I do. I want you to leave so badly I could scream it at the top of my lungs. But with my next breath? I want you." He grabs my braid in his fist. "I'm half-mad with the wanting of you." The pressure on my scalp doesn't hurt, but it's close. "But I should let you walk away."

"So do it, then." Frustration surges through me as I try to shove him away. I'm not some stupid toy for him to play with because he's bored and alone.

He loosens his hold, but then lunges forward, burying his face in the top of my head, breathing deep. My hands, pushing against his shoulders, begin to do the reverse, cling, pull him closer. I can't have him touch me and not do the same.

"Stay the night with me," he mutters into my hair.

Oh my God. This is it. An invitation to Pound Town. My lungs don't work, as if I've fallen in the deep end of the pool. This isn't an asthma attack. This is a life attack.

I stare at him. "Yes." My whisper is barely audible.

He draws back. "You will?"

"It's New Year's Eve." My stomach throbs. "The perfect time to embrace new adventure." It's tricky to smile with this huge lump settling in my throat. His irises are the exact same burning yellow that licks the edge of a flame. Inside, I'm scorched down to bare earth, but not empty, rather primed, as if now, at last, I can grow.

He hesitates a moment before brushing his palm over my hair. "You can back out. No harm, no foul."

"You're trying to discourage me?"

His gaze darkens. "Auden, I'm asking you for one night of no-strings sex. No' exactly a romantic proposition."

He's right, but I'm going to agree anyway, because the part of me that wants this is overriding the part that cautions. "Yeah, Prince Charming could probably spin a better line."

"Don't want to give you any lines. I've nothing to lose, so I'll speak plain. Most people? I endure them. But I like you. I want you."

"You like and want me?" Jesus, my heart is two seconds from hulking out of my chest. Pretty sure a vein or two has popped from the pressure crushing my internal organs. "Or you like that you want me?"

"Can't it be both?" His half shrug coupled with the hint of a playful grin twists my stomach into a pretzel. My insides are an honest-to-goodness mess at this point. Jesus, I'm even biting my nails. Time to stuff my hands in my pockets and hope my courage is hiding next to the lint balls and random pesos.

"I want..." My knees quake even as heat radiates up my thighs. My body is stuck between fight-or-flight mode, or rather more to the point, fuck-his-brains-out-or-flight mode. "I really, really, really want to say yes."

Pretty sure he growls, and the sound is so primal and unabashedly needy that I start to get wet. I can feel it, illicit and wicked, pooling against my underwear's thin cotton.

"And you understand that tomorrow we'll go back to being near strangers?" He tilts my chin and leans down, his bottom lip grazing the side of my jaw.

*Strangers who are intimately acquainted with each other's baby makers?* My laugh is doing this Jerry Lee Lewis "Whole Lotta Shaking Going On" impersonation. Great, I'm getting propositioned for afternoon delight and giggling like a middle schooler. I clear my throat and try to rearrange my features into something a little more alluring and worldly. "I won't even shake your hand after."

"Let's get this crystal clear. I'm asking to use you, Auden." Those words should be ugly, selfish, disrespectful, but they don't match the promise in his face.

*Jesus H. Christ.* My brain has officially exploded. "Maybe I want to use you, too." And that's the truth, in more ways than one. I drop my hands from his shoulders to the bottom of his shirt, let my fingers steal under, and holy shit, yes, good-bye, misgivings about his story, and hello, stomach. My own muscles are strong and compact, but over them is a sense of softness, of give. Rhys is forged from stone and iron. I could crash against him again and again until nothing remains but rubble.

I slide his top up farther, and he pulls away, fists it off, and throws it behind him. There's a rustle in the bushes from where it lands.

"Not big on shirt wearing, are you?" I murmur.

"Rather feel you, lass." He tugs my shirt up, wanting to undress me in the forest. "Look at your body. You're gorgeous." He rests his forehead against mine, gaze fixed on my breasts. I look down, too, and it's strange to see all my familiar curves and dips. My shape has always seemed so normal, and yet suddenly it appears wanton and impossibly erotic.

"Will you let me touch you here?" He circles a thumb over the rise of my breast, sensitive even behind the sports bra's thick fabric. My nipple hardens, aching to be rolled between his clever fingers.

"Yeah," I manage to whisper. "God, yes."

"And here?" He grabs hold of my waistband, slides a knee between my legs, and angles up to grind against where I need him most.

I hump him like a wild animal and don't have the shame or good sense to stop. The thin layers of cotton between us might as well not exist. "Please, keep going."

"I imagined your taste all morning. What it would be like to drag my tongue over that sweet pussy." The way he says "tongue" with that gravelly lilt, I could die now and be happy. But I should petition whoever's on duty at the pearly gates for a few extra minutes so Rhys can put that dirty mouth to extra-good use.

I whimper something that starts as the word "Please" and ends in a jumble of consonants.

"You've the look of a girl who hasn't been properly kissed in a long time."

I can't control a shiver. "Maybe ever."

He nuzzles the side of my neck. "Better make it good, then."

A lick of unease cools some of my heat.

*What are you doing?*

Here I am, hooking up with Rhys MacAskill, and I haven't said a peep about the fact that I figured out who he is or that I'm interested in his story. He said he wanted to use me, and I want to use him, but not just physically. This is a mega conflict of interest, right? A rough, frustrated confusion wells within me.

But then he's there, bold lips covering mine like this gesture is the most natural thing in the world. It's a whisper of a kiss, a flashlight in the dark, a faint taste of salt. He teases his tongue against my lip seam, and when I open, we circle each other until I'm consumed by the taste of him, the lingering hint of currants and Earl Grey. All other thoughts, anxiety, and better judgment are thrust away by the wet, hot heat.

The stream babble fills my ears. His tongue works like a slow eddy, pulling me into a natural rhythm. Kissing is usually something slightly desperate, as if I'm trying to get somewhere, chasing an elusive feeling hinted at in great movies and love songs, something that transcends flesh and saliva. He's taking me there, to that place.

My nails sink into his shoulders and he doesn't flinch. I can't stop. I want to leave marks, as if engraving my initials in a tree with a penknife. His exhalations take on a raspy edge. Maybe I really can do anything if I put my mind to it, so I put my mind here, into this kiss, this give-and-take.

It should be simple, so simple, a touch of tongue, a brush of lips, but it's as if the forest crashes down around us. Guilt and desire collide, each emotion sharpening the other. He might be saying my name. He could be reciting the entire encyclopedia. In this kiss, there is nothing, and everything. We've stumbled to the place of secrets, where lovers through the ages have sneaked away. We can't stay here. No one can. But that's what makes it better. Knowing that you'll lose a thing sharpens the sweetness.

A kiss should be the simplest thing in the world.

Not this gentle stirring, like wind through the underside of leaves, inexorable as the glacier grinding behind us. So hot and yet it doesn't scorch. No, with every breath, with every touch, his kiss carves.

When he's finished, my landscape will be forever changed.

# 13

## RHYS

*J* stifle a groan of need as Auden grinds against my leg, losing herself in the back-and-forth hip rock. Doesn't take much imagination to predict how she'll move when I'm inside her, and the knowledge is bloody brilliant.

"That's it, lass. Use me. Use me how you need to," I whisper in her ear.

She trembles, halting the sensual motion with a jerk.

"Are you OK?" I should be asking myself the same question. What the hell just happened? Fuck, I've kissed more than a few girls, but nothing has ever come this close to undoing me and we haven't even really begun.

"Guess I'm a little nervous." Her teeth chatter.

"Shite, you're cold." Not to mention the fact we're beside the trail. Anyone could walk up, see us, see her. I turn to grab her shirt. A shame to cover those lush curves, but an animalistic jealousy rises in me. I don't want anyone else to have the privilege of glimpsing her skin, at least not today, while she's mine.

"Thanks." She shoves her head and arms through the holes, pulling the hem down over her stomach.

"Are you sure you're all right?"

"I told you I'm nervous." She doesn't hold my gaze. "You're the first new guy I've been with in a long time. Guess I'm out of practice."

"Aye. Me, too. Out of practice, that is." The last time I tried to hook up with a woman ended in disaster. I went to a bar in Colorado while Dad was at Bible study and the silence of his house grew oppressive. The girl was sweet enough, cute, good for a laugh. But when we kissed, nothing happened. I couldn't get hard or bear having her close.

Even sex's fleeting oblivion had been denied me.

Then Auden popped in as unexpected as a ghost, slipped under my defenses before I had time to mount a counterattack. She's got me at her mercy, with a mad wish to please her. This is a bad idea. With every kiss I become more and more certain of that fact, and more drunk with anticipation.

"Come." To hell with the consequences. I want her naked, panting, and wet beneath me. I want her in all the ways she can give. Aye, I made it clear that I intend to use her. But how did she respond? "Maybe I want to use you, too."

Bloody hell.

"Rhys!" she shrieks as I scoop her up in my arms.

I stop her laughing protest with another kiss. One that almost takes the strength from my legs, tempts me to drop us both to the earth and rut her senseless.

When I get her in the tent, she still responds, but the tenor's changed.

"I need to tell you something," she whispers.

"What, are you a virgin?" It seems unbelievable, but what else could be making her so uneasy?

She shakes her head with a grimace. "No, that's not it."

"Then let's talk later." I coax another kiss. Outside, by the stream, she'd responded without fear or reservation, but another sort of game is at play here, and I don't know the rules. "If you want to, we can stop," I murmur against her. "We can stop anytime. I'd never force a thing on you."

"I know." She threads her fingers through my hair.

"Want me to put my shirt back on?"

"No. God, no. Pretty sure you break a couple of different laws of nature whenever you wear one." Her hands splay my lower belly. "I mean, you're ridiculously beautiful." She shakes her head. "Forget me. I'm being stupid. We're using each other. This is all that's happening here, right?"

"Right." My cock twitches, ready to start doing just that. Using.

"And it's New Year's Eve after all. Might as well start the year off with a bang. All puns intended."

"You're sure, then?"

She nods slowly. "I have a chance to be ravished by a sexy-as-hell Scottish mountaineer in a tent in the middle of nowhere. If I don't make that happen, later I'm going to kick my own ass."

"So I'm to be your adventure—is that it?" I undo her pants.

She slides her hands around to my shoulder blades and down, nails grazing their way toward the base of my spine. "There are condoms in my bag. I brought them on a weird impulse, in case I had a chance for some rebound action."

That's not what I want to be, but I don't flinch. "I knew you had them."

She pulls back with a frown. "How?"

"Saw them last night when I was getting your inhaler."

She snorts. "You must have thought 'Today is my lucky day.'"

"Nah. It was more, 'Christ, I hope this chick doesn't die on me.'" What do I care, if she wants me for a rebound? It's not the worst thing in the world. It's not like this is ever going to be anything more.

"Wow." She slaps my skin. "Mr. Sensitive is in the house, or tent, whatever."

"Well, I would no' have much minded giving you mouth-to-mouth." I go in for another kiss, take my time about it.

Finally she stops, reaches into her backpack, and pulls out a foil.

Everything moves fast after that, clothing dispensed with, an increased urgency of tongue, lips, and touch. I raise her on top and she freezes. Fine. She wants me to take charge. Not a problem. I settle her beneath, my body casting a shadow on her pale skin. She presses the condom in my hand, and I'm acutely conscious of myself as I slide it on, that she can see me, all of me, for the first time.

I spread her legs, settling against her center.

She stills. "Do it," she whispers, a little desperate. "I don't want to think. Do it now."

Give the lady what she wants. My head enters her, just the tip—so fucking good. I'm determined to watch her face but halfway through the thrust forget entirely. Forget everything. *Jesus God. Jesus God.* I sink deep and for a moment don't move, can't move. I brace my weight on my elbows, not wanting to crush her. When I withdraw, there is a sucking sound as the sweat sheening our stomachs comes apart and slaps together again at my return. I must be nervous, too. Shite, my hairline is damp.

I don't know the way of her, so I start off with a slow rock and glide, see if that's good. Her soft, breathy sounds rocket me to the brink despite the gentle rhythm.

"Harder." She wraps her legs around my ass and slams me to the hilt again and again, but I'm not hitting her clit.

I shift, ready to do just that, when she begins to moan.

*Already?*

"You're close, lass?" I keep pumping, press my tongue against the roof of my mouth, struggle to hang on.

Auden throws back her head. "Now. Come."

*Fuck.* I fill her with a last heavy thrust. She cries out as I empty myself, but it isn't until I finish that I know for sure.

All her sound and fury signified nothing.

She fucking faked the whole thing.

I might be an idiot, but I know the few key signs to look out for, like contractions against my cock—a law of physics I worked out before my eighteenth birthday. Perhaps not every guy pays attention, but that's what I do best. My greatest strength and biggest curse is having single-minded focus.

*Shite.* I roll onto my back, a pain spreading through my gut. The late-afternoon air replaces her heat, the sweat cooling on me.

She's quiet, too. What did I do wrong? Everything was so good by the stream. It felt real, realer than anything I've ever experienced.

And now this.

My cock softens, and I don't bask in any afterglow. Shame steals around me as my heart rate slows to normal. Should I say something? I don't have the first clue as to what.

"So, um, that was good." She speaks first. The way she pronounces the word confirms my suspicions. It's as if she is trying it on, hoping it fits.

"Yeah," I find myself responding in turn. "Good."

"Happy Almost New Year." She rolls and gives me a soft kiss on the shoulder before crawling into her sleeping bag.

"Aye, you, too." I glance over, but she's already turned and her back tells no tales.

Every muscle in my body screams in protest. Why didn't she just tell me what she was after? I'd have done anything to please her. Instead, she played me, and there are no winners in this sort of game.

I peel off the condom and set to work cleaning myself. Every noise is magnified, highlighting what I've done, that I've been the chump who came while the girl faked it. This doesn't make me unusual. All across the world right this second are thousands of assholes thinking they're getting their girl off when she'd rather be watching the telly or eating an ice cream.

I collapse on my mat, but for once, my tent is the last place I want to be. I reach to touch her back and freeze. My hand, the one that did the deed I've spent the last six months hating myself for, continues to be useless. It remembers every inch of Auden's hips, the exact geography of her small frame, but it can't do a damn thing to improve the situation.

I close my eyes and cross my arms tight to my chest, remembering the last woman to ever share my tent. Sadie, a base-camp emergency doctor who specializes in high-altitude medicine, respected the fact that the mountains are my true love, which is part of the reason we lasted three years. We met on my twenty-first at an expat dive bar in Kathmandu. I'd gone out to a pub with Cameron after a successful Himalayan expedition. She leaned in from an adjacent barstool, sexy as hell, and whispered in my ear, "Want me to make you a man, darling?"

And she tried. But beyond her easy smile and her unblinking acceptance of my addiction, she was older, past thirty. Our age gap never bothered me none. She was beautiful, confident, with a posh London accent that drove me a little wild, but eventually her mind traveled to the next inevitable steps: marriage, a child.

At twenty-four, I wasn't ready. That's the easy answer, the one that looks good on paper. It's also not the whole truth. The thing of it is, I could always forget her. When Sadie was around, we were good. The sex was adequate, our interests similar. But whenever we were apart, I couldn't recall the finer details of her face, the notes of her laugh, the way she tasted or gasped in my arms.

Shouldn't that be part of true love? Remembering such specifics? Taking the time to cherish the little things? I hadn't even thought of it until she'd proposed. Yes, she'd been the one to ask for my hand, not that I minded. I've always preferred strong women, ones who make their wants plain. Better than the alternative, the endless guessing games I watched other blokes put up with.

We'd been at Everest Base Camp having breakfast in the expedition canteen. She was working there for the season, and with bad weather keeping people off the mountain, she didn't have much to do, except me, and treating the odd case of altitude sickness.

"Darling, we should get married," she'd said nonchalantly, like she was giving the time.

At first I'd laughed, and she'd joined in, before leaning back in her chair, crossing her legs, still smiling.

"I am serious," she'd said, and I'd choked on a currant. "Rhys, I'm thirty-four. That thing they say about biological clocks? It happens. Mine's ticking away."

"I don't know what to say." I opted for the truth. A few other mountaineers entered, sitting nearby.

She'd leaned in, steepling her fingers. "Yes does seem like the best answer."

"But I…It's…" I'd stood, abandoned my bowl on the table, and walked outside. Fresh air and open skies were a sudden necessity.

Everest hid behind a shroud of thick gray cloud, the summit socked in since my arrival. No one moved on the mountain on account of the unexpected spring storm.

She walked behind me, and I spoke first. "Think I'll meet up with Cameron after all."

There'd been a long pause as the reality of my unspoken decision sank in. Was I being a dick? Absolutely. But I was also scared as shit, my gut clenching with anxiety.

"But, darling, you'd decided against that climb, said you were going to…" She didn't finish her sentence. The idea had been for me to stay the month with her. And here I was breaking the plan before the first week even finished.

"Sadie—" I turned around.

"No." She held up a hand. "Please. Don't say another word."

"I…"

"I know." Her small smile belied the tears gathering in the corners of her eyes. "You're not ready."

We'd left it at that. She came to me during the night, and I let her take what she needed. It wasn't so much a joining as a severing. As she fell apart in my arms, I knew this was my last chance to put us back together, but I didn't. Instead we rolled apart and spent the rest of the night staring at the ceiling in silence. The next day our good-bye was short, businesslike, a peck on the cheek and a promise to stay in touch. I'd started the hike out back to civilization and a week later caught a flight to Cameron in Pakistan, where he was getting ready to lead an expedition.

If I'd stayed with Sadie, tried to make it work, nothing that happened next would have ever occurred. I don't regret our breakup but would gladly endure any sort of penance to turn back time and have missed that damn plane. I thought letting her down was bad, but that was only the start of my fall.

Turns out anytime I care about anyone, all I do is let them down.

I glance to Auden's back and lock my jaw. Looks like my new year is starting out much the same as the old.

# 14

## *AUDEN*

*C*ameron!"

I bolt upright, the hairs on the back of my neck standing on high alert, heart choking my throat. The light outside the tent is dim and the time is definitely early evening. We must have passed out post-sex. Rhys jerks inside his sleeping bag, gripped in the throes of another nightmare, one that sounds worse than before.

"Hey?" My hand hovers over his shoulder, unsure if I should touch him. Stupid to be tentative given everything we've just done, but them's the apples. "Wake up. Please. Wake up, Rhys."

"Shit," he grinds out. The tendons on his neck tighten, stand in sharp relief. "Fuck it. Answer me. Cameron!"

"Shhhh." I wipe sweat-soaked hair off his forehead. "Shhhhh. Hey, it's OK. It's all going to be OK." I keep a running monologue of meaningless words. Everything is nowhere near fine. He's sweating. The sharp tang of fear fills the tent, makes my own skin prickle in alarm.

I'm the last person who deserves to witness something so private about him. Guilt tightens my throat, the same sensation that gripped me when he slid into me. Turns out I'm not big on taking advantage. I wanted him, but not at the cost of my own moral code. I messed up by not sharing the truth of myself. Turns out sex without honesty is a lady boner killer. The only relief is learning that deep down inside I'm not Harper; I'm unable to use people like the consequences don't matter.

He yells, a frustrated cry tinged with pure anguish. I push my own misgivings away, focused on getting him back from wherever he's trapped.

"Wake up." I shake harder. "Rhys, I said wake up right now. Come on. Wake up, Rhys."

His eyes open, wide and unseeing, and he flies to sitting, his forehead crashing into my nose.

"Ouch. Holy shit." I fall back, cradling my face as white stars cascade across my vision. My stomach gives a sick roll. Dampness spreads across my upper lip. Crap, I'm bleeding. "Is my nose broken? Did I break it?" I flinch from his outstretched hand. "Never mind. Don't touch. It hurts too much." Warm wetness splatters my chest. Excellent. I'm shirtless, with blood dripping onto my bare breasts. *Texas Chainsaw Massacre* isn't the sexiest post-coital look.

I pinch my nose and rock my head back. Intense copper flavor fills my mouth, and it's gross to swallow. "Can you get something to clean me, please?" I mutter stiffly, determined to hang on to any loose thread of dignity.

He presses rough wool into my hand, and I glance down. "A sock?"

"I don't have a tissue at the ready." His cheeks flame. "Don't worry. It's clean."

"Fine." I dab at my chest. Not sure it's helping. If anything, I'm just spreading gore across my body.

"Why were you up in my face?" His dull monotone is a sharp contrast to the anguish that strained his voice moments ago.

"You were having a nightmare, screaming. I wanted to snap you out of it."

"Sorry." He kneels, giving me his back, rummaging through an orange waterproof gear bag. "I didn't mean to hurt you."

"It was an accident. You freaked me out though."

There's the sound of a lid unscrewing followed by a quiet splash. "Here. I remembered I have a bandanna. There's some cool water on it. That will wipe the blood easier."

The initial shock of pain fades and I am able to hold still while he pats around my nostrils. "Do you think it's broken?"

"No, but I got you good. Might have bruising."

"Wow, get busy with Rhys MacAskill at your own peril." I mean it as a joke, to smooth over the awkwardness in the situation, but he doesn't laugh. If anything, he folds into himself, drawing up the hatches and shutting me out.

"What were you dreaming about?" The pain from my nose spreads through my forehead, settling into a tension headache. If he unloads his whole story right now, while I'm sore between my legs, I don't know what I'll do, but he's hurting. And even though I barely know him, I want to ease a little of that suffering.

"Nothing." There's finality to the word. The turn of a key. The door locks. I'm on the other side of the moat with no way to cross.

"Please remember, I am here for you." God, even saying such a phrase out loud makes me cringe. So generic and cheesy. I want to reach out, to touch him, but can't bring myself to, not when he's built the Great Wall and I have the world's most dubious motives.

He was honest about wanting to use me, while I couldn't find the way to be truthful in return. "How's your head?" I ask. "My nose is kind of big."

"Thick as ever." His voice softens a fraction. "I truly am sorry if I worried you."

"It's fine." *It's not.*

He's quiet except for a ragged exhalation. "I want to go back to sleep."

"OK." It isn't, but we're trapped in this weird politeness spiral. He's been inside me, and I still have no idea what's going on inside him or what I can do to repair the situation.

I burrow back into my own sleeping bag. It's not dark, and I'm positive I'm not going to sleep another wink. From the sounds of Rhys's breath and subtle movements, he's wide-awake, too, but the gulf between us is impassable.

Heck of a way to start a new year.

Eventually though, the exhaustion from the day's stress causes me to drift off again. When I awake, it's well and truly twilight, and Rhys is gone. I crawl outside and sit on the rock where he cooked breakfast, fed me porridge from a spoon, and afterward licked it clean. Then I realized who he was and what he represented. A way to advance my career. And what did I do? The stupidest thing possible.

Sex.

I had sex.

I had sex with Rhys the scruffy Scottish God. I had sex with Rhys MacAskill the Infamous Rope Cutter Whose Story I Covet. Oh dear God. I bury my face in my hands. The whole situation is ridiculously awful.

What's worse is that I even faked it, as per usual. That's what I do because I can't manage to get off when a guy's inside me. I know what works when I'm alone, but with another person? Yeah, that's way more complicated than a showerhead.

A sickening realization takes hold, a sensation like riding backward on a train. I have this feeling Rhys knows I didn't really come. But how? Brett never suspected anything. All I ever had to do was make a few breathless moans, arch my back, and it's like I was a normal girl, experiencing sexual magic. It's not that the motions don't feel good. It's always nice, in the same way that eating carob is pleasant, or gluten-free baked goods. But it sure as hell ain't the real thing. There were a few moments when it seemed like Rhys could give me chocolaty goodness, but then my guilt took over, barring the path to the great and mysterious O.

I'm in over my head here. Rhys will go on to bigger and better things. Climb impossible mountains. Marry a former Victoria's Secret model. Me? I'll be fine with my life partner, the showerhead. Maybe when I'm thirty I'll have a commitment ceremony, make things official, not to mention squeaky clean:

*Do you take this nozzle to be your committed and devoted partner, for better or worse, even if the hot water runs out?*

*I do.*

*You may five-speed-massage the bride.*

The sound of whistling carries through the trees. That's not Rhys. Someone is coming. My ears prick as I rise on alert like Bambi's mother right before she says, "Man has come into the forest." A stranger entering the valley shouldn't be a surprise. After all, the stream has receded enough for me to cross and the trail runs both ways.

The whistle grows louder. The tune is "Eye of the Tiger."

"Oh no," I whisper, dread knotting my belly.

"Auden? Ha! Incredible. It is you! I wondered what became of my favorite American!" Diedrick the annoying Dutchman emerges into the clearing, hands on his hips, still dressed in those same tiny shorts, beaming.

"Oh, come on. You've got to be kidding," I mutter. Of all the backcountry campgrounds, this guy walks into mine?

"Sorry!" Diedrick cups behind his ear. "What did you just say?"

I use my hands as a megaphone. "I thought you would have almost finished the trail by now." The W trail we'd been hiking on takes around four days to complete. He should be almost done, not here, bringing his indecent khaki shorts into my strange little Eden.

"There was all that rain! Such a storm, hey? And wait…" He scrambles up toward me like a khaki-loving mountain goat. "At the refugio, I heard a most interesting rumor."

"Oh."

He looks around at the forest, gloomy in the fading light. "Who else is here?"

For some reason, the avid expression in his gaze is off-putting. "Why?"

He leans in with a stage whisper. "I'm looking for Rhys MacAskill, the guy who cut the rope. You know that story? Of course you do, everyone does. Have you seen him?"

I give an involuntary shiver. "He a friend of yours?"

"No, but I would like to make his acquaintance very much." He points to the camera equipment slung around his neck. "See if he'll share his story. Imagine selling that puppy freelance?" He mimes pumping a cash register. *"Ca-ching, ca-ching!"*

A protective instinct wells inside me. Rhys stands six foot two, and his muscles have muscles. He's in no way weak, but an intense fragility surrounds him. I might not be able to protect him from the world, but I can keep a single mercenary Dutch dude at the gate. "Sorry. You're wasting your time. He won't talk to you."

Diedrick shrugs, nonplussed. "Oh, I do not think that's for you to decide."

I bristle, annoyance blazing through my chest, when an idea occurs to me. "Did I forget to mention that I work for *Outsider* magazine when we were hiking? Sorry. I've already secured exclusive dibs on the Rhys MacAskill story and his attempt on La Aguja. You're too late." I wave my hand toward the trail behind him. "Scoot now. Nothing else to see here."

"But I—"

"I said, you're too late. This is my story now." I summon my best Harper face, the one that's the perfect blend of arrogant and contemptuous. My heart beats faster. Any second Rhys could appear. No amount of guilt can change the fact that I did the exact same thing Diedrick is now doing—considered my own benefit to writing the story over the man living it.

"Go. For real, beat it," I repeat in a cold tone, clenching and unclenching my fists. "You're too late."

Diedrick waffles before ultimately backing down, retreating a few steps, perhaps remembering my scro-tack threat from the other day. I'm pretty sure he calls me a bad name under his breath, but I don't stick around to listen. My mind is made up at last and relief quickens my pace.

No way can I stomach doing an exposé on Rhys. I'm not Harper, happy to step on people to raise myself. His story would make my career, no doubt about it, but if that is the way to catapult forward, I'd rather inch along. At least he'll never know what I considered, what I was willing to stoop to. There's no point in telling him.

I almost did a bad thing that would have rendered me a less than decent human, but in the end I stepped back from the point of no return and stayed true to myself and my own values.

No harm, no foul.

# 15

## RHYS

$\mathcal{U}$ndergrowth closes in, prickly heath tugging at my legs. White flowers streaked with purple appear and the tiny blue-black Calafate berries. I pluck a few, place them between my lips, and chew. Sweetness spreads through my mouth even though my stomach is as contorted and twisted as the surrounding beech trees. At the stream, there's a downed tree over a small waterfall. I cross it easily, striding until the earth falls away. The cliff edge provides a viewpoint to Glacier Frances below. Across the craggy ice field, the eastern wall of Cerro Paine Grande rises.

To the naked eye you can't see a glacier move, but it is, grinding away at the granite, relentless and inexorable as memory.

"Rhys! Rhys!" Auden calls for me through the forest.

I could stand still and she'd never spot me. The dying light of the sun is right in her eyes and I'm cloaked by shadow, camouflaged in a black jumper and dark green pants, blending into the forest. I know how to keep my body perfectly still. But sod it. I call out to her despite my better inclinations. Why? Because I'm a bloody idiot where she's concerned. No sense of self-preservation.

"Here," I say. Once. Loudly. If she hears and finds me, it's meant to be.

There's thrashing through the brush, and her beautiful face pokes from the forest a few meters away. "I followed your footprints. The ground's muddy and..." She pulls up short, staring at the scene. It's beautiful. I know this in an abstract way. The interplay of ice and rock is captivating. But despite the view, she's the thing I can't stop watching, even as my jaw clenches. She lied about me getting her off, and my wounded male pride hasn't recovered. Not by a long shot.

"I woke and you were gone," she says softly.

"Aye. Needed air." *Space from you.* What a bloody joke to have had the best sex of my life be completely one-sided.

"Want to talk about what happened earlier?"

A bitter taste floods my mouth. "What's there to say? You faked an orgasm."

Her eyebrows vanished beneath her thick, side-swept fringe as color steals up her cheeks. "How did you know?"

A small brown bird flits through the low-hanging branches. I was born into the wrong species. I'd be happy living out here in the forest every day, where all I need to do is peck around for a nut or a berry. Fly above the tree canopy. That would suit me fine. "I could tell," I respond at last.

"How, though?" she repeats, as if that part actually matters.

I glance to her, then away. It hurts to look for too long. "Glad to see you're no' denying it."

"I..." She clears her throat. "No, I'm not. But no one has ever noticed before."

"This wasn't your first time?" That's important for some reason.

Now it's her turn to study the dark woods. "It's every time."

"You fake it every time?"

"I've never come during sex." Her mouth grimly twists into an approximation of a smile. "No idea why."

"So you've never...?"

"God, you want to know it all?" She throws her hands in the air. "Great time to start asking all the questions. Look, I can get myself off or whatever. I figured that out a long time ago. But I can't"—she pantomimes the distance between two points—"leap the divide with a guy."

I drag my hand through my hair. "Why don't you ever say anything? Give the one you're with a chance to make it better?"

"Because I...feel like a fraud." She hugs herself. "Who wants to be with a girl who can't orgasm? It's humiliating. Guys want to be able to feel like they are with a girl who is a sex kitten in the sack. Not a no-hoper who is bad in bed."

My laugh comes out a bark. "You'll be bad in bed when pigs fly. No one who kisses like you could ever be otherwise."

I wish I could say her startled look leaves me unaffected. That I'm not tempted to take her again right here and show her how good it can be if she will only teach me the way of her. "I'm no' sure if I like you, but I still want you."

"Sorry?"

"Me, too." I know that's not what she meant, but I'm still pissed as hell. "I'm sorry I met you. Sorry out of this entire park you came into this valley. Sorry I'm not thinking about my climb. Sorry that instead of focusing on La Aguja, all that I can think of is how badly I want to fucking kiss you again. Not like in the tent, but earlier by the stream."

She bites the corner of her lip, worries it a moment. "What are we going to do?"

"We?"

She points at the gloom. "It's almost dark. I can't leave. I don't have a tent. I'm stuck with you now, like it or not."

"What bothers me is that you weren't honest." My voice rises, self-control slipping through my hands.

"I'm sorry, OK?" She is pacing now, her expression agitated. "I don't know how to make this situation better." She steps within reach of my arms—arms that outstretch of their own volition and bring her gently against me.

I can't help myself.

"Me either." And then I'm kissing her, trust be damned. Hell if I know why, but I'm not sure I'll ever be able to be this close and not kiss her.

"What are you doing?" she murmurs, holding me tight. She couldn't possibly hurt me—her arms don't have the strength—and yet she brings me to my knees, wages holy war on my insides.

"Told you, I'm a fucking masochist." I hate how she makes me feel, but I can't walk away. The pain's too sweetly addictive.

# 16

## *AUDEN*

*I*t's hard to break free from Rhys's consuming kiss, but there can be no more physical contact until we've talked this out. "It doesn't feel like you've forgiven me."

"I haven't." Rhys grabs my face, his palms nearly covering my cheeks, his broad fingers grazing my temples. "But I don't care as much now." He removes one hand and slides it under my shirt. Everything about how he looks, breathes, and touches is tinged with desperation.

"Stop. Please." I try to control my shaking voice and trembling limbs. "We need to sort a few things out before this goes any further."

A shiver passes through him as he withdraws abruptly, cool air replacing the heat from his body. "I should no' have cursed at you." His expression is troubled. "Mum didn't raise me to speak to a woman in such a way."

My feelings are in turmoil. I wasn't honest when we had sex. And I still can't be completely honest, not about how I almost stabbed him in the back. He'd never forgive me.

Almost doing something isn't as bad as doing it, but still…

Rhys concentrates on the empty air before him with single-minded attention. "Come with me."

"Where?" I freeze. It's nearly pitch-black, and we're alone in the forest.

"Do you trust me?" he asks me in a strange voice.

"More than you trust me," I murmur.

"Down this rise." He points into the gloom, to the glacier spread out at our feet.

"We can't walk out on that!" My heart clogs my throat. "I'm serious. There are crevasses in those things. One wrong step and it's game over, fall down a crack and break your back, never to be seen again."

He gives a low rumble of amusement. "There aren't crevasses down there. Well, there are, but not in the area below us."

"Well, we could also slip and fall on the ice," I say lamely. "Fracture a hip."

He cocks a brow. "Or get struck by lightning."

"Twice," I say, finally smiling. "OK, I'll go if you hold my hand."

"Gladly." He folds his fingers over mine and leads me with mountain-goat grace down the steep hillside. It's as if his eyes are secretly night-vision goggles. I can barely see a single thing, and yet his every move is practiced and sure-footed.

When we get to the bottom, my heart pounds, not from exertion but pure adrenaline. "I can't believe we didn't fall."

"I wouldn't have let you," he says softly, and I believe him. He holds my hand too tight.

Somehow in the last twenty-four hours, the story he lives and the story I live have merged. The words are scrambled and I suck at anagrams, but I don't need to solve a complicated riddle to understand this guy is a walking, talking cry for help.

"What do we do now?"

He unzips his vest and settles it against the earth. "Lie on this, but put your head on the ice."

"Um, OK." I awkwardly sink to my knees, crawl over his polar fleece, and position myself. It takes me a few seconds before I realize what he's trying to show me. "Oh, Rhys. Look at that."

He lies down beside me. "Good, hey? Before the storm I came here a few nights, listened to the ice."

Below us is a frozen river, popping, crackling, and groaning in discordant rhythms, and overhead is another river, one made entirely from starlight. The Milky Way seems poured out tonight in all its sparkling splendor.

"I'm sorry," he murmurs quietly, taking my hand again. "For losing my temper with you. Da used to carry on poorly when Cameron and I were lads. He was born in Scotland, but his father, my granddad, was a Methodist pastor transferred to a position in America. Da returned home in his twenties to rediscover his roots and met my mum. But something bad is inside him. Something that eats at him. In those days, he'd drink to deal with his darkness. That's when he'd take up the yelling.

"One Sunday afternoon, he lifted a hand against Mum and she'd had her fill, threw him out and said never to return unless he was keen to be stuffed and mounted on the lounge-room wall. He found his way back to sobriety, but she never forgave him. Eventually, in some Colorado backwater town, he discovered a new cause to dedicate himself to and replaced whiskey with God. He wasn't going to be content with being anything as mundane as a Methodist minister though. Da always needs to go a step further. He founded a church, the sort that handles snakes, natters in tongues."

"Are you serious?"

He nods absently. "Religion's no' my thing. Or Mum's or Cameron's for that matter. But he's still my da." His thick brows draw together as he rises to pace with that deceptively lazy, loose-limbed gait. A casual bystander might be fooled into believing he was relaxed, but his jaw flexes tight, so sharp it could scratch glass. "I'm my father's son. We share a bent for fanatical tendencies. I just so happened to have turned my capacity for zealotry to the mountains. Climbing is my obsession, keeps the worst parts of myself at bay." His jaw clenches and releases. "But then…even that…Ah, never mind."

He's retreating again, going back to his dark places, the secrets I'm not supposed to know about. There's only one way I know to move us forward. And it's a risk—a big fucking risk. I turn and prop myself on one elbow. "I don't want to be harsh, but stop and listen to yourself. Are you a character in a Brontë novel or something?"

"Excuse me?" His breathing slows, eyes fixed on me, not in anger, but shock.

"Hey." I stand and clutch his arm. "I'm not trying to be a bitch. Really I'm not. But the best thing you can do is return that broody Heathcliff self-destructive act to the moors, stat."

I don't want to be all tough love when he is saying things that tear my heart, but he's right about one thing. He's lost, and the only thing I know to do, that might help, is to barge in from left field and use twisted humor against the angst.

A raspy breath huffs out of him. "Finished?"

I swipe a wisp of hair off my cheek. "Yeah, I think so."

"You're mad; you know that?"

I pick up a tiny piece of ice and lob it at him. "Maybe we're all mad here." Last night I jokingly asked if he was the wolf or the woodcutter. I still don't have a clear answer. Rhys is dangerous, reckless, and more than a little wild. But I'm hooked, dangling on the end of this stupid line, and even though there's little chance of our situation ending anywhere good, I don't want to be anywhere else.

Something is happening here and I'm not sure what to label it. I like him, more than like him, but that's crazy, right? Why am I even asking the question? Of course it's nuts. This is a rebound, or at least a simple vacation infatuation.

That makes sense.

Not this other feeling growing deep inside me, pressing against my rib cage, heating me from the inside out.

"Aye, mad indeed." He flashes a brief, rueful smile before running his mouth along my jaw. His kiss includes a graze of teeth, as if he wants to eat me whole.

I shiver from more than the ice. I can't tell him that I am developing feelings. Or that those feelings mean I'm unable to betray him.

I can't even tell him I know who he really is, because if I do, he'll pull away, and I'm not ready to lose this. Whatever this even is.

"You're an unwise idea." He leans in to me, and his thickness presses just above my hip. At least one thing is out there in the open. He wants me. That part is growing increasingly obvious. "This is all terribly terribly unwise."

"Yeah, probably." My body gives up the fight, unable to resist reacting to his proximity. I'm wet, so extra sensitive that even the skim of my underwear feels like too much pressure.

He laughs then, and this time I don't join in. I look up instead. Twilight is gone. Replaced by stars. The day is officially finished.

The end of the year.

We're on a threshold, and maybe spending the next few days

with Rhys will be a mistake. In fact, it's most definitely going to be one. But I don't care. I never chose the reckless road before this trip. Why not see what's awaits further down that path? Besides, regardless of what I choose to do in this moment, I'll be making all sorts of missteps next year, no matter how carefully I tread on the straight and narrow. Errors are inevitable. Maybe, in the end, our whole lives are nothing more than a sum total of blunders. So if I'm going to fuck up, let my mistakes be huge.

Let them be stunning.

Let them change my entire world.

———

We return to the tent, and despite all my expectations to the contrary, Rhys doesn't touch me again. Instead, he falls asleep, hard and fast, like a log, rock, or any other big, hulking, inanimate object. At first I can't believe it. Outside, furtive animals scurry in the undergrowth, and the deep hoot of an owl follows, the haunting call vibrating through the air. It isn't until he jerks, in the way people do when falling asleep, that I know he's really gone, no doubt mentally exhausted.

"Happy New Year," I whisper to the night, to Rhys, to myself.

No nightmares visit him, and I'm willing to bet I didn't sleep a wink, except that suddenly it's light again and he is promising me coffee.

I crawl out of the tent, rubbing my eyes, and take the proffered mug.

"A peace offering," he says.

I take a sip and nearly moan. The coffee is perfectly brewed. God bless this man. My thighs clench under the intensity in his gaze.

He's set for us to go, backpack fixed with climbing rope and helmet strapped to the outside. I eye the coiled rope. Warmth spreads down my back. Hmmmm. Getting tied up by this guy wouldn't be so bad. Tying him up might be even more fun. Imagine all that pure male virility under my free-roving fingers.

*Whoa, whoa, settle down, homeslice.*

The notion flounces to the back of my mind. But it does have a certain appeal. All the appeals. Still, I have to be able to make polite eye contact, and it will be awkward in the extreme to do so while having light bondage fantasies. *Refocus.* The mountains are pretty. The glaciers, yeah, super cool. But my lips traveling the ridges of the abdominal muscles hiding beneath his thin T-shirt—

"Auden!"

"Huh?" I jerk to attention.

He narrows his eyes. "Where's your head at?"

"Um . . ." *Up your shirt.* "I don't know."

"You're off with the fairies. I've been saying your name these last twenty seconds."

"Sorry, yeah, I was way far away," I mumble. Images of ripped, bearded fairies in loincloths dance through my head. I officially have a problem. A six-foot-two-inches-of-strapping-Scottish-man-flesh problem.

"Ready to go soon?" He finishes taking down the tent in quick, efficient motions. The campground is still empty this early in the morning. No one else had ventured into the valley and no more signs of Diedrick. Hopefully that rodent has gone well and truly underground.

"Yeah. Just need a few minutes. I'm going to be brave and take a quick splash in the stream." If we're spending a few days together, the outlook seems good we'll get handsy. His hair clings to the back of his neck in damp tendrils. Looks like he's cleaned himself up, and I need to do the same.

"The river water's cold but bracing. Wakes you up in a flash."

"Noted." I grab a mostly clean change of clothes from my bag and beeline toward the creek. What have I gotten myself into? Who is letting me hike with the cool kids? When will Rhys wake up and realize I'm Queen of Joe Average? Harper is the one with all the mad skills. When I first announced I was going to major in journalism, my sister had snorted at the dinner table before saying, "Congratulations."

My parents acted like they didn't hear the sarcasm, kept chewing their chicken casserole and discussing the weather. That night, while I was brushing my teeth, Harper appeared behind me in the bathroom, our faces the same in the mirror.

"Funny you'd go for a career where you'll spend all your time watching things happen to other people," she'd said in a tone that was anything but humorous.

Enough with this. I remove my clothes and wade resolutely into the water. "Motherfucker," I grind out. Snowmelt is an excellent distraction. No more brain space is available to devote to what to do about Harper and her everlasting enmity. After all, I don't know what I'm going to do today, and that's right in front of me.

A sudden idea strikes me. I'm tempted to reject it out of hand, but it has serious merit. The more I don't outright deny it, the more I think it's exactly the right way to start the next chapter in my adventure before getting to La Aguja's base camp. "Hey," I ask Rhys as I return to the clearing. "Before we go, will you do something for me? Even if you won't like it?"

"What is it?"

"Well, here's the thing." I pull my plastic comb from the top of my backpack and tug it through my loose, wet tangles. "You'll say no if I tell you."

"All right, I'll save you the effort. No, then."

"Where's your curiosity?" I throw back. "Your spirit of adventure?"

"I can be adventurous."

"Yeah, yeah, that's what they all say."

"You're asking for trouble, lass." His voice deepens, and I'm pretty dang sure my panties just melted. I'm afraid to look down in case I'm standing in a puddle.

"Pretty please with a cherry on top?" I bat my eyes, mostly as a joke.

"Very well. One."

"One?" Does eye batting really work?

He holds a single finger. "You get one unequivocal yes from me. That's it."

I can't repress a triumphant grin. Perhaps I don't have magical powers, but I just bent Rhys MacAskill to my will. Good enough. "I want to use it now."

"You're sure?"

"Do you have scissors?"

"Aye." He frowns slowly. "On my utility knife."

"OK." I take a deep breath. "Here's the deal. I want you to cut my hair." Time to start the New Year as my own person. The fact that I almost stooped to Harper's level scares me, and I want to put more distance between us. I've never looked drastically different from her, and this is a perfect opportunity.

"What?"

"You heard me."

"But why? You have beautiful hair," he says crossly.

"I look exactly like someone I don't like or respect."

"Your sister."

"Exactly. And I'm ready for a change. More than ready."

"I can't cut girl hair," he says. "I'll cock it up."

"Come on, please. I would do it myself, but I can't see what I'm doing. Anyway, you promised."

"Thought maybe you were after a shag." His smile is wolfish, pure feral magnetism.

Imagine him taking me Animal Planet style, thrusting from behind, biting my neck as he takes his pleasure. *Whoa, mama.* Looks like lust has seriously rewired my brain. Is *lust-washed* a word? Because it totally should be. "You have a high opinion of yourself." As soon I say that, it strikes me as the worst possible thing I could have uttered. Rhys has this complex from me faking it, a crazy complex considering the problem is all with me. "That was a joke."

His posture is stiff again. Back to retreat. "My humor must be off with my pride."

It's strange to have had sex with someone and know nothing about him. I suppose people do this all the time, hook up, wham, bam, and then that's it. But I'm like human Velcro. Stuff sticks to me. I get attached. "Please. I just need to do this for me. You have your own crazy ideas. Let me have this."

He shifts, and visibly relents. "Very well. How short do you want to go?"

OK, we're in business. "I actually haven't thought that far ahead. Hmmm. Not too short. I don't want to look like a fat little boy or anything."

He stares at me like I'm insane. "That's not a danger."

"You're kind, but I'm serious." Bad haircuts can do worse things. "Maybe a bob."

"Right then, a bob." Twin lines appear between his brows. "What's a bob?"

"Like the hairstyle?"

He blinks with a blank expression.

"God, men." I mimic a length right below my jaw. "Maybe somewhere in this area would be good. Do you think that will give me mushroom head? Like a poof? Because poof isn't a good look."

He gestures to his shaggy hair and scruffy almost-beard. "Do I look like an expert in personal grooming to you?"

"Um, maybe not. The whole mountain man look is sexy, no doubt. It works for you, but...you're sort of starting to creep close to a hermit in a cave."

He tips his head back. "Pardon?"

"Right now that beard is perfect, but give it a week or two and little birds might start building their nests in it," I tease. "Or you could start running around in a pelt and people will definitely give you space. Rumors will spread that the Valle del Frances is haunted by the ghost of Cro-Magnon Man."

"No' a bad idea." He give his chin an exaggeratedly musing rub.

"How about this—you cut my hair and then I'll shave you? I'd love to see your face." And that's the truth, God as my witness.

He shakes his head. "The beard stays, but I'll do you."

*I'll do you?* Can he see that I'm turning five different shades of red? I duck my chin and sit on the stump, combing my hair out with my fingers.

He picks up a lock and rubs it between his fingers. "I'm nervous," he admits. "Once Cameron made me pierce his ear when we were lads. With a safety pin."

"And?"

"He bled and I spewed."

"Good thing hair doesn't bleed." I close my eyes. "Go on." This could be a terrible idea, or a chance to be more me, myself, my own person. Escape Harper. Hair is a trivial first step, but as he begins to tentatively snip with his Swiss Army scissors and long strands fall over my lap, I feel no different from a butterfly emerging from a cocoon or snake shedding its old skin. "How's it look?"

He makes a shushing noise.

I open one eye. "Did you just seriously shush me?"

"Aye, stop talking. It makes your head move. Don't muck up my line."

"Whatever you say, Vidal Sassoon."

He snips, and I'm lighter every time a new tendril of hair falls to the earth. I needed this, distance from my sister, from looking like someone who enjoys making me suffer. "There. Finished." Wind licks my neck. I reach up to run my hands through my hair and the feeling is disorienting.

"It's all gone."

He's staring.

"Do I look weird?" Self-consciousness replaces relief. "Am I a fat boy all of a sudden?"

"I would no' have thought it, but you look even prettier this way. Your eyes are bigger."

His breath is a little ragged, as if he's as affected by my proximity as I am to his. It would be nice to think so. Optimism isn't my strong suit. Not that I fall into the glass-is-half-empty camp either. More like, "What's exactly in the glass and what's the outside temperature? LET ME CALCULATE THE DAMN EVAPORATION RATE."

He points in the opposite direction from the trail we'll take out. "Follow me."

I make a show of balking. "I don't make a habit of following strange men into the woods."

"It's a little late for that, ken."

"I'm not sure what I ken." I give him a wink. "Maybe some haggis?"

"That's it." He throws me over his shoulder. "Now you're in for it."

"What are you doing!" I tilt precariously as he adjusts his grip.

He moves through the woods, finally setting me beside a fallen tree well out of sight of the main trail and still-empty campground. He takes off his fleece vest and splays it over the wood before setting me on top of it with one easy lift. The moss underneath is damp, soaks into my pants, making my ass a little cold. "Hey." I wiggle. "My—"

He cuts me off with a bruising kiss, nothing slow or gentle about it. He conjures my response before I can question whether this is a smart idea. When he slides his tongue against mine, I taste his essence, a hint of coffee and a trace of dried pears, and moan a little, the hum rising through the back of my throat.

He savors the hollow of my neck. Takes his time to ensure every square inch of my throat receives attention. Through the tree canopy, the sky is overcast, but it doesn't matter when I blaze inside.

"Take off your pants," he whispers. "I want to feel you."

I give a shaky laugh and lift one of my boot-clad feet. "That's going to be hard. There's a lot to untie here. I made a triple knot."

"Aye, fitting." His next kiss takes what's left of my breath. "Seeing as you've tied me in one hell of a knot, too."

# 17

## RHYS

*T*he skin on the inside of Auden's elbow is soft, and I can't quit skimming my finger over it even as she trembles. When she's close, I feel better. More settled. I'm never comfortable in my own skin unless I'm pushing myself to the limits. This girl's a shot of novocaine, dulling the gnawing, relentless grief inside me. "Before we leave, I want the truth from you."

"Ask me anything," she whispers.

I take my time studying her face. "Was no' intending to talk."

"Oh?" Her gaze gives nothing away. No small feat with those expressive blue eyes.

"Although saying 'Yes, good,' 'Right there,' or 'Rhys, you are a fucking god' will be acceptable."

"Sorry, Charlie." Her lips form a ghost of a smile. "My condoms are in the clearing with my backpack."

I shake my head. "We moved ahead of ourselves yesterday, and I'm easily jealous. I want you mentally with me, not wandering back to your past."

She wrinkles her brow. "I don't understand."

"Forget what you think you know about sex, lass, how it can be between a man and a woman. All those past failed experiences. You are going to show me the truth of you, right here, before we take one more fucking step out of this valley." I unbutton her pants and she cants her hips, allowing me to tug them to her knees. I could strip them off. No doubt she expects me to, but the idea of restricting her movement appeals. This way she can spread for me, but only a little. She'll need to focus down to the micromovements. Pay attention to every detail.

I step back and take my time looking my fill. Her head is down, turned shyly away. How can she not understand that she's stunning?

"Look at me." Let her see how badly I want her.

She doesn't move. "Um, I feel a little exposed over here."

"Because your pussy is bared to me."

She flinches, a bolt of hectic color shooting across her cheeks.

"You don't like me talking like that?" I press.

"Um." She clears her throat. "I've never had anyone talk dirty to me. Especially not using *p* . . . You know, those kinds of words."

"*Pussy?*"

She makes an uncomfortable face.

"Do you prefer *cunt?*" I ask softly.

Her head snaps back. "Jesus. No. God."

"You didn't strike me as the type. What about *fanny?*"

She chokes on a giggle. "Sounds like someone's grandmother."

"*Muff?*"

"Cute, if you're a poodle." She tries to close her knees, and I catch them, keeping them spread.

"So what, then?"

She shifts her weight. "If you insist, I guess circle back to *pussy* because I can't hang with *vagina* even though it's probably the most mature."

"*Vagina* comes from the Latin word *vaginae*, which means 'sheath,' or 'scabbard.'"

"A sheath for a sword?" She sounds incredulous.

"Exactly."

She lets out a huffy breath. "Why can't women get the equivalent of *cock*? It's not fair. You can't go wrong with *cock*. The word is like a little black dress, always ready to party."

"We're off subject." Her pussy, cunt, muff, whatever we're going with, is in plain view, and I haven't come remotely close to looking my fill.

"Let me close my legs?" There's a pleading note in her voice.

"Hell no." My cock strains against my boxer briefs at the sight of her soft curls, the hint of slickness between her lips. "Touch yourself."

"No." Her eyes go wide. "No way."

"Go on, for me."

Her mouth twists. "I'm not your puppy. I don't play fetch on command. And forget about telling me to roll over."

"Stop joking and do it." I keep my voice soft but insistent.

"You do it," she responds petulantly, tapping the back of her boot against the wood.

"So it's like that, is it?"

She twists a lock of her hair. "Look, I think you've got me pegged all wrong. I'm not the kind of girl who does this sort of thing."

"What about all that talk about saying yes to new experiences?"

Her glare is formidable. "Breaking out the heavy artillery, huh?"

"Simply reminding you of your resolution. 'Yes' is your word this year."

"I can't say it to everything. What if you ask me to kill someone?"

"Masturbation isn't murder."

She rolls her eyes. "Insert a rubbing-one-out joke here."

"Can I tell you why I want this?" Fair's fair. I want her to give of herself, so I need to offer something of myself.

"Please."

"First, I can't think of anything hotter than watching you pleasure yourself. Second"—I lower my voice—"I don't ever want you to be false to me again."

"So this is punishment?"

"Reframe it as pleasure. Show me a sexy, beautiful, gorgeous girl getting herself off."

"What if I fake it again?" She sounds half-cheeky and half-peevish.

I brace my arms on either side of her thighs and lean in, sucking the lobe of her ear in a slow, wet kiss before whispering, "You won't."

"How do you know?" She gasps.

"Because I'm going to give you something."

"Which is?"

I pull back and hold her gaze. "My trust."

Her mouth forms this perfect little O.

"Go on, then."

Her fingers slide up her knees, travel her inner thighs, and my brain flatlines even as my pulse pounds harder and harder. Though I thought she'd do it, seeing her in action is a whole other box of dice. Fuck me, she looks good—better than that, bloody incredible.

"This what you want?" She eases two fingers into her slit, pupils dilated like she didn't think she had it in her. I don't get that about this girl. She doesn't recognize how special she is. No one's ever looked at me like this. She's not intimidated. Maybe a little nervous, but hell, so am I.

She's working herself properly, fingers glistening.

"How do you normally do this?"

"Alone." Her teeth latch to her top lip. "In the dark."

"I meant fast or slow."

"Slow. It's not like it's going anywhere."

I laugh long and loud, which is something I'm not sure I've ever done with a hard-on before. Auden's brand of sexy is fun, and I've never known that was possible. It's good to be turned-on and smiling.

I really meant to make her do this—touch herself, come while I watch—but fuck, my plan unravels with every rise and fall of her breasts. I could tell myself it's pride at work, that I want to have another chance to assert my manliness, that she isn't going to fake it with me again, but there's something else more simple happening here.

I want to touch her.

So I do. And it's bloody brilliant. I set my hands in the small of her back and before lowering my mouth to hers, say, "Don't stop."

She parts her knees a little more and gives me a clear view of dusky pink slickness. Fuck. Never could I tire of such a sight.

"What about pressure? Hard or soft?"

"Light first." Her voice cracks. "So light it's almost not touching. Only use the tips of my fingers."

I glance down as she flicks herself. "Like that?"

She nods distractedly.

I'm transfixed, undone by her small circling movements.

"This is something you're into?" She breathes. "Watching?"

"I've never done this before."

"Not something you make all the girls do?" She arches her back, gives her breasts a subtle thrust.

"I've never asked any girl for this." My voice is husky as hell.

"Guess I better make it memorable."

She already has. This girl's put me under a sort of spell. Despite the fact I'm not even sure if I fully trust her, I find myself hoping, though I'm not even sure what for.

"You can't control everything—you know that." She pants.

"Maybe no', but it's worth a try."

She pauses what she's doing. "But if you're always in control, then you're never surprised."

I swallow back a frustrated groan. "Don't like surprises."

She pops one of her fingers in my mouth. I jerk in surprise as her flavor spreads across my tongue. Before I can grasp what's happening, she's palming my cock straight through my trousers. She drags her thumb along my shaft, and it responds like she's its high lord and master. "That's nice?"

"Aye." I'm reduced to single syllables.

"See? Surprises aren't all bad." She winks, smug as the cat who ate the cream. She moves her hand over mine, and her wet heat is better than anything.

"What if I do this?" I ease back her hood and brush my thumb over the exposed bud.

"Oh, God." Her thighs give an inadvertent twitch.

"I'll be taking that as a yes, then." I do it again and her legs jump, and she's laughing and then I'm laughing, but our kiss intensifies. My tongue thrusts with as much fury as the fingers I've added inside her. This is good, incredible even, but I need more.

I fall to my knees between her spread legs and tug her pants to her ankles. When she's open enough, I lean in and tease with my tongue, a slow lick up and down before she can gasp. Her taste is incredible, tangy and addictive. My hands roam to her hips, holding her, and I don't just lick. I kiss and add a soft bit of suction until her hips buck, keep it up until she's coming, hard, right on my face. I want to pull back, finish her with my fingers, watch her fall apart, but can't bear losing the taste of her.

Afterward, she collapses, limp and spent against me, rubbing her still shivering thighs. "They won't stop."

"Elvis leg?"

She looks puzzled.

"I get it climbing sometimes. Cameron and I called it 'Doing the Wild Elvis.'" I shake my own in an impersonation as I rise back to standing.

She is quiet a moment, her ribs rising and falling through her shirt. "I wish I could have that effect on you."

"Don't think for a second you don't affect me. How are you? Want to go again?" I'm as greedy as a kid in a candy store.

She gives me a lazy smile and stretches over her head. "Sorry. I think Elvis has left the building. You, on the other hand—"

"Me?"

She reaches, skimming my hard-on again, and I hiss, sucking in a breath. "I owe you one."

"There is no debt."

She makes a little *tsk-tsk*. "That was just my way of saying I'm going to fondle you now."

"Fondle?"

She smirks. "You prefer 'pat'?"

"I no' a dog," I grind out as goose bumps march down the furrow of my spine.

"Sex words really need an overhaul, don't they? 'Rub' isn't good either." She shakes her head.

"You are such a fucking romantic, lass." I give a hoarse laugh as she eases her hand beneath my waistband, tracing my shaft with a light, teasing caress. I tear open my trousers and boxers, until my cock thrusts out.

She lifts the length and gives it an assessing look.

"You're beautiful."

"Cocks are no' beautiful." I know that, but it doesn't prevent me thickening even more. It's a good thing to please her.

"I'd normally agree, but you really are."

"Careful. You'll give me a big head."

Her smile is crooked. "All right, your turn. I'm ready to see how this whole voyeur thing goes."

"I don't know if I can." My abdomen flexes, and swallowing is suddenly impossible. It's different having the tables turned.

She gives me a coy smile. "Don't be shy. I just jilled off—"

"Jilled off?"

"Like instead of jacked off." She waves her hand as if trying to conjure the perfect explanation. "More PC."

My brows smash together. "Sex is PC?"

She gives me a look. Her look. "You want to argue semantics?"

She wants to fight fire with fire? Fine, let's burn the forest down. I go for it, don't hold back, work myself fast and furious. Her breath grows ragged, as does mine. Undercutting each exhalation is the friction I'm creating. My head glistens, and when I circle the tip, a slow press of my thumb, the flesh is slick with my need. That's when she rips my hand back and takes me for herself.

"Harder," I growl, pushing into her palm.

She increases the pressure. "Better?"

"More."

"Won't that hurt?"

"I like a tight grip."

"You asked for it." She squeezes, and I'm almost there before she glides back to the base.

"Fuck."

"Good fuck or bad fuck?"

"Good, fuck, oh, fuck." My voice is husky as she brushes the sensitive underside of my head. "Bad fuck, too."

"Why?" She frowns, pausing.

I rock my hips again. "Because I'm going to come."

"This fast?"

"It's no' my normal style." But it's true. Intense pressure radiates through my tightened sac. I bury my face in her neck and come like a shot, so violent blue stars burst behind my closed lids.

"Did you like—"

I shut her up with a wild kiss, my cock meshed between us, still half-hard. Her laugh is gentle, and I'm seized with a sudden instinctive sense of rightness.

This was the strangest sexual experience of my life, funny, forceful, and brilliant. For a few minutes, I forgot my remaining anger toward her as well as my more constant anger at myself. The world became a good place, good enough at least. And even now, the feeling lingers, which suggests this wasn't a purely lust-inspired activity where the brain rationalizes all sorts of dumb-arse ideas to justify getting off.

Voices drift through the woods. Not close enough anyone is going to come near, but I shove myself back in my pants while

Auden straightens herself up. In takes only a moment to erase the evidence. We could have been bird-watching or indulging in botanical pursuits.

"Think you can keep your hands to yourself for the rest of the hike?" I say, cocking my brow at her.

"You are a regular funnyman, aren't you?" She pulls her top lower, covering the exposed sliver of belly. I want her back the way she was before, spread bare, squirming with desire, giving me everything and holding nothing back.

I shrug as my abs go rigid. It's dangerous to give a name to what's happening inside me, how deep she is under my skin and how I don't mind; if anything, I want her even deeper.

But I can't think such thoughts. Not consciously. If I do, the spell could well break.

# 18

## *AUDEN*

*T*he hike up into Campamento Britanico took me three times as long as the hike out. When we reach the main trail, my feet are a little boot sore, but thankfully the fit is good so no blisters threaten. I yank the map from my backpack's side pocket for a quick consult. "You're sure you want to stop in just a few hours? It wouldn't be hard for you to reach the La Aguja climbers' camp in a single day."

"This pace is good."

"I feel like you're holding back because you don't want to push me."

"That's where you're wrong," he says with an oh-so-insinuating grin. "I'd like nothing better than to push you, or at least push into you." Rhys doesn't give lovey-dovey speeches, but even his frank— and frankly cheesy—dirty innuendos do it for me. As much as I want to roll my eyes, I'm too busy not passing out as blood races from my extremities to pool between my legs.

We're bound for a designated campground near the Refugio Cuernos, not far down the trail, my original destination the night

I turned in to the valley. According to the guidebook, there are fifty campsites there, and given the high season, it should be pretty near full. Still, Rhys doesn't seem to care about crowds for once. He ignores a large, raucous German hiking party pausing to take pictures of a delicate waterfall. Instead, he stares as if the world's distilled to one person—me.

"Tell me a story," I say.

He frowns. "You haven't had enough of my stories yet?"

"I want to get to know you better." I plow right through his misgivings.

"That's what I'm afraid of." He makes it sound like he's joking, but I know he's not. He hasn't just folded his arms over his chest; he's locked them tight like a Viking shield wall.

"What's something else you are afraid of?"

"Nothing." He bristles. "I do whatever I'm afraid of."

I'm tempted to call bullshit and respond with *No, you actually don't, because you're prepared to face a deadly mountain rather than have a simple conversation with your brother.* Hmm. Yeah, not the best tactic. Maybe I'll go for the more subtle approach. A skeptical eyebrow raise.

"Dogs," he responds curtly. "I'm afraid of dogs."

"Dogs?" My hearts sinks. "But I love dogs." I'm devoted to Gog and Magog, our family huskies. Not that it matters. This is hardly going to be a relationship where pet views are called into question.

"I didn't say I don't like them, only that they scare me. A little." He coughs into his fist. "Once, when we were lads, a great German shepherd chased down Cameron and me like a hound of hell. It lived near our school, and the owner was a mean old sot who kept him on a short lead. Every day we'd walk by and it would bark, growl, and do a grand carrying on. One morning, the chain snapped and he barreled at us."

"Oh my God, what did you do?"

"Told my brother to reach in my schoolbag, fetch the sausage rolls Mum baked, and give them a good hard throw. He did, and we scrambled up a nearby tree fast as you please. Hung tight until a neighbor walked by and noticed." He gave a rueful smile at the memory before shaking his head. "What about you, Auden Woods? Time to fess up. What are you afraid of?"

"Drinking fountains."

He stops in his tracks, and I almost plow into his back. Two dreadlocked girls come around the corner from the direction we're headed. One gives me a head nod before her gaze slides toward Rhys like he generates his own gravitational pull. I swear to God a little bit of drool appears in the corner of her mouth.

My old friend self-doubt slips in for a visit. Seriously, how can a guy of Rhys's caliber be into me? It's like that scene in *The Hobbit* where the hot elf falls in love with the dwarf and everyone in Middle Earth goes, "The fuck is this?"

*Stop.* I haven't gone on this whole journey to end up back at the start, believing I'm not good enough. I've got to remember to keep choosing the different path, the one that says, "I'm here and enough."

Besides, Rhys isn't even glancing in the other girls' direction. Instead, he steps to the trail side, braces his hand against a wind-blown tree, and his repeated question, "You're afraid of drinking fountains?" yanks me from my racing mind.

"Yeah, and there's no good reason like a childhood trauma or anything to conveniently pin the blame on," I respond, trying to refocus on the conversation. "But whenever I lean over one, I'm gripped by sudden inexplicable terror that someone will creep up from behind and slam my face into it. Break my nose."

"That's the strangest thing I've ever heard."

"Welcome to my world." *Creepy fears and inadequacy issues—it's a hoot.*

We resume hiking, and I concentrate on keeping my shoulders back, posture straight, and head high. Lead with the outside, and the inside will follow—I hope. The trail is flat and boardwalked in this section, and we can walk side by side, almost as if strolling along a sidewalk. When the lake comes into better view, we pause, checking out the distant black dots, guanacos grazing on the far south shore. "Also, lately, I keep having those dreams where my teeth fall out."

"Hate those."

"I know, right? They all start wiggling and then—"

"Stop. You're twisting my guts." He slings his arm around my shoulders and plants a casual kiss on the top of my head.

I like this version of Rhys—the fun and playful edition. Maybe this is what I bring to him, because today the yellow streaks in his eyes don't seem as intimidating. He's more woodcutter than wolf. He's just a guy, and I'm just a girl, and we're having a hard time keeping our hands off each other.

Shoving any professional interest to the side, why does he want to climb La Aguja? It's too dangerous to be explained away by a flippant "Because it's there" sort of answer. What drives him, especially after his accident last spring? So many questions and none that I have the right to ask. All too soon we're going to be at the La Aguja base camp and it will be time to pursue our individual dreams.

A ripple of unease passes through me.

I am willing to let Rhys's story go, but what about others? Hopefully Diedrick made fast tracks out of the park. It's a little strange he left us alone, almost too easy, but maybe Rhys is finally due a bit of luck.

Guess I am, too, because I got away with it. I never have to tell Rhys that I put his puzzle together, that I considered using him for my own gain.

He plucks a white wildflower and twists it between his fingers. "About your job, being a journalist."

"Yes?" I jump as if he can read my thoughts. He tucks the flower behind my ear before gently lacing his fingers with mine.

"Why?"

"Why what?" I keep my voice light. This is dangerous territory.

"Why do you want to be a journalist?"

I snort. "You mean terrible pay, shrinking newsrooms, and long hours doesn't sound like reason enough?"

His intense gaze lets me know deflection won't get me off the hook.

"Well." I loop a hand behind my neck. "I love to meet new people, ask questions, dig deeper and see what makes them tick."

"I wouldn't have guessed that," he says wryly.

I poke my tongue out at him. "I love to write and want to go out and find great stories to tell. But the story I'm doing is only part of an internship. That's why I need it to be great, because if I kick butt, then I'm in contention for a real job." I pull from his hand to bracket the word *real* with imaginary quote marks. "Those are as elusive as Moby Frigging Dick in my field, but if I fail and don't get the job, I'm still considered lucky to have six months of super-glamorous grunt work and a stipend that will allow me to subsist on ramen noodles. I'll probably have to supplement my diet by sneaking into

McDonald's and stealing ketchup packets. Add some hot water and voilà—tomato soup."

"Disgusting." He feigns gagging, or maybe he is for real gagging.

"Stick with me in a zombie apocalypse, baby." I mockingly flip my hair. "I have mad survival skills."

"Raiding fast-food joints?" he deadpans. "That's your brilliant Armageddon strategy?"

"You've got a better one?" I take in his build, the red climbing rope coiled on his back, the indisputable fact that he's completely at home outdoors. "OK, fine, you probably do. So you'll protect me when the zombies come for my brains?"

His look is impenetrable. "You'd trust me?" The only give-away that the question means something to him is barely detectable hesitancy.

I lay a hand on his shoulder, my jokey smile fading. "Trust is important to you, isn't it?"

He bows his head. "More so than anything else. When you're on a mountain with someone, you aren't alone. Your fate rests in others' hands."

"I've never had to do that, trust another person with my life."

"It's no' easily given. I've only ever completely trusted my brother." There's danger beneath his quiet words, like a trap waits, lined with pointed logs, waiting to spear anyone who wanders too close. "Our relationship is complicated of late. We…we…aren't speaking."

"I'm sorry." I increase my grip. "Have you tried reaching out to him?"

"No. It's complicated." His eyes glitter as a ruddy color spreads across his throat. "But he sent a letter. It arrived at Da's place right before I left last week."

I count to five, but he doesn't appear in a hurry to cough up the rest of the story. "What did he say?"

His lips press hard against each other. "Don't know."

"You didn't open it?" I remember the first night, when I bumped into his book and a sealed envelope fell on my chest before he whisked it away.

He doesn't respond. I'm guessing the lack of reply means no, but that he knows that is the wrong answer.

"Rhys MacAskill. You need to read that letter."

"What do you care?" His gaze snaps to my face, and I don't have time to hide my reaction. I don't know what he sees there.

Maybe I should just confess, tell him I know who he is, but he seems to need this brief time to be "normal" again, not the guy who starred as the villain in the year's most famous accident. I've only just regained his trust. I'm not ready to lose it again.

"Because I have a terrible relationship with my sister," I say, giving him only the tiniest, unrelated part of the truth. "Because I'd do anything to repair our relationship if given the chance. Even though she's treated me terribly, family is family, and I don't want holidays to be like venturing into an enemy camp."

He gives an inward sigh, shoulders dropping. "Let's keep going, lass."

We slowly make our way down the steeply descending trail. The forest is different here, more dense and dark, no longer providing expansive views to the distant grasslands. The wind's picking up again, whipping through the branches.

"Guess I'm afraid of more than dogs after all," he says at last. "But you don't know how it is, or was, with me and Cameron. Da left a long time ago, and Mum worked long hours to support us. He and I were inseparable, until Amelia. His wife."

The way he says that name is a little off. "Were you jealous when they met?"

"No, at least not of her. I just missed his company. Amelia's a good sort, but I didn't see why they needed to rush into marriage. They are both so young. But then he said a thing about her that has stuck with me ever since. When you know, you know. Nothing particularly profound, but he knew that girl was it for him. He just knew."

That's the moment I know, too. It's as if my body encases pure sunlight. This grumpy-ass, hot-as-hell guy in front of me? I'm falling for him, and it's more than a pull to the magnetism he exudes. Of course I'm physically attracted to him, but there's something deeper at work here, as if I'm tapping into a subterranean current. For all his broody bluster, I see him, the real guy—the good guy—who's unsuccessfully hiding one hell of a heartache. And he sees me, understands that I'm up for adventure with the right person, that if I'm pushed and encouraged, I'll take leaps I'd never attempt on my own.

"I get being afraid of that letter," I say tentatively, unsure if he can see what's hiding in my heart. "Maybe it has bad news. Says the opposite of what you hope for. I am afraid of things, too, like asking for help. When I had to go to your tent a few nights ago? That was almost scarier than not being able to breathe. I haven't climbed mountains, but I know it's hard to put trust in people."

His whole face shifts, the muscles doing a weird thing where he looks exactly the same but everything rearranges. All his latent hardness softens a fraction as his eyes blaze. "Who placed you in my path?"

"I put myself there."

"Thank you, then." He cups my face in his big hands and rests his forehead against mine. "I'm glad you asked for help."

I kiss the tip of his nose. "Got to say, you didn't make it easy."

"No." He grimaced. "Not my finest hour."

"But I'm glad, too."

"At the La Aguja climbing camp"—Rhys traces the side of my bra through my shirt—"it won't be like things were back in Valle del Frances."

"In what ways?"

"We won't be alone. There will be others, hard to say how many. Could be twenty, maybe more. People have been gunning for this mountain for a long time."

"Do you know anyone who will be there?"

He takes my hand as we continue down the trail. "Three Australians—Psycho, Goonbag, and Murray. We've never been on the same team, but we've done other climbs at the same time. I arranged for my supplies to be shuttled in with theirs on horseback with a gaucho team they hired, South American cowboys." He patted his pack. "Can't carry all my provisions and equipment in here. I'll need more rope, crampons, an ice ax, extra clothing, food, and the like."

*Psycho? Goonbag?* "Are those actual names?"

"Murray is a surname, I think. Lots of nicknames get thrown around camps."

"What's yours?"

"I don't have one."

"Why doesn't that surprise me?" I fail to suppress a grin. "You probably scare everyone."

He returns my smile despite himself.

*Ooh, a challenge.* I put my hands on my hips. "I'll come up with one for you."

"What's yours?"

"Um, I don't have one either." I'm betrayed by a blush. Great.

He gives me a deeply suspicious look. "It can't be that bad."

"Au contraire, it can. Awful actually."

"Now I must know."

"Woody," I mutter with as much dignity as I can muster.

"What?" He bursts out laughing.

"See?" I give his chest a playful whack. "That's why I didn't want to say anything."

"It's apt, truth be told, seeing as I've had one since meeting you."

"God, here we go." I throw my hands up in mock aggravation. "And to think I hoped traveling thousands of miles would put enough distance between me and Woody jokes."

"A woody can stretch a fair way."

"I appreciate your attempts at joking." My tone is a little acerbic. "And that smile? It's a good look on you. But make another Woody crack and I'll cut a bitch, and by 'bitch' I mean you."

"Cut me?" If he intends to peeve me by ruffling my hair, mission accomplished. "With what?"

"I haven't forgotten you have a utility knife somewhere in that giant Santa bag of yours."

"Santa bag?" He gives me an incredulous stare.

"You know what I mean." I point to his huge backpack.

"Half the time I don't have a clue what you're talking about." He draws me in tight, his murmur warm against my skin. "But nothing about you makes sense, so perhaps it's fitting, eh?"

Overhead, through a gap in the trees, a mountain rises in a bold granite thrust of rugged cliffs. "Isn't it beautiful here?" Easier to look at the overwhelming natural beauty than feel half the things I do.

"Aye, that it is." His stare bores into me.

I skim his scruffy jaw with the tips of my fingers, allowing myself to explore his thick hair, then dip down to travel his
brawny back, reveling in his unabashed male beauty. "That sounds
strangely like you're giving me a compliment."

"Auden, two days ago, I didn't want to see anyone. Talk to anyone. Hear anyone speak. I wanted to climb La Aguja, and that was
my sum total." He leans down and kisses the place where my neck
meets my shoulder. "Then you came along, and I don't know…
Things don't seem half as bad."

"I…" I don't have words. I don't have thoughts. His lower lip
drags along my skin until I'm distilled to a hard beating heart. He's
gruff and awkward as hell, but there is something about him that's
charming the pants off me. Literally. I'd drop trou right here and
let him go to town if three Israeli backpackers weren't gaining on us.

"On your left," calls one, and they plod by single file.

I'm so wet I can barely stand it. Can these strangers tell from
the look on my face? Can he? The way he watches me—yeah,
he knows. I knock the toe of my boot into his. "I bet you don't get
passed on trails normally."

"Not really."

"See, I am slowing you down."

"Nothing about you makes me want to go slow." He clasps one
of my hands between his, rubs the pad beneath my thumb in the
intimate way he has of making every touch half-sexual and half-
tender. "Faster? Harder? More? Those are the words that come to
mind."

I smile and squeeze his hand. "I like being with you."

"Aye, same." He tugs a wayward lock of my hair, reverently
threads it between his fingers as if he's handling something priceless.

My body grows tense, concentrated. I wish I could stay with him, in this fantasy lovey-dovey space, but the real world hovers around the corner. The expectations related to my dream job are mounting, and my panic is rising in conjunction. What if no climbers want to talk to me?

"Why that sudden frown?" he says.

"I'm flying home in a week. What if no one speaks to me at base camp?"

"Is this the part where you ask me for help again?" He doesn't stiffen, but I know this is a test.

"No. I'm not giving you a big hint." I let out a sigh. "But I do need people to interview."

He grimaces. "I'm sorry I can't be the one to assist you, truly I am, but don't go worrying none. Once the lads at camp get a whiff that you work in media, you'll be beating them off with a stick. Everyone likes to hear themselves talk."

We're going up a steep incline, and he holds up a hand, suddenly distracted. "Stop. Wait here."

"Why?" I'm still in fretting-about-the-future mode.

"Let me check something."

He doesn't pause to see if I obey. It's a little annoying the way he barks commands and expects I'll follow orders without question. But before I can get too worked up, he's back.

"Follow me," he says, even as he raises a warning hand. "But careful, mind the edge, and don't venture too close. It's a trifle steep."

I gingerly pick my way down the escarpment, trying to avoid tripping on the roots riddling the small footpath. I duck under a low-hanging branch, but I don't squat enough, and the top of my backpack wedges against the wood until Rhys reaches and tugs me free.

"Thanks," I say, straightening before vertigo sets in. "Steep? Whoa, that's a bit of an understatement." We're on a four-foot thrust of rock, and beneath us the ground disappears. There's no sloping gradient, just boom, earth gone. Far below a blue river runs through the green, like an open vein. "I knew we were at altitude, but not that we were so high."

"Do you see?" Rhys stands right on the edge, casual as anything. He might as well be standing on a curb, pointing out an interesting city landmark.

It takes a moment before it's possible to swivel my head in the direction of his outstretched hand. When I do, my heart does this weird swelling thing but also plummets off the edge. I'm full and empty at the same time. Because Rhys is showing me a gorgeous stone tower, rising against the distant sky like a pointed finger, wider at the base and tapering near to nothing at the top. The peak is crowned by a thick band of snow. At least I think it's snow, because a last layer of cloud is still covering it.

"Look, the weather is clearing just as predicted," Rhys says, excitement animating his voice. "La Aguja, isn't she something?"

"You can't do that," I say, aghast to see his plan come to life. There is a world of difference between hearing about a legendary, dangerous mountain and seeing it firsthand. I wanted to go to the camp to profile climbers, see what drew them to put their lives at risk to achieve their dreams, but this mountain isn't a dream maker; it's a death maker. Suddenly, getting to the camp feels like my worst nightmare. "Rhys, you can't climb that thing solo. This is insanity."

The way he sets his mouth is three kinds of stubborn, like he's about to do a Cartman "I do what I want" impression.

Holy shit. I'd be terrified if he said he was doing that climb with a team, but at least then he wouldn't be alone. This mountain doesn't look the sort to fuck around. There has to be a better way.

"How long until we get there?"

"At the rate we're going?" He frowns, considering. "Tomorrow afternoon." The way he rocks on his heels, all repressed energy, I know if he could, he'd bolt right now, take off running. He probably thinks that offhand smile is reassuring, but he doesn't even see me anymore, staring instead at the peak as if it's an enemy to vanquish.

I want to tell him that the demons he fights are on the inside, that if he does this climb, the stone will be just an innocent bystander to his private battle, but what's the point?

He can't hear me. I could jump up and down and turn cartwheels and he wouldn't notice.

The same hypnotized gaze slides over my sister's face before a competition.

I've gone from being his total focus to a ghost, sidelined by the force of his ambition.

# 19

## RHYS

*A*uden's quiet after we leave the lookout and remains so for the short distance to the campground. I wanted to stop here for the night because it's the last chance before we get to La Aguja and there's more at stake now than my shot-to-hell focus. Once we arrive at the climbing camp, it will be damn near impossible for her not to learn the truth about what happened to Cameron on that lonely mountain in the Himalayas. I should be grateful for this stolen time, the opportunity to have spent a few days not haunted by the past.

What if…? What if she somehow understands how the situation occured? Doesn't hate me like everyone else. What if, someday, our paths cross again? I come through the States on occasion. She doesn't live far from Da. It could happen.

*No.*

I try to stamp out the whim, but it persists as a stubborn little flame…Maybe.

*All right, wise guy, think it through,* my inner voice pipes up. *Imagine if the best-case scenario happens and she learns about the*

*accident and doesn't hate you. Decides your sorry ass is still worth pur-*
*suing. Isn't it better for this moment to be all you ever have rather than*
*facing the real world, the eventual drudgery of the day-to-day, inevi-*
*table fights about how you'll want to go for a climbing trip and she'll be*
*after a beach-bound holiday to Hawaii? And either way you'll lose. At*
*least she will. Because you'll go.*

Aye. I will.

There will always be another mountain. It's selfish, but at the
end of the day, that's what we are—selves. If we don't look out for
our own interests, there are plenty who'll be more than happy to
chip away at our core, piece by piece, until we forget what we ever
wanted.

Cameron's headed in that direction. Amelia is from the California coast, not much vertical there outside of climbing gyms. But then,
he doesn't have a fucking hand anymore, and whose fault is that?
I grit my teeth as bitter self-loathing floods my mouth. It's a nearly
impossible effort to swallow it down, keep from losing my shit.

As we set up the tent in a clear, flat space, other people lounge
in front of their tents, reading paperbacks or playing Hacky Sack. A
couple pauses to give us a friendly wave, but I keep my nod as curt.
I'm not after a "how do you do" chat with the neighbors. I don't
give a fuck if they come from Boston or Toronto, Sydney or Paris. I
haven't come to this place to shoot the breeze with people I'm never
going to see again. Auden's my exception, the only one I'm prepared
to make.

Simply watching her is its own form of foreplay, the way she
snaps poles together and threads them into the nylon. Each thrust of
her wrist is an invisible stroke on my cock.

"There, all done." She sinks the last peg into the earth, her
round ass showcased by thin hiking pants. "Home sweet home."

My brain flashes to the night we met and those damn captivating underclothes.

"Good. Now, get in there," I rumble, unzipping the door, "and get into those kitten knickers."

"Kitten?"

"Take me off right meow," I say. "Put them on."

She shakes her head slowly. An expression close to disbelief takes hold. "Are you going to say the magic word?"

"You've a magic word?" My brain isn't equipped for riddles right now. "And just how am I supposed to guess it?"

"Holy God." She half laughs and half looks like she's about to smack me upside the head. "Did you grow up among trolls? Were you raised by wolves? Here's a hint. It starts with *P* and ends with *lease*."

I mash my lips together, rolling them a little. "Please, Auden, please put on those sweet fucking little knickers. They drive me mad."

She averts her face, gaze dropping to my climbing rope coiled to my pack. "Have you ever tied anyone up?"

She's the master of a well-played diversionary tactic. My cock thickens at the thought of binding her. "No."

"Have you ever been tied up?" she asks.

I fold my arms. "Of course not."

"Of course not?" Her mouth quirks.

"I prefer to remain in control."

"And I think I'd like taking it away from you," she murmurs.

"You want to tie me up?" I say slowly, her words sinking in as my cock gives a sharp twitch.

She wrinkles her brow. "Yeah, I kind of do. I'll give in to your weird underwear fetish for a chance at tying you up—those are my terms."

"Your terms?" I allow a shred of amusement to enter my voice.

"Yeah," she says softly, before clearing her throat. "Yes."

*Yes*...such an innocent word for a wicked proposition.

I run my thumb over my jaw. Giving up control doesn't sound appealing, but when you layer in the idea of Auden naked, it's got a certain level of appeal. The girl's clearly in league with the fairies, working strange magic, because I'm actually considering letting her do this.

Fuck it.

Maybe she's right and not all surprises have to be bad. Plus kitten knickers. "Very well, Miss Woods. You have got yourself a deal."

"Really?" She blinks once, twice, three times before retying the blue scarf in her hair, the one that's a near-identical match to her eyes. "OK. OK. Yeah. Um, let's do this." She rummages in her backpack and tugs out a pair of small black shorts, swinging them around one finger with a shy smile. "These are what you are after?"

That's it. I'm done for. I grab her hand and my rope in two efficient movements. "You, in the tent, now." I zip the door closed behind us and sit on my heels.

In a few short seconds she sits across from me, hands braced on her knees, lips parted in anticipation.

"Remember the knot I taught you?" I ask.

"Yeah. More or less."

"That should work." I drop my chin, sensing she's got another request. "What else?"

"Would you mind...? Um, is it cool if you...?"

Her blush drives me mad—makes me want to care for her and at the same time pound her breathless.

She traces a circle on her thigh. "Can you take off your shirt? It does all the things to me."

I fist off my shirt and drag my hand through my hair a few times. "All the things?"

Her gaze pierces mine before dropping to spread over my chest with open fascination. "So many things," she murmurs, picking up the rope and turning it over in her hands with a private, wicked grin. "Lie down."

I do without protest. This isn't something I'd normally consider, and perhaps that's the appeal. Auden is new terrain for me; it's fitting we try new things as well.

She gathers my wrists and fiddles about. Her tongue pokes out in the corner as she falls into deep concentration tying the knot. "How's that?" she asks at last.

I twist my hands and the rope slips away.

"Shit," she mutters.

"You'll have to go rougher."

"I don't want to hurt you."

She hurts me every second we are together. The sharpest, sweetest stabbing pain. "Not all hurt is bad."

She mutters something like "You asked for it." This time the rope winds tight, chafing my skin.

"There," she says with satisfaction. "Better?"

I test, gingerly at first and then with a stronger attempt. "Aye. Holding fast."

"Good." The air charges between us, palpable and hot.

She moves to my ankles. "I want you at my mercy."

She wants a game, and I've indulged her, but everything feels different. I'm on my back, arms raised over my head, legs strapped together.

She pulls her gaze from the erection tenting my trousers and tugs the scarf free from her hair, moves to drape it over my face.

"But then I can no' see those knickers."

"I said that I'd put them on, but not when." She sounds smug even as uncertainty crosses her fine features. "Now, should we establish some sort of a safe word?"

"A what?" I splutter, unable to believe she got the better of me and admiring the hell out of her for doing so.

"Safe word," she repeats. "Like the thing you're supposed to say if you want me to stop."

I arch an eyebrow. "Stop what?"

She blushes straight to her hairline. "Well, the thing is, sometimes people want to say stop while, you know, fooling around, but they don't mean it."

"How the bloody hell do you know all this?" Maybe I've read her wrong. She's not an innocent, not in the least.

"My, um, e-reader has given me quite an education in kink," she mumbles. "I've just never tried any of it in real life."

If my arms weren't tied over my head, I'd pull her into my arms and give her a proper education in all sorts of things. "I don't need a safe word."

"So stop will mean stop. But can I blindfold you?"

"Fine."

"Don't sound so thrilled." She settles the scarf over my eyes, and the world veils. I can sense shadows when she moves, but that's all.

She blows over my stomach before giving my nipple a slow, circling lick. I arch like a bow.

"You're sensitive there, huh?"

"Looks like it," I gasp, and she does it again to the other one. Such an eager little thing.

"You prefer it this way?" She circles me lightly with her tongue, the pressure increasing as she switches to the flat of her tongue. "Or a little harder?"

"Aye." I swallow. "Just so."

"Good to know." She pulls away, and my senses heighten. Who knows where she'll go next? The waiting drives me mad, but it also feels goddamn incredible.

"You have such an unbelievable body, Rhys," she whispers, running her hand over my abdomen.

"So do you."

"Like art." The tips of her nails graze beneath my navel, raising my internal temperature twenty degrees. "I love your hardness."

"I love your softness." I groan when she undoes my trousers, tugs my boxers, and takes my cock in her wet palm. Fuck, she must have licked her hand first. She slides down my length without resistance as her tongue flicks against my lips. Jesus, the way she works her hands. When her teeth return to close on my nipple, she grazes hard, just as I'd asked, just as I need.

"Jesus-fuck-damn-Auden."

"Hmmm. You're not so articulate when I do that. What about this?" She cups my sac, presses a thumb to the base of my cock, and a garbled sound tears from my chest.

"You wee witch," I gasp, every muscle in my body taut, steel hard.

"Or this?"

"Mary and Saints." Now I'm thrumming, as if the place where her skin touches mine is overlaid with live wire. The thing she does with her mouth—good, so fucking good.

My breathing is loud. Lust rises, hard and fast, relentless as a floodwater. Losing control is hard, and a part of me, a large part, rails against it, screams to be released. But there's also curious relief. For the next few minutes at least, everything is out of my hands. I can do nothing, nothing but feel everything Auden gives. I twist against the rope and my wrists chafe, but the hurt is good, not because I like pain but because I like Auden. The girl has me smitten. I've given her pieces of myself that I've never shared with anyone. In return, she's taking me to places within myself that I didn't know were there. Around every corner waits something new, unexpected, and—

"Ow. Fuck."

"Oops. Sorry. That was my teeth; got carried away." There's the furtive sounds of her undressing, and then she crawls astride me, thighs bracketing my waist. The heat of her sex is slick as she rubs me, her silky inner skin hot as it slides across my shaft. She's not entering me, just teasing with the promise.

"Oh." She grinds harder. "Oh, yes." She is using me, and I don't mind. There's a part inside me that rages, says I'm nothing, worse than worthless, and it might be true, but for right now, I can lie here and let this beautiful girl make another of those beautiful breathless sounds against me.

If my skin is fire, hers is an inferno. Heat radiates through my lower belly in a series of slow pulses that gather in the center of my sac. I flex, desperate to touch her, and yet the rope holds firm. I jerk my head to the side, knocking off the scarf, and the sight of her naked above me tightens my throat. Her face is upturned, the angle exposing her throat's creamy white skin, the dark line of her erratically pulsing vein.

"Look at you," I mutter.

She opens her eyes and stares down, freezing. "You can see me."

"Aye." I swallow hard. "That I can."

She ducks her chin to her chest and moves to cover her breasts.

"No!" I want to grab her but am held in place. "Don't shy from me."

She glances through her lashes. "I'm not sure what to do next."

"Touch yourself again."

"You're very bossy for someone tied up."

"Do it." I hardly recognize my voice. "What you did earlier was the most fucking beautiful thing I've ever witnessed."

She moves a hand between her legs and gives a few soft swirls. "You're easy to look at, too." When she strokes my chest, her wetness sheens my skin, and that's it; I'm at the end of my own fucking rope, and grind myself free of the bindings.

She lets out an amused shriek as I pull myself loose and tug her against me. "You're a crazy girl, you know that?"

"Crazy as a fox." She kisses my cheek.

"Very foxy."

"A foxy lady?"

"Come here." I kiss her slowly, stroking the rise of her breast, then along her stomach, and lower still. "You like a light touch. I remember."

"Sometimes. It can change."

"So right now, is this good? What I'm doing here?"

She gives a little shiver, her toes curling against my calves. "Yeah. Really good."

"And when I touch you here?" My fingertips skim her inner lips. I want to press my whole hand up against her heat, but this isn't about my wants. It's about her. Her needs. I want to give her everything.

I've barely begun to touch, and yet she responds, growing wetter by the second. Her breathing takes on a ragged edge.

"Slower," she pants.

"No. Don't think I will."

"I don't want to come yet," she pleads.

"Why? You can come and come again."

"I've never been able to."

"This is a new year, remember?"

"A new year of multiple orgasms?" She grabs her hair in two fistfuls. "I can get behind that."

I keep up the light, skimming strokes, but with my other hand ease a finger inside, one slow thrust. When I find the soft ridge above her entrance, I press hard while increasing the pressure on her clit.

"Rhys."

I do it again and again, until her muscles clamp around my fingers and she comes in a drawn-out shuddering climax.

"How was that?"

She opens one eye and gives me a dazed grin. "Pretty sure I need to phone the president and ask him to award you a Congressional Medal of Honor."

"The smile on your face is reward enough," I murmur gruffly.

"Really?"

"No." I chuckle despite myself. "But it sounded good, didn't it?"

A laugh slips out of her. "You're awful."

I crawl back on top. "Awful enough to see if you can go again."

She pouts her sexy mouth. "Am I an experiment to you?"

"No, but you are quite a lot of fun."

Her mouth curves against mine as she presses a condom in my hand. I roll it on without breaking our rhythm. As I slide the tip of my cock into her heat, fear strikes out of nowhere, anxiety sinking into my muscles like venom. What if for all my big talk, I can't please her this way?

"I need you inside me, Rhys," she whispers. "All the way in."

The way she watches me with such desperate helplessness weakens my own resolve. No more waiting. I reach under her ass and jerk her hip to better get the angle that hits her clit. My reward is her walls tightening. She rocks against me, and I keep on her until she is close, almost there, but not quite, not quite.

"What else? What else do you need?" I'll do anything for this girl right now.

"Not sure." She closes her eyes. "Maybe a little talking."

"Dirty?"

"Yeah, no one's ever done that to me."

"I've no' done much myself." Fuck, her pussy tightens fractionally, and I'm conscious of every inch of her.

"We'll be each other's first. Just go gentle, cuddle after, and remember to respect me in the morning."

"I can do that." I smile into the side of her neck. "You're so soft and warm, I'd cuddle you after any day."

"That makes me sound"—she gasps before finishing—"like your teddy bear."

"Nah. I wouldn't do this to a teddy." I flip her over onto her hands and knees, checking that the condom is still snug. "Look how ready you are for me," I say, sliding to the hilt. "Taking you this way, I see the arch of your back and"—I finger her wet clit—"have easy access to all this sweetness."

She pushes back to meet my thrust. "Love the way you smell," I whisper hoarsely. "Loved tasting you earlier."

She offers up a moan.

My hand moves to her throat, her pulse frantic under my hand. "Tell me," I say. "Tell me how much you want this."

"So bad."

"You like this?" I slam balls deep. "Being taken hard?"

"Yes, yes." She keeps repeating the word.

"You know what else I can see? Your sweet, sexy ass. That's it, lass. Spread those thighs wider." She's stretching around me, and fuck, the fit is glove tight. I know this sounds cliché, but inside her, it doesn't just feel good; it feels right, like I'm where I am meant to be. The only other time I've come close to the same sense of belonging has been on a mountain.

"What are you doing to me?" I lift her to my lap, stay buried deep, peppering kisses along the base of her neck.

"Same thing you are doing to me." She reaches back to brace herself against my hips.

"God, look at you." I stare over her shoulder at her breasts, the softness of her stomach, the delicate curls between her legs. "I feel your wetness on my thighs."

"Take me. Don't hold back." Her nails sink deep. "You feel incredible."

I go hard with a fleeting hope no one has wandered close to our tent, because the sounds she makes, it's like she's forgotten herself, and then I'm gone, too. For a guy who never makes noise during sex, I'm unleashing rough groans. Sweat slicks my body and hers until there's no clear line of either of our beginnings or ends. Two becoming one isn't some bullshit thing. I know that now, because while I'm inside her, she's just as deep inside me.

"Rhys. I—I—Rhys…" She is past speech, and it doesn't matter because I feel her words instead. She's coming for me, and I'm right there, too. Tomorrow everything is going to change and she has no idea. I'm not ready for this to be over, for her to pull away, look at me with new, hard eyes, and find me lacking.

I'm not ready to give this moment up.

Never has it been this way with anyone, and when she drops her head against me with a shuddering sigh, I hold her tight, so fucking tight.

How do you ever let a girl like this go?

## 20

## *AUDEN*

*I*'m amazed that I can still hike. Hand to God Rhys screwed me sideways. We got halfway through my condoms, calling it quits only when the friction started hurting. He took me again and again like a desperate man, as if he were soaking me up, as if we wouldn't have another day. I wonder if the mountain is getting under his skin, if he is beginning to be aware of the danger he faces.

This morning we woke early and packed while avoiding eye contact with the nearby campers. Rhys forwent a hot breakfast because I couldn't choke down porridge while people gaped as if we were sex fiends.

Apparently we weren't quiet.

On the bright side, it doesn't look like I'll be pledging my life to a showerhead. Turns out—surprise—I can come during sex with the right guy, just need a little patience and focus. Two characteristics Rhys possesses in spades. We make good miles through the morning, despite the increasing heat and our smoldering chemistry. We take lots of kissing pit stops. Is kissing even the right word for it? It's more like we fuck with our mouths—I don't have a better term for it.

With every touch, with every breath, Rhys shows me I'm special, treasured.

It's silly to think this way about someone I've only just met. Insta-love has always been an unbelievable concept conveniently suited to Hollywood romantic comedies. I was with Brett for almost all of college and he never made me feel this way. Rhys and I didn't do a whole love-at-first-sight thing, but the intensity between us after a few short days is almost palpable.

Everything I thought I knew about anything is being challenged.

Except I still haven't actually given him the one thing he demands above anything else—truth. And the fact of the matter is, he hasn't told me his story either. So is all of this simmering between us ultimately fake, even though it feels realer than anything?

I can't believe that.

Hooves strike rock behind us. A weathered gaucho in a worn jean jacket and a wide-brimmed black hat comes around the bend, leading a line of three small brown and white packhorses, while a young boy who resembles him enough to be identified as his son brings up the rear. They give nods and wide smiles as we step off the trail to make ample room.

Rhys calls out in halting Spanish, asking who he's delivering gear for, and the man answers with "Nick Goodall." The name is unfamiliar even as Rhys nods in approval.

"Some of this gear is for me," Rhys tells me.

The man glances over his shoulder with increased curiosity, asking about his climbing plans.

"La Aguja," Rhys answers simply.

*"Conchetumadre!"* The man whistles. *"Eres loco."*

Basically: Holy shit, you are crazy.

Rhys avoids my stare. No doubt because he senses the gaucho echoed my thoughts exactly.

I don't want him to risk himself, but neither can I ask him to give up his dream so that I don't have to face my fear of losing him up there.

They clomp up the hill and vanish into the tree tunnel, hooves fading as the regular forest sounds return.

"Who's Nick Goodall?" I ask.

"I told you some friends are at the camp, from an Australian team."

"Right." I nod. "The ones with the crazy names."

"Nick Goodall usually goes by Goonbag."

We are closer and closer to our goal, the base camp, but my heart is as plodding as my pace. I don't want to get into it with him about the climb. If I start sounding like a broken record, it will only make it easy for him to tune me out, believe I am anxious because of my own lack of climbing skills.

Instead, I change the subject entirely. "You don't happen to have a can of Fanta in all that gear, do you?" I ask dreamily, clasping my hands together. I want him to think I'm less nervous; hopefully, that way he'll listen to my concerns more open-mindedly when the time is right.

"Fanta? As in the soft drink?" He wrinkles his brow. "Can't say I do; I have plenty more porridge though."

"Dang." My shoulders fall. "I've started having this fantasy about orange-flavored soda a few hours ago. Weird because I don't even really like anything carbonated as a rule. But since this morning, the idea of a pressing a cold can against my neck, letting the condensation cool my skin, then that little hiss when you flip the top—"

"Fuck." He drags a hand over his scruff. "Auden, you canno' talk like that. You've gone and gotten me hard."

"Sorry, not sorry. But can we please stop a second? I think this is a sign that I need some sugar." I swing off my backpack and balance it against my leg. "I have a couple candy bars stowing away in the top pocket."

"Aye, next to your inhaler and condoms."

"You see where my priorities lie. Maybe that could be my big story instead. 'Hiking in Patagonia: A Tale of Chocolate, Asthma, Broken Tents, and Scottish Monkey Sex.'"

"I'd buy two copies."

I laugh, unwrapping a chocolate. "Want a bite?"

He recoils his head. "No, thank you."

"What?" I glance between him and the bar. "Who in their right mind turns down chocolate?"

"No' a big fan."

"But how can you be my soul mate if you don't love chocolate?" I need to quit speaking before thinking. Obviously, I'm kidding, because calling Rhys my soul mate is borderline crazy talk, but the way he's staring, it's like I'm not jokingly waving around a half-melted candy bar, but offering my heart.

In truth, the metaphor kind of works, seeing as love is sticky, delicious, and makes one hell of a mess.

"Fine. Give us a bite." Looks like he's going to give me a hall pass for that gigantic foot-in-mouth.

I hold out my hand, and instead of biting the bar, he nips my finger, slides his tongue to the join of two of my fingers.

"Oh, you fight dirty." My breasts ache and there's an answering pulse between my legs. How can he turn me on this much with a single naughty tongue-lashing?

He bends and lifts my pack. "Get this back on." His expression is dead serious. "We need to reach camp. I want to be inside you."

Why do I feel like there is an unspoken second part to his statement? "I want to be inside you, one last time."

It's not raining, but the mountain is fast disappearing again beneath a thick blanket of clouds. "The weather is so changeable down here. You don't like it, all you have to do is wait five minutes."

"Southern Patagonia is at the bottom of the continent, farther south than any other landmass except for Antarctica. Winds come screaming across the ocean and slam into the other side of those mountains, where a large ice field spreads, the Hielo Sur."

"That's what's behind the mountains—an ice field? I'd wondered."

"The great southern ice cap runs through the heart of the range, so vast it generates its own weather."

"La Aguja doesn't look like it wants to come out and play," I say. The peak is shrouded again. The mountain is almost completely lost to view by a thick swirl of cloud.

"Aye, no' a big surprise. It's positioned to attract the worst weather, part of the reason attaining the summit will be such a challenge."

"It's not as high as many others. What makes it famous?"

"The difficulty. Look at Everest. Is it a test? Sure, it's the highest mountain on earth, but it also comes with all the support and infrastructure, not to mention paid guides. As long as the person has coin and is fit, they stand a fair to decent chance of standing on the top of the world."

"I mean, I don't think I could do it, but I guess I see what you're saying. Climbing is expensive, right?"

"Can be. Some of the lads you'll meet have spent half their year doing menial labor to get a fix here."

"Is that what you do? You and you brother?"

"Aye, worked construction between trips. I had two years at university, studied geology before dropping out. Figure I can go back and study when I'm older and less fit. Cameron and I paid for many trips ourselves, but oftentimes costs such as gear, transportation, Sherpas, even oxygen, mount up. If you can get anyone else to front some cost, it's a help. Get some money in return for corporate branding, or sell an image. Occasionally wear certain outdoor gear and get photos snapped in places people recognize."

"It sounds like a lot of work to keep it all going."

"Once you're on the mountain, everything is worth it."

He pauses in front of small wooden trail sign. The words are scratched out above the mile marker 0.5.

"This is the way," he says, turning up the fainter trail.

"Why's the name crossed out?" I ask, joining him.

"To keep punters from wandering up and bothering everyone. The main campground is another kilometer in that direction." He points east.

"You sure...?" He scratches the back of his head.

"Am I sure what?"

"That this is the story you want to do? Profiling a bunch of climbers?"

"Absolutely," I say firmly.

He lets out a sigh. "So you're coming with me, then."

"Don't sound too excited," I joke, even though my throat is tight. Doesn't he want me here? Am I not badass enough to enter the hallowed climber sanctum? Hair prickles on my upper arms. Rhys is impressive enough on his own. What will happen when he's among his tribe, those larger-than-life men and women? Will I end up starring in that old "one of these things is not like the other" game, same as whenever I'm around Harper and her teammates?

Jesus, these old thoughts are like gophers popping out of holes—impossible to rein in.

"Hey, hey, hey. G'day, cobber, didn't expect to see your ugly mug this arvo." A guy saunters out of the forest ahead with the ease of a woodland sprite, that is, if a sprite had shoulders broad enough to build a skyscraper on. The guy's ash-blond ponytail falls to the nape of his neck, and he sports a deep cleft in his chin—a textbook butt chin if I wanted to be rude.

Wait. He's not looking anywhere near the vicinity of my eyes. Instead he ogles my chest like my boobs are trying to shake his hand. I'm tempted to say, *Yoo-hoo, up here.*

Ugh, never mind. Butt Chin is a perfect name for this butthead.

Rhys notices the googly-eyed boob stare, too. His jaw looks like it could crack walnuts.

"And who's this?" Butt Chin asks, practically rubbing his hands together.

"Psycho, Auden. Auden, Psycho," Rhys says curtly, taking my hand.

Aha! Rhys's Australian climbing pal. Psycho is some name. I'd even take Woody over that one.

"You've been holding out on me, mate?" Psycho slugs Rhys's biceps.

Rhys doesn't say a word. He doesn't have to. He exudes an aura of "touch me again at your own peril, dickweed," to the point where even my stomach flip-flops. I'm glad this guy is on my team; he'd be a formidable opponent.

"We just met," I mumble, trying to clear the air.

"Aw, shit. Picking up on the trail, you sly dog?" Psycho flashes me a leer that makes it sound like what I actually said was *Why, hello. I plan to be whoring myself off to Rhys and all his compadres. In fact, packed inside this little ol' backpack is a travel-sized stripper pole and an extra-large bottle of personal lubricant.*

For the record, I don't mind being Rhys's good-time girl. That currently seems like a viable career option, or at least a respectable side business, but no way am I going to stand here and be drooled on by a douche nozzle. Nor am I going to be a wet dishrag while Rhys fights my battles.

"Let's do a little more formal introduction. I'm Auden Woods." I take off my sunglasses and affect a brisk no-nonsense attitude. "I work for *Outsider* magazine."

"*Outsider?*" Rhys says with a start.

*Shit. Shit. Shit. Way to blurt that out.*

I'd told him I was a journalist but never the specifics of where I worked. *Outsider* is the same magazine that ran a cover story on his accident last summer.

I avert my gaze back to the Australian climber and see that my gambit has paid off. The vast majority of people aren't Rhys "Don't Fuck With My Privacy" MacAskill. They are more "Hey, look, Ma! I'm on TV!"

Immediately, Psycho snaps from eyeing me like a plate of sizzling bacon to an opportunity for personal advancement.

"*Outsider?* No shit." He wipes his hands on the front of his shirt. "And you're doing a story on this drongo?" He eyes Rhys. "Thought you weren't talking to the media."

"Nothing's changed on that front," Rhys responds brusquely. He's already taken five steps away from me.

"We should go." Enough talkie. I need to get him alone, explain everything.

"So what are you working on?" Psycho flashes what I'm sure he imagines is a charming smile. Instead, I'm coated by invisible slime. "A piece on Alpine-inspired fashion? Pretty girl like you? Yeah, that be about right."

Oh. My. God. Such a sexist dick. I busted my ass through journalism school: late nights at the university paper, missing parties and all-you-can-drink-for-$1 nights. I suffered through First Amendment and Journalist Law, Ethics and Trends in News Media, whizzed through classes on reporting, and fell in love during Magazine Writing. And not because I wanted to write puff pieces on the cutest down vests or trail shoes.

"Wow, no, but what a great idea." Sarcasm drips from my words like a swamp monster emerging from the deep. Maybe I could do a story on sexism in mountaineering. If asshats like Psycho abound, I'll no doubt find plenty of ladies willing to go on the record. "For your information, I am doing a series of profiles on—"

"We're going to get settled in," Rhys says, pulling me away without a trace of subtlety. Guess he's got things to say to me, too.

"I'll catch up with you crazy cats later," Psycho calls after us, giving a bro-like nod. "We'll be convening in the hut for dinner and no doubt partying a bit, seeing as visibility is shithouse. Weather window my ass. Bring Lois Lane here. She can do a story on my balls."

"You're out of fucking line," Rhys snarls, dropping my hand and storming toward the smaller guy.

Psycho doesn't lose his easy smile, even though Rhys is nearly a foot taller and appears willing and able to tear his smirking head off. "Easy, mate. I'm just having a go—you know me."

"Aye, I do," Rhys says tensely. "Here's some advice: keep a distance from her." He turns, and as he storms past, he barks, "Come. We need to talk."

I exchange a look with Psycho. He winks, clearly enjoying that he got a rise. I fight the urge to stick out my tongue before turning away.

# 21

## AUDEN

*R*hys, about *Outsider*—"

"I don't want you talking to Psycho," Rhys says as I
trot after him, trying to keep up with his furious pace.

"Aren't you two friends?" It's taking me three steps to match
his one. I have no idea where to drive the conversation.

"I never called him that." Rhys's tone is brusque. "I said I knew
him. I'm friendly with his climbing partners."

"How did you meet such a charmer?"

He makes a rude sound. "Our paths first crossed in New Zealand,
ages ago. Cameron and I did a climbing trip on the South Island."

"So you—"

"*Cooee!* G'day, mate." Another Australian waves from the
clearing ahead. This one is older, with graying temples and a griz-
zled face that's seen more than its fair share of weather. He's as lanky
as Psycho was stocky, but still Rhys tops him. I'm only now fully
realizing how big he is, seeing him in comparison to other men.

"Hey." He greets this guy more easily, does one of those dude
clasp handshakes. "How's it going?"

"It's not." The new guy gives a low whistle. "All we're doing is sitting around with our dicks in our hand. If it's not rain, it's wind, but word is things should be improving." His curious smile is aimed at my face. No skeez vibe coming off this guy.

"Hello," he says. "I'm Murray."

"Auden," I say, accepting his handshake.

"You two climbing together?" He sizes me up.

"No," Rhys answers abruptly. The tension radiating off of him is nearly palpable.

Uncertainty tugs my insides. What do we even have in common? Since I arrived in Torres del Paine, the unknown has been exciting, but it's also exhausting. I can see why so many people get hung up on predictability. It's easy, and easy isn't always bad. Maybe you don't grow as much, but it's comfortable, like right now I could be back at my parents' house sipping hot chocolate while logs crackle on the fire, trolling my iPad for news while watching costume dramas or the History Channel.

Not about to be forced into admitting uncomfortable truths.

The forest opens into a meadow. A dozen or so tents in colors ranging from orange to red to blue cram into sheltering heath wherever possible. In the center clearing squats a crude windowless wood hut. The wind must blow fierce through here if the thick ropes holding the tarpaulins in place are any indication. Large stones keep ground cloths fixed to the earth. Slacklines stretch between various trees, and gear is everywhere: ropes, helmets, ice axes. A man is doing a yoga headstand near a rusty water pump; just watching makes my neck hurt.

Off on the far left, a massive boulder rests in a clearing, dislodged from the mountainside. One guy is spotting another beside a thick crash pad. The one bouldering is three-fourths of the way up the rock and has a heel hooked at waist height as he leverages himself over an overhang.

Someone calls outs, "You sure you know what you're doing?" to general laughter.

"Piss off," the guy huffs, scrambling to his feet on the top and wiping his hands on his pants, leaving chalk streaks on his gray pants.

"You're so fucking hot," shouts another, who's wearing a ratty T-shirt that reads MOUNTAINEER in the same font as the Mountain Dew logo.

"Think so?" The climber on the boulder grabs his crotch. " 'Cause you've got a face a sledgehammer would love."

More raucous laughter.

Where are the women? I expected at least one or two. So far there's not a single one in sight. I don't like feeling as if a bull's-eye is fixed to my body—specifically between my belly button and chin. Guess Psycho wasn't alone in the boob fixation, or maybe Murray is the sole Boy Scout.

Guys keep coming up to us, each wanting a word with Rhys, obviously respecting him and intrigued by me. He exudes the air of someone comfortable in charge.

At last he breaks away and says, "Come on, Auden. We'll go this way." He takes my hand, leading me to the camp's edge. The gaucho we saw earlier on the trail sits opposite, drinking something clear from a milk jug while his son ties up the horses. He gives a cheerful wave. Someone smokes a joint nearby, and I hasten to get downwind from the smoke, not in a hurry to mess with my lungs.

Most of this crowd has probably heard of my grandfather, but while that's a perfectly acceptable conversation starter, I'm nothing impressive. I haven't made first summits or kayaked the Northwest Passage while surviving a polar bear attack.

Once, I braved Black Friday sales, and even that was a little too much excitement.

Rhys unshoulders his pack and removes the tent.

"It seems a little heavy on the testosterone up here," I say. "Where's the estrogen?"

"Sometimes there are more women. More often than not, none."

"These guys act like they haven't seen a female in weeks."

"Some probably haven't." He gestures to Murray, who is in a huddle with Psycho and another ginger-haired guy on the opposite side of the camp. "Murray is a good sort. But as for Psycho, like I said, stay clear of that one. He likes to stir shit."

"Can't say his name inspires much confidence."

Rhys gives an absent frown. "He's reckless on the mountain, takes big risks and can endanger others. Sometimes his boldness pays off. He's built an impressive résumé, but he has a bad habit of putting people in danger."

"Wait a sec." I drop my voice as my belly clenches. No one is close, but I don't want to risk being overheard. "You are going to be on the same route as a guy you don't trust?"

"I've been on mountains with him before. My plan's to get a head start. I'd rather be in front of him than behind."

I glare at the rust-colored wall of granite before me. The base of La Aguja has no scrap of vegetation on its menacing flank. My cheeks tingle as my head tips back, the low cloud blocking any further view. "Can we please talk about the fact I work for *Outsider* magazine? Back there, on the trail, you had a reaction."

"I'm going for a walk," he says, hammering in the last peg. "Go in the tent; don't move until I return."

"That's a joke, right?" I know he likes to control situations, but this isn't the military, and he's sure as hell not my drill sergeant.

"Wrong."

"You aren't the boss of me." I should add a foot stamp for good measure. Or lie on the ground and kick my legs. "We need to talk."

"Fine. Talk. So you work for *Outsider* magazine." He rocks on his heels. "Am I supposed to believe that you didn't know who I am? That you hadn't heard about the accident?"

"OK, OK, look. I didn't put it together at first. It wasn't until the next day." I hate the look on his face. The look I put there.

"Stop." He scrubs his face with his hands. "I need space before I say something I'll regret," he says. "I don't want anyone bothering you, so if you stay in the tent, you should be unbothered."

"Fine," I say flatly.

"Good."

"Great. You know what, I do want to talk to you, like an adult. There is a lot to say, so let me know when you're ready for that. In the meantime, I'm going to go fill up my water bottle." I grab my Nalgene and storm off for the tap.

I know I'm in the wrong, at least partially, but damn it, so is he. For years I put up with Harper's attitude and bad behavior, and what did I get but fucked and over? I can't take that from anyone anymore.

I go to grab my hair and twist it into a messy bun, but I can't. It's all gone. Instead, I rub my temples, as if that's the way to infuse myself with inner calm. If he would just relax, stop and take a breath, I could try to explain the situation, how everything got so messy, but the stubborn set to his jaw as I left didn't seem promising.

I can fuck Rhys's brains out, but I can't knock any sense into them.

———

No one is around the water tap. I turn the handle to the left and hold my bottle under it, pausing to take a few greedy gulps. It was a long, hot hike today, and a cold drink sends a jolt of optimism into me. Rhys and I both got heated, but we'll work it out. Our connection is undeniable, and if this situation is as real as it feels, this should all sort itself out.

I'll tell Rhys I figured out who he was. But I didn't want to tell him because…

Because…

Fuck.

Because that means admitting to the part where I almost screwed him over.

There are footsteps behind me and I brace myself. He must have come after me. I'll have to tell him the truth. Will he understand?

I spin around and squeak with shock. It's not Rhys approaching me, but Diedrick the Dutchman.

Am I hallucinating?

"What are you doing here?"

"Oh, just a little thirsty." He holds up a water bottle and gives the dregs a swish. "I saw you come in a little while ago with a big fellow. That's him, isn't it? That's Rhys MacAskill."

"It is, but please, leave him alone."

"You made it clear back in the valley that he is your story." He imitates a cat hissing, batting a hand like a mock claw. "I wouldn't want to go stepping on those pretty toes."

"Good," I snap, flouncing up the trail. The walls are closing in. I'll have to find Rhys and tell him everything before things get worse than they already are.

A twig snaps on my right. I jump, expecting to see an animal. Instead, Rhys stares at me through the filtered forest light.

"Oh." I pull up quick. "I didn't know you were here."

"Aye, I got that idea," he says without any trace of emotion. "I came up here to apologize."

My heart drops to the soles of my boots. *Shit.* From the way he looks, it's clear he overheard that whole conversation, or enough to think—

"Rhys. Wait. Please. Let me explain."

"Is that guy for real?" His nostrils flare. "You are doing a fucking secret story about me?"

"No! At least it wasn't a premeditated plan." My left eyelid twitches. "I meant what I said earlier, that I didn't even put it together at first, who you were. My asthma was bad and I was scared. It wasn't until I tried to leave that I remembered why your name sounded so familiar."

"That's why you came back." He rubs his chest as if in pain. "To write about me."

"No. It's really not. The stream was high; you saw that yourself." I stare helplessly at his face. "Rhys. Look at my eyes. Will you please look at me?"

"No." His gaze stays fixed on the ground between us.

"You aren't sleeping with the enemy, OK?"

"I'm no' so sure."

"I'm not someone who can use people for my own gain."

He shakes his head, resignation taking hold of his features. "I said I'd use you, and you promised me in turn. Guess I walked right into it."

"Please listen. I changed my mind."

"So you did think it, then? That you could get the story from me without me knowing?"

I duck my chin, hating the truth, but owing it to him anyway. "I did consider it for a few hours."

His top lip curls. "Do me a favor, Auden."

"Yes? Anything." Tears well beneath my eyelids; his face blurs like an impressionist painting. "What can I do to put this right?"

"Get fucked." It takes only a few strides before he vanishes into the shadows.

# 22

## RHYS

*I* tear under a low-hanging tree branch without slowing pace, my mind unable to form coherent thoughts.

Auden.

She knew.

She knew who I was all along.

Who I *am*.

The guy who cut the rope.

She knew.

Everything between us these last few days was a ploy to get my story.

These are the only words my brain can string together. Someone calls out in the distance. Not her, though. The voice is male, even though it's high-pitched.

"Mr. MacAskill! Excuse me, Mr. MacAskill!"

I freeze. Who the fuck wants my father? It takes a second to realize that it's me. I'm Mr. MacAskill.

I turn slowly, and a tall, wiry guy rushes through the forest. He's dressed in khaki shorts, ready to scamper off on some African safari, and breathing hard enough to scare away any animals within a five-hundred-meter vicinity. The camera swinging around his neck must not get much use. "Ah, very good. Here you are! Mr. MacAskill, allow me to introduce myself. Diedrick Overbeek at your service." The guy pants, bracing his hands on his knees. "And, wow, you move fast."

Auden appears. "Leave him alone." She's not talking to me, but him. Her voice is uncommonly cold. "You said you would."

"Oh, well." He gives a high-pitched laugh. "Looks like I lied."

"What do you want?" I snap, already knowing. I heard Auden's whole conversation play out like my worst nightmare a few minutes ago. Clearly I'm a fucking masochist to want to listen to a replay.

"Only a few moments of your time." He straightens and removes a blue handkerchief to loudly blow his nose. "I have many questions for you."

"'Few' and 'many' don't pair well together. You're another journalist," I say flatly. If I watch the two of them fight over me like hyenas with a fresh carcass maybe that will be enough to purge her from my system.

"I'm freelance," he says, clicking his heels together and issuing a salute. "Here to be of service."

The laugh that comes out of me is laced with bitterness.

Diedrick clears his throat, ready to make his pitch. "The world thinks you're a monster—"

"Stop. Enough. Just...shut up, for Christ's sake," Auden breaks in. "Rhys, you don't have to talk to him."

"Aye, I know." I don't spare a glance in her direction.

"Go back to our tent," she pleads. "Wait for me there. I'll take care of this."

Half of me never wants to see her again. The other half, the daft-as-shit half, wants to ask her why.

Why would she lie to me? Did she not feel the same?

"Are you together?" Diedrick frowns at her. You can almost hear the wheels turning over inside his weasel-looking skull.

"I'm not fucking around here," Auden snaps. "You aren't asking him a single question."

"Stop talking about me like I'm not here," I shout, the sound bringing them both to full attention.

Diedrick only increases the speed of his chatter. "Your brother, Cameron MacAskill, crawled for three days through crevasse-infested glaciers. His right hand was so badly frostbitten, it had to be amputated. He has the survival story of the year, the decade. I hear they are making a movie of it."

"Stop. Stop talking right the fuck now." I don't know how it happens, but somehow I've moved, gotten right in this guy's face.

"What're you going to do? Punch me?" Diedrick taunts. Either I've lost all ability to intimidate, or he has no sense of self-preservation. "Go right ahead. Hit me. One way or another I'll have a story."

"You sneaky little bastard." Auden looks ready to leap on his back like a spider monkey.

"Go," I say to him. "If you go now, nothing will happen. I give you my word."

"What does that mean? You're a man of honor?" Diedrick spits on the ground. "I do not think cutting your own brother loose to save your life is honorable." He's baiting me. A part of me understands this. He's realizes I'm not giving him what he wants, so he's trying to generate his own material. Not much different from when paparazzi harass stars in Hollywood for a behaving-badly shot.

But I'm not a star—quite the opposite: I'm the human equivalent to a black fucking hole.

My fist aches to connect with his chin, but that's only playing right into his slimy hands. Still, I shouldn't have done many of the bad ideas I've had in my life.

What's one more? My hand twitches.

"Rhys." Auden's voice demands my attention even when I don't want to give it.

My fist doesn't land in that prick's face with a satisfying thwack but is held back in her grasp. I outweigh her by at least four stone, could break her hold as easily as cracking an egg. Yet I allow her to restrain me. I close my eyes, and her touch feels so good even as it makes me hate myself.

"Go on." The guy's openly taunting. "Slug me all you want, but you can't escape the truth. You left your brother for dead."

"I thought he *was* dead." The words shred my throat.

He cocks his head. "A new piece to the puzzle. Come on, then. This is a chance to clear your name. Clear the air."

I can never escape the past. It's a shadow that I'll never be rid of.

"Hit him and you're giving him exactly what he wants," Auden murmurs. "Don't be stupid. Think, Rhys. Think."

Her words appeal to some rational part of my brain, but Jesus God, I want to hurt someone.

"Go. Walk it off." She shoves me toward the trees ahead. "Get out of here. I'll deal with this."

She's got a lethal look on her face like a tigress mid-hunt. Strange, she's half my size and is defending me. She's right, though. I need space. Otherwise I'll do something stupid. I'm already accused of being a wannabe murderer. Adding actual murder to my reputation wouldn't do me any favors.

As I stalk away, Auden's voice drops to a menacing hiss. "This is your second strike with me, Diedrick. One more, and you're in serious trouble."

*Second strike?*

"Rhys! Wait! Hey, listen, please," she says, catching up to me, once it becomes clear I'm going to maintain a stony silence. "You don't have to say anything, but I meant what I said back there. I'm not going to tell anyone your story."

"Why not?" My hands drop to my sides, forming two fists. "It's a good one. And while you're at it, throw in this afternoon. How you got to screw me in more ways than one."

Her head rocks back with force, as if I've struck her, and for a moment I'm ashamed but anger wins out. "It's the oldest trick in the book. But if I'm such an idiot as to fall for it, maybe you should get your reward."

"Please." She's crying now and still I push forward, my voice sharpened to a point.

"Last May, I reached a...a...crossroads, for lack of a better word. I had a woman, a doctor who spent the Everest climbing season working at the base camp. She wanted to get serious, get married, have children. Sadie was older, ten years older; that's where her head was."

"You don't have to tell me this."

"Maybe it's festered long enough." I give a halfhearted shrug. "When it came to Sadie, my head wasn't in the same place as hers, nor my heart. Making a long-term commitment with her didn't feel right, and so things ended. Instead of spending the season at Everest together like I'd planned, I decided to meet up with Cameron, who was going to the Karakorum." It's strange talking about this, like I'm telling a story about a person who is me.

"Cameron was in Pakistan. Highest concentration of tallest mountains in the world. I barged in on his show, but he didn't seem to mind letting me join the team at the last minute, despite grumbling from the others. He never minded my moods. He was unusual in that way. My brother is the one everyone likes. He has that way about him. He's a troublemaker, but when he smiles, you forgive him anything. I'm more..."

"Difficult?"

I arch my brow.

"Sorry." She gives a short laugh, wiping her eyes. "I can't believe you are still talking to me."

"It isn't hard. In fact, it's dangerously easy. You act as if climbing La Aguja is reckless. That's nothing. This, right now, remaining here with you? This is me at my most reckless. This story is a knife placed in your hands. You can cut my throat with it." I tear off a leaf from the bush beside me, shredding it in my hands.

"Why do it?" Her eyes scan my face as if my features are a narrative she wants to read and reread. "Why tell me anything?"

"Maybe I'm a fucking masochist, like I said. Or sick of evading. What's the cost of privacy in a digital age? More than I am willing to pay. Thought if I kept my head down, everyone would leave me alone. Instead, it's the opposite. People want what they can't have. So take it." My last sentence is no more than a harsh whisper, but it hangs in the air as if I've roared the words. "Go on, take what you came back for."

"Stop." Any trace of her tentative smile erases. "Please stop."

I jab my finger at a boulder. "Sit." Her legs fold at my command. "You wanted the story of why I cut the rope. Here's your big chance. Have a fucking front-row seat."

Her tears start fresh.

I should care more that her cheeks are wet. Stop and fight

for calm. But I'm a rock on the steep slope, rolling without care toward who or what I hit. I tell her how I joined Cameron. How he and I were picked from the group to lead the ascent. The weather window was predicted to be short, and we moved the fastest. We'd been in the mountains together since we were lads, knew what each other was thinking without needing to muck with words. "If anyone on the team could make the summit, we had the best shot.

"We climbed quicker than anticipated, up into the death zone, high enough that acclimation was impossible. You can't stay at such heights for long. The storm came in faster still. We made it to the summit, ken, but the weather was upon us before we were close to camp. It got to near whiteout, slow going. The wind, it screamed in such a way as to take the heart of you. What happened next was so quick. Cameron was there. And then he wasn't."

"Oh, God, Rhys—"

"He'd gone, disappeared over a ledge below. His weight drew on the rope, and at that angle, in those conditions, I couldn't down climb. Despite my efforts, I couldn't reach him. It was impossible to haul him back up, and since he didn't reappear, he clearly wasn't in a state to climb back himself. My body was connected to his dead-weight, sliding me inch by inch toward the precipice. I called again and again. For hours I tried everything I could think of to save him. Then an avalanche came down, a great wall of ice and snow. It missed me by a mere foot, wildly careening over the side. I knew if he wasn't dead already, he'd surely be dead after that. Still, I pulled with everything, and nothing. I thought my brother was gone. He'd only just married. I imagined what I'd tell his wife, Amelia."

I cleared my throat, the words coming harder now. "I was half-stupid from cold and assumed I'd soon be dead, too. We'd go out together. Seemed fitting. We were brothers, and best friends. Why should I make it if he didn't? But survival's a strange thing. I swear in the wind I heard his words telling me to cut the rope. Let him go. Not to let Mum lose her two children in one awful night. Getting out the knife wasn't easy. My fingers had no feeling. Took ages to reach it and longer still to open the blade. Cutting the rope was the easiest part—too easy. A back-and-forth grind of the wrist and then only me, alone on the fucking mountain."

She gasps, but I don't want her pity. Nothing will make this easier to bear.

"Hell isn't fire. Hell is ice that needles your eye sockets, burns any bare trace of skin. I've no idea how long it took to work myself back through a glacier riddled with crevasses. A thousand times death crept close, but each time something spared me. It wasn't until the next day that I reached camp. Hadn't even felt this." I massage the thick scar splitting the back of my skull. "Falling rock or ice must have struck me. Didn't notice until base camp. I credited my survival to Cameron, as if his ghost looked out for me. Even took comfort from the idea. The satellite phone was broken, so no one, not his wife, Amelia, or Mum or Da knew he was gone. And then, as I gathered his few belongings, my mind fixated on mounting a search party to at least find his body to bury, there he was."

"He survived," she whispers. "Despite everything."

"He was a shade, caught between the world of the living and the dead. One of his hands was completely black with frostbite. That's the one he ended up losing. Then there was the broken ankle, concussion, and fractured clavicle."

"How do you think he lived through the fall and the aftermath?"

"Sheer stubbornness. He couldn't say much, just how he'd hung there off the cliff, dangling like a fucking pendulum on a clock, waiting." My voice breaks. I'm seconds from losing control. "He said he'd made peace that I'd eventually have to cut him. There was no other option. That he had to survive the fall and what would come after, and live for Amelia. He landed in a crevasse and had two choices, to lie down and start dying or get up and crawl, hoping it would eventually lead him out."

"It sounds like there wasn't an option," Auden says. "And he understood that. Didn't you talk to him?"

"He was no in a state to speak. I got him to the hospital in Islamabad. Figured out how to get Amelia to him and told my parents what I'd done. Word spread fast, and news stories leaped on it. Within a week I was world famous for being the prick who sent my brother to his death."

"You thought he was already gone."

"I deserve what I got. I lost faith. In being tested, my true nature was revealed." My hands clench into two fists. "I've a coward's heart."

Auden shakes her head. "I don't buy that, not for a second."

"You weren't there. You don't know. You can't make it better."

She approaches me warily. "You can trust me."

"I can't."

# 23

## *AUDEN*

*J* try not to flinch at his words, but it's hard. "You said he wrote you a letter. Have you really not spoken to Cameron for all these months?"

"Not since he was in hospital," Rhys says in a monotone. "He was in rough shape, so we didn't exactly have a heart-to-heart. Besides, I don't have anything to say."

I tilt my head. "I don't believe that." He left before his brother could react. Rhys isn't giving Cameron a chance.

"What I mean is that I haven't the right." He takes a shuddering breath. "An apology won't return his hand. I ruined his career, stole away the same joy in his life that is the core of mine. He can't climb again, at least not like he used to. *Sorry* is a weak fucking word. People say it when they spill a glass of milk."

"You thought he was dead."

"I lost faith." His tone is stubborn. Nothing I say is going to change his mind.

Still. I have to try. "Climbing a mountain and risking your life isn't the answer." My ears fill with the panicked throb of my own pulse. "You matter, Rhys. You matter a great deal."

"I don't believe you came into this valley by accident," he says softly.

I bristle. "You don't have to believe me, but I had no idea you were here."

"That's no' what I mean." He grasps one of my hands, holds it tight in his own. "Don't you see? You are brave, braver than me."

I laugh. At first, it's somewhere between a snort and a guffaw, but it spreads to a cackle. His dubious expression makes me convulse all the harder. How can he be so perceptive and yet peg me so wrong?

"I'm not brave." I gasp, wiping my eyes. "That's like calling the Cowardly Lion courageous."

"You don't see what I see." He leans forward and whispers in my ear, "You followed me here. You didn't run away."

I swallow hard as a rush of heat runs down my spine. "There's a funny thing about running. You can't do it forever." I'm talking to myself as much as to him. For years, I've tried to rationalize my sister's toxic behavior to keep peace. Accepted blame and punishment for things I had no control over. I've been running from the truth, too, that maybe the burden of Harper is too much to bear. But how can I cut that relationship loose? What will that mean for my family? For me?

His arms tighten around me. "I didn't know what to do after the accident. And that's not me, how I live. I always have a plan. For months I was lost, holed up at Da's, avoiding the reporters, listening to his fire-and-brimstone talk. Finally, one night, half pissed out of my mind on bourbon, I got an e-mail about the La Aguja weather window. I had enough in my bank account for the trip and figured, why not? Might as well see if the legend is true. What I want most in the world could be there." He looks away. "Who knows, right? Stranger things have happened."

"Forgiveness," I murmur, realizing. The look he has, it's someone eaten inside out by guilt. "That's what you most want, isn't it?" He hopes this crazy climb will help him find atonement.

He casts his eyes away as color splashes over his high cheekbones. "You think I'm daft."

"Not at all," I answer quickly. "But there's got to be an easier way. Reading the letter for starters."

He looks as if I've suggested he volunteer to be cannibalized.

"Stay inside the tent, lass," he says. "I told you before, I don't trust the others here. People are getting impatient with the weather. Twitchy. The mood is off, and I don't want you to face any trouble. But I need to get away and think."

———

Rhys has been gone sixty-five minutes and I'm attempting to assemble the camp stove. Brewing a cup of tea isn't a big adventure. In fact, it's probably an unconscious act for most of these guys. But I've never done it before. I screw together the different components, and yeah, hmmm, don't think that's right.

My fingers tremble as I reassemble the various finicky parts, and my vision blurs with tears whenever I try to read the directions. I hate that I hurt Rhys. The look on his face, the look I put there, sad, vulnerable, ashamed, and full of self-hate? I helped send him back down the rabbit hole.

I take out my frustration on screws and metal. My jaw tightens.

No way will this stupid stove be my Waterloo. I've got to get this right, if only for the vague superstitious inclination that if I can fix this, I can fix everything.

While no one approaches, I get the distinct feeling that I'm surrounded by a pack of African hunting dogs. Guys swivel their heads whenever I glance up, but the minute I look away, gazes bore into the back of my skull.

The two standing beside the slackline keep nodding in my direction and snickering. Maybe I'm being paranoid and they're simply making jokes or sharing puns. Yeah, just a pair of punny guys, and I coincidently happen to be in their line of sight.

Or it could be the reality, which is that it's awkward as hell to be a single girl among badly behaving testosterone-fueled guys. While I don't feel unsafe per se, I do need to prove that I'm doing stuff, hanging out, and comfortable in my skin, not crying because my heart is threatening to split down the middle. It's my own posturing. I tuck back my shorter hair behind my ears, and for some reason that gives me confidence.

I'm breaking away from my old unconfident self, stepping outside my sister's shadow and forging my own way.

In my fantasy, Rhys will come out of that forest any minute. I'll cradle a mug between my hands, steam lazily rolling from the top. *You're back*, I'll say casually. *I know we need to put things at ease. Come sit and have this tasty, tasty cup of tea I brewed using my mad outdoor skills.*

*I realized something out there. You are a good person, Auden Woods,* he'll respond in a gruff yet oh-so-tender tone. *The best person. The sort who stared temptation in the face and turned away for higher moral ground. May I escort you into our Tent of Pleasure and ravish your lady parts with my tongue? And look at that stove that you oh-so-competently erected.*

His face would twist in a mix of ardor and admiration. *Auden, you gorgeous, capable woman, how will I ever be parted from you?*

That's when he'll bend me over and plunder my mouth with his fervent tongue. My bodice (yeah, I'm wearing a bodice) rips. My bosoms heave. His manhood is turgid against my quivering swollen folds, ready to invade my womb and—

"What's that? A bloody modern-art installation?"

I blink up, the sexy imaginary Rhys replaced by Psycho's butt chin. My fantasy comes to a screeching halt, like dragging a needle across a still-spinning record. I can't control my grimace, and my reaction only makes his leer widen.

"I'm fine," I snap, sitting back on my heels, studying the stove and trying to figure out what I've done wrong.

"I'm sure you are," he says. "But that stove? Not so much."

"I've never done this before." I am forced to admit the truth.

"How did you meet Rhys anyway?" He stretches his back muscles. "We've all been wondering."

We—as in the other guys.

"Don't you have anything better to do than sit around and gossip?" I twist a screw and, shit, the whole damn stove falls apart. I swear under my breath, back to square one. "Thought you had a mountain to get ready to climb."

"Waiting for this weather window is boring as buggery. You're an improvement."

"Rhys is my friend," I say tightly, digging out the instructions and reading them for the fourth time.

"Who is he climbing with?" Psycho is poking around for information. As much as I hate to play dumb for this ass clown, I'm not willing to sell Rhys down the river, despite my annoyance.

"Don't know." I shrug. *Himself.* "Why do you care?"

"I don't." A barely restrained flicker of annoyance skims his features as his butt chin clenches. His lower jaw protrudes a bit. His eyes bulge like a pug. Yep, he's a pug with a ponytail. All he needs is a snaggletooth to complete the pretty picture. He spits on the ground. "Just trying to have a little friendly conversation. You putting the stove together to make anything particular?"

"It's cold and windy, perfect tea temperature."

"Walk with me. I'll fix you a cuppa back at my tent."

"That's OK." The last thing I want is this guy doing me any favors.

He saunters away with a snort, and I eye the woods. *Come on, Rhys. Where are you?*

I need to pee and have to locate the bathroom, or whatever outhouse passes for one in these parts.

It's a little way past the tents, and after, as I come back into camp, guys are congregating in front of the hut, which is a perfect word for the dilapidated structure that looks like it's that twig house the second little pig built. It must be deceptively strong because Patagonian wind does more than huff and puff.

The three Australian climbers are there, joined by two others. They get out a deck of playing cards, and Murray opens a bottle of pisco, the ubiquitous South American form of brandy. The gaucho is still around, next to a bedroll, sipping maté from a silver bombilla. It looks like he and his son will stay the night.

"Hey, girlie, have a drink with us," Goonbag calls out.

"Nah, that's OK," I return, still walking.

"We're playing Asshole," adds another climber, this one with a thick Southern US twang.

Asshole? I hesitate—I do love that one. But I'm not in the mood for fun and games. Plus, Psycho's there, and even though I don't know him, there's a large part of me that's put off, that senses danger, and I need to trust that vibe.

"It's good fun." His pug eyes dare me.

"Fine," I say, and just like that I realize, as much as I want to say I'm different, that I'm changing, I'm not. Harper could always get under my skin. Push hard enough and I'll cave.

I need to be better at keeping my own power, letting haters hate and all that.

But how do you let someone hate you and not care? If I can figure out that life lesson, I'll be more than halfway to a functional adulthood.

But for right now, I'm sitting down and being dealt a hand. When Murray passes me the pisco, I take a swig.

I'm not drunk when Rhys finally strides back into the camp after the two-hour mark, but I have a pretty good buzz going. He doesn't look left or right as he goes to the tent, opens it, and freezes, registering that I'm not where he told me to be.

"Your boyfriend's back," Psycho says, calling out as Rhys approaches us. "You want to play, mate?"

"Auden." He focuses all his attention on me. "I need to speak with you...please."

I scramble to my feet. "Yes, of course." I have no idea what could have happened, but he appears genuinely freaked out.

His back is ramrod straight as he stiffly walks toward our tent. He carries himself as though if he drops control, even for a moment, he'll shatter. And if he falls, he'll break.

I squeeze his hand. Can I be strong enough to hold him? I never expected to find myself in a situation where the hero clutches me, clasping tight as earth gives way, the entire world distilled to our tenuous grasp. I don't really feel like this great bastion of strength, but right now I'm all he's got.

So I'll do my best. He won't fall. Not on my watch.

# 24
## RHYS

*A*uden crawls into the tent after me. "Listen, Rhys, I'm so sorry we fought. I'm sorry that I didn't—"

"It doesn't matter. I was taken by surprise, but I'm no' angry. No' anymore. I know that I don't make it easy for people to open up to me. And the most important thing is, you didn't stab me in the back."

"I—"

"Please, wait." I hold up my hand. "There's something else." The words that I need to say are hard, nearly impossible to find.

To her credit, she sits back on her heels, patient, not grilling me with a million and two questions. Normally, I don't mind her doing that, despite what I pretend. I like that she's not intimidated by my attitude and blasts through my defensive walls like they don't exist. But at the moment I'm at an honest loss.

So I decide to do that, be honest.

"I…" I clear my throat. "I took your advice and read my brother's letter. I read what Cameron wrote."

"You did?" she asks, touching my knee.

I cover her hand with mine. "You don't sound surprised."

"I'm not. I knew you'd eventually get the courage. But I am happy, really happy. Do you feel better?"

I stare at her disbelievingly. "How did you know the note would be positive?"

"Because you said your brother knows you, right?"

I nod slowly, still in a daze. "Aye, better than anyone."

"Rhys, you don't seem to get this, but to know you is to…to…" She wrinkles her brow like she's solving a puzzle. "It's to care about you. You are one of the good ones."

"That's almost verbatim what Cameron wrote."

"He knew there was no other solution after his accident. You didn't have a choice. You thought he was dead, and if you hadn't cut him, you certainly would have been."

I stare into space, still seeing his words. "He said—he said he blames himself. Says that he made the error that led to his fall."

"Maybe he did. But more than likely no one is to blame." She comes closer, kneels before me. "Or if you must point a finger, point it at bad luck."

"Here. Read it yourself." I remove the letter from my pocket and pass it to her. Any anger I had toward her is vanished by this revelation. It's as if an anvil has been lifted from each shoulder. I've memorized every word, having read it at least fifteen times in the last hour. He wanted me to know that he felt responsible for the accident, that he knew I was blaming myself and that I needed time. Da told him about my plan to come to La Aguja for the solo climb and he decided he needed to be here. We had planned on climbing in this region together since we were lads, and he wants to be here with me.

"Wow." Auden's eyes scan the page. "Wow. Wow. Wow. Wow.

Holy shit." She lowers the letter. "And you are going to be an uncle? Congratulations!"

"Aye." I laugh despite everything, and it feels brilliant. "My brother is going to be a father. I can't get my head around it, but I can't think of anyone who'd do a finer job."

"He's really coming here? To the La Aguja camp?"

"So he says. You see his planned date for arrival."

"Tomorrow."

"Yeah."

"So you'll hold off and wait for him?"

"Looks like it."

"Good. I'm still nervous about you, but I feel a lot better knowing you aren't going solo." Her top teeth latch onto her bottom lip. "But you guys need time to connect, and that doesn't include me. Do you think the climbers would let me move into the hut? To sleep at night until I finish my story?"

What she's saying makes sense. My brain accepts it even as the realization of her walking out of my life, cutting free this connection, hits me in the gut. I lace my fingers with hers and the gesture anchors me. In mountaineering, an anchor keeps the climber and their rope attached to the rock, breaks any fall. That's Auden. That's what she's done, stopped my headlong descent into self-destruction.

That's not what I tell her, though. The idea of saying such words out loud is terrifying, has the potential to change what's currently an easy thing. My thoughts flash to the trail, my bravado when I said I always do the things that scare me.

I'm a fucking liar and need to grow a pair.

I clear my throat and say, "Please stay close."

Her eyes widen, the brightness increasing.

I love her eyes, love her curves, love her thick hair.

Shite. Panic scalds my throat. Words that start with *l* and end with *e* are dangerous.

"I am grateful for you," I continue, my voice rough, still clinging to her damn hand like it's a talisman. "The last few days, since meeting you…" How do I say this? My brain spins in a mad kaleidoscope as a grand declaration builds in my chest. "Auden, I like you. No, it's more than that. I feel like I'm…like I'm…"

"Yes?" Her anticipatory whisper turns the blood in my veins to hot, thick lava. Sweat breaks out across my chest. She absentmindedly bites the corner of her lip, and the gesture wrecks me.

"I like you," I repeat more firmly, because what the fuck do I say? *I am falling in love with you, Auden?*

How do I even know the first thing about love?

"Good thing I like you, too," she says.

I kiss that place she keeps biting on her lower lip, soft and slow. It's good, and I do it again and again. I've never had this sort of infatuation before. Kissing, for example. I could kiss her all day. My tongue slips into her mouth, and she shivers. This is also new, carrying on a silent conversation with eyes closed, heads tilted, bodies pressed flush. Our hands rove, weaving a connection that binds us closer.

Last night I woke from a deep sleep, not a nightmare, nothing of the sort, but the simple heavy oblivion that only strong drink has afforded me during the last long months. Her deep, slow breathing filled my ears, and even as the wind blew outside, her presence kept me secure from black thoughts.

Anchored.

Safe.

What the hell are we?

*We.*

Not me.

I've never used that word with regard to a woman. Not even Sadie. Never given serious consideration to my plans in accordance with another. How do people do that? Go from *me* to *we*? Before Auden, it always seemed that relationships make people compromise, and that begins the slippery descent to losing themselves.

When Sadie indicated she wanted to settle down, that's all I could think. She'd want stability, to quit high-altitude medicine and take a solid job back in England, a position where she could have kids, and that makes sense. I get why she'd do that. But for me, I couldn't imagine giving up so much of myself.

But what if love doesn't have to be losing yourself? What if instead it's about realizing that here is one person who I can be real with, who can see me in all my good and more important, my bad, and realize despite my flaws, I'm worth being connected to?

I tell her all this with my kisses, easing her against the ground, her pants tangling around her ankles, and I'm between her legs, flooding my senses with her sweetness. I work over her wet, sensitive slickness like a man consumed, because that's exactly what I am.

When Cameron arrives, he's going to take one look at me and laugh his fucking ass off.

*I told you, brother*, he'll say.

He was right. When it happens, you do know. The first moment I heard her voice outside my tent, a part of me knew that my life was about to veer off course. I didn't want to admit it then, but when she crawled inside, smelling like rain, with those big blue eyes, I felt I'd known her forever rather than five minutes.

She comes in that quick, sudden way of hers, no slow, rolling climax, but the sudden ferocity of a mountain storm, and I'm shaken bare at the realization.

*I am falling in love. I am falling in love. Fuck, I am falling in love.*

Terror and peace make strange bedfellows. She should be the last person I let in, and yet there isn't a choice. She's already inside me. Her legs wrap around my neck, and I rest my cheek on her stomach, her navel in my line of sight, my hands splaying her inner thighs, still damp from her and my own mad kiss.

"Wow." She laughs this low, delighted sound. "That's not enough of a word, but seriously, *wow* is all I'm left with."

"Glad it was good." I trace the outline of her hip. What am I going to do?

"Good?" She caresses the top of my head. "That's like calling the Sistine Chapel a pretty picture." Her fingers sink into my hair. "It's never been like this for me before, with anyone."

"We're…" *We.* The word has a rightness, a certain mouth feel that's almost as delicious and addictive as she is.

"We're pretty good together, aren't we?"

"We're bloody brilliant." I rise up over her, bracing my weight on my forearms, resting my forehead against hers.

The truth is, I'd rather be here, with her, than on the mountain. If the weather cleared this very moment, I'm not sure I could leave her.

None of this makes any sense, but then Mum always has said I had as much sense as a chocolate teapot. Here I am, crazy in a crazy moment. Auden's got this pink-cheeked look; a wayward lock of her hair rests diagonally across her forehead.

*Go on. Don't be an arsehole. Get up the nerve, lad. Tell her how you feel. That she's more than a shag. She is… She is…*

"Hey, Mac, get out here," comes a voice. Murray, by the sounds. "New report came in. Weather window should begin tomorrow."

*Shite.*

Auden glances toward the door, breaking our gaze. *Mac?* she mouths. "That's the best nickname they can give you?"

"Looks like it," I say, rolling free of her and turning to the tent entrance, feeling less alive, less vital, with every inch that separates us. This is too much, too quickly. There is almost a purity in the pure hopelessness taking root in my chest. She has her own dreams to chase, and I have mine. These last few days are the kind of magic I'll get only once in a lifetime.

A brief light in the long dark.

# 25

## AUDEN

After Rhys leaves to speak with Murray, I lie, panting, the tent smelling of sex, of my need. I press my palms into my closed eyes as each thought bleeds into the next. How has this guy filled me so utterly, to the point where my heart is close to bursting? This is crazy. And it's crazy to be mourning the idea that soon, all too soon, I'm leaving here, him, and this alternate world we've existed in the past three days. Might as well be three lifetimes.

Rhys entered my bloodstream. The effects are mind-altering, and the idea of detoxing cold turkey makes me a little woozy. How am I expected to return to real life after this? I'll be back in a familiar landscape, everything unchanged, except me.

I don't know how to do that.

I've scrambled back into my pants by the time he returns and am rubbing my face like I can scrub sense into my thick head.

"Climbing starts tomorrow," he says. "There's something of a celebration going on in the hut. Would you like to go?"

No is my initial impulse. Our time is unraveling to hours. But if I hold on, it's not going to stop the fraying. Time continues relentless and unyielding. Being around others might give me space from our intensity. Make the inevitable parting easier. "Sure," I say, plastering on a bright smile. "Sounds fun."

When we enter the cramped hut, guys are everywhere. The space smells like body odor and alcohol. Someone has an iPad set up, playing fast-paced indie rock. Everyone is laughing and most look spaced-out.

"Hey, check it out. Rhys Dog is in the house," some guy calls out, another American by the sound of the accent, his features blurred behind a veil of pot smoke. Anxiety licks at me. I'm not going to be able to hang out long with that going on. I linger by the open door, averting my face to the fresh air outside.

"Here you go, love," Psycho says, advancing toward us with two mugs. "Told you I'd make you tea."

Rhys ignores him, a little awkward considering we stand right in front of him. I take the mug, sip, and restrain myself from making a face. It is as bitter as witches' brew. Is this the maté everyone drinks in South America? It must be an acquired taste.

Psycho gives me a wink before returning his attention to Rhys, grilling him about the climb. Rhys answers in monosyllables, omitting the fact that Cameron is on his way.

I take another gulp of tea. Gross. This stuff seriously tastes foul. The smoke starts to get to me. I cough, and Rhys looks alarmed.

"Are you all right, Auden?"

"I—I—I'm fine. But I don't think I can stay in here. Need fresh air."

"You'll feel better in about twenty minutes." Psycho snickers.

*Huh?*

Rhys looks around the room, grabs the tea from my hand, takes a swallow, and spits it on the ground. "What the fuck?" His fierce look strikes like a sudden squall as he flings the mug's contents in Psycho's direction.

"Bloody hell, mate. That's not on," Psycho says, wiping his T-shirt. "What a bloody waste of perfectly good shroom tea."

Shroom tea? Wait. My stomach gives a sickly roll. "Did you give me mushroom tea?"

Psycho laughs, and others join in. That's when it starts to click. Everyone in here is laughing because they're all tripping balls.

I've never taken drugs. Smoking is out of the question, and I've always been way too paranoid about hallucinogens. I press a hand to my forehead, my throat tight. What the hell is going to happen to me?

My blood is a river of ice, and it's only when I taste the copper tang of blood that I realize how hard I've bitten the inside of my cheek.

"You fucking imbecile," Rhys growls. He's drawn himself to full height and looks as if he's going to transform into a grizzly shifter. His lips curl, revealing clenched teeth as his fist draws back.

"Wait, no. Rhys. Wait." I grab his arm. Sure, I want him to punch Psycho. Fuck, I want to punch Psycho. I don't know why that weasel has it in for me, but I can't deal with him now. His beatdown can come after I figure out how to get this crap out of me.

That's when a most unwelcome face appears behind us in the doorway. This guy turns up as often as a bad penny.

"Hello, Auden." The Dutchmen waves brightly. "You had some of my mushrooms, yes?"

"You brought them?" I say.

He nods and laughs, clapping his hands together. That manic giggle is nails on a blackboard.

"What are you still doing here?" Rhys's voice is flint striking. Sparks are practically visible. He's incandescent with rage.

"If at first you don't succeed, try, try, again," Diedrick says with a satisfied smile.

"What is that supposed to mean?" Rhys growls.

Psycho shrugs. "I'm working with him. He needed a source, someone who knows you."

Rhys stares incredulously. "And you spoke to him?"

"Free speech, mate." Psycho bends to retrieve the mug Rhys threw.

"Seriously, deal with him later." I tug Rhys's hand. "I need your—"

*Thwack.*

The sound of Rhys landing a punch to Psycho's jaw vibrates through the hut in a big, wet wallop.

Psycho grunts, stumbles onto his back foot before using the stance to switch momentum, barreling toward Rhys, head ramming square into Rhys's chest. Rhys is taller, but Psycho is built like a brick house.

This is not what I need.

People stare, some vacantly, others frightened or amused.

My stomach twists, really hurting. This isn't a dull, hollow ache, but a slow recoil, like my insides are encountering the mushrooms and going *hell no*.

"Stop!" I shout. "Please, Rhys, stop."

Hard for him to respond when he's fallen to the ground, tussling with Psycho. Their low grunts and swears are overshadowed by the other guys laughing, as if this is all absolutely hilarious.

I don't want to leave Rhys, but he chose fists while hallucinatory mushrooms circulate my system. Going all WWE won't solve a damn thing. It's gross, but I have to take matters into my own hands and make myself sick.

I push past Diedrick and stumble outside, beelining toward a grove of trees. Can I induce throwing up? A shudder runs through me. I hate being sick. I haven't done so since I had an awful stomach bug at sixteen. I loathe it so much that I've never even drunk much. I have honestly planned to never vomit again. Ever. And here I am getting ready to force the feeling on myself.

More cheers erupt inside the hut.

Stupid men, always so quick to deal with their problems through fists and tempers. Women should just rule the world. Psycho is jealous of Rhys and trying to get under his skin, and Rhys has basically set up a welcome mat to be mind-fucked.

My stomach lurches as if my intestines are playing a game of cat's cradle. Sweat beads my hairline. Seriously, can I stick a finger down my throat? The idea makes me gag all on its own. Good. I mean, terrible in that gagging is an awful feeling, but good in the sense that maybe I'll be able to force this tea out through sheer strength of will. I refocus and speak out loud. "Throw up. Do it. Rid yourself of that nasty stuff."

Turns out that I'm one shitty Jedi. No mental powers here. How much time left do I have? I don't know when the effects will start or what's going to happen. The unknown scares the crap out of me. I shove my finger into my mouth, reach for the back of my throat. Ouch. It hurts, and there's a vaguely uncomfortable tickling sensation. After that?

Nothing.

A whole lot of nothing at all.

What the hell?

I try again and still nothing. I'm crying now, my finger down my throat, and when I look up, there it is, La Aguja, the summit breaking free from the cloud's hold long enough for me to glimpse it. Way up high is the mushroom-shaped ice cap that makes the peak so treacherous.

"Goddamn it," I yell, slapping the tree beside me. That's when I realize that my arm doesn't feel connected to my body. The idea is scary but also hilarious. I sit down and laugh in hiccupping chuckles. The trees start giggling, too, softly in the wind.

The sun is setting. Whoa. I've never seen a sunset like this. How do you feel a sunset? That's what's happening. My cheeks are wet; for some reason I'm crying. The colors intensify, and the sheer beauty wraps around me like an invisible rope, squeezing my heart.

There are voices.

Someone is talking.

I know that voice, but I can't respond because I think I lost my mouth. I feel for my face and there it is. Yes. Two lips. A tongue. Teeth. I count my teeth. I can't say anything, but I like hearing my name.

There are footsteps nearby.

"Fuck, can't find her."

"Your girlfriend will be fine."

"She's not my girlfriend."

"Fuck buddy?"

"Do I need to pound your fat head again?"

"So it's not serious?"

"She's nothing, you ken? Back off and forget about messing with her to get to me."

That's Rhys. He says I'm nothing.

I'm nothing.

I'm nothing.

And I should move. Follow him. Chase him down and tell him to say it to my face. But I can't move.

Nothing doesn't move.

Nothing has nothing to say. All nothing does is curl into a ball and rock.

*I'm eighteen and home from my first semester at college. Harper greets me at the front door with an unexpected hug. The only other time I remember her touching me willingly is when she pinched me in the bathroom after our tenth birthday party. She'd pointed at my reflection in the mirror. "You are nothing," she whispered. "You are me, but I am already here. You're the leftovers. Nothing. Don't forget it."*

*I screamed and Mom found us. Guess who got yelled at for upsetting her sister? Me. Because Harper had her ears covered and was saying, "Auden is crazy, Mom."*

*Tonight, though, she's acting more or less friendly. Mom makes a welcome-home dinner, and it's normal, at least normal for my family, which means that we stay surface level, but still, there were actual questions about my classes, Harper's new coach, Mom's marathon training, and Dad's work. We are able to communicate like we have a cordial grasp of the English language, not like we individually spoke Russian, Chinese, French, and Hindi and are expected to hold a conversation.*

*Harper keeps smiling, and it lowers my defenses. Then, right as Mom offers chocolate ice cream without her usual "once on the lips, forever on the hips" disclaimer, the doorbell rings. I get up to answer it, and there he is.*

*Jed Royce.*

*My ultimate high school crush.*

*Oh. My. God.*

*Soft snow is melted in his thick dark hair. I shut my mouth. Wouldn't do to have drool splash on the toes of my pink Ugg boots. My heart beats so hard that I swear if he looks down, it will be forming one of those cartoon-shaped imprints through my shirt. This was the moment I waited for during the four long years at Aspen High, the moment that prevented me from really being able to crush out on any of the guys at the University of Colorado.*

*How do you compete with a guy who looks like he's starring in his own Patagonia ad?*

*"Hey you," he says with a flirtatious smile.*

*This is my moment. He's driven over in a passion-fueled frenzy my first night back from college because at last his love needs to be shared. He needs me.* Come, take my hand, Auden, *he is about to say.* Come to me and let me make you a woman, treat you to all the physical pleasure you can stand.

*He takes a step forward, and that's when I hear, "Dude, that's Auden."*

*Behind him stands Brett. Another guy from my high school, also a student at the University of Colorado, his features as bland and indistinguishable as a glass of water.*

*"Oh. Hey." Jed clears his throat as his gaze searches over my shoulder. "Is your sister home?"*

*"Here I am." Harper appears, shoving past me to fling herself into Jed's arms. I watch my mirror image kiss my first love. I think you could call it kissing. It might have been attempted murder through tongue strangulation. My sister does a few moves that might be better suited to soft-core porn than on the front step while Brett and I exchange awkward waves, clear our throats, and look up at the night. The snow is falling, but not hard enough to bury me.*

*That's when Mom appears, beaming. Granted, Harper has quit doing the crazy hip thrusts and is now just burrowed up against Jed like he is the ratty old bunny she used to carry around. The bunny that*

*had been mine, from Grandpa. He'd given Harper a reindeer, but she*
*wanted Bunny and I let her have it. Just like now I watch her go for the*
*guy I love. Or at least kid myself that I love. As unpredictable as Harper*
*can be, in one way, she demonstrates remarkable consistency.*

*She is never sorry for her actions.*

*She watches me from Jed's embrace, and the hatred on her face*
*frightens me.*

Afterward, I went for Brett, because he was there, mostly, and
seemed to be OK with me. And I was fine with him. He road biked
so his calves were nice and his grade-point average respectable.
We didn't have anything approaching a grand passion, but people
would refer to us as Grandma and Grandpa with some affection.
What we lacked in passionate intensity, we made up for in easy. We
didn't have a handsy stage when we couldn't get enough in the bedroom, rather skipped to the get-along-without talking stage.

He didn't ask me to check him for hemorrhoids or anything,
but within a few more decades, the idea wouldn't have shocked
me. Everything with Brett was simple, boring, like, "Eh. Good
enough." Eventually, Harper decided even good enough wasn't
enough for me.

Although she says I'm nothing, she still wants all my some-
things. Her coach raves about her "killer instinct," but as soon as
the Olympics are over, I'm not so sure she won't land herself in jail.

But maybe she is right.

Rhys thinks I'm nothing, too. And why wouldn't he, after
everything I've done?

And haven't done.

He's a guy who lives at the peak, and I'm lost, wandering
valleys.

Nausea rolls through me. There is a light from a star, and it's glowing, lasering between my eyes. I want this to stop. I want to be normal. How can I get back to myself? I place my forearm in my mouth and bite. It hurts, and I bite harder. The pain keeps me anchored in some form of the present.

"I'm not nothing. I'm not nothing. I'm no thing. No thing."

Then Rhys is there. "Auden? What are you talking about?"

I start laughing because all I can think of is that W. H. Auden poem, "Musée des Beaux Arts," where the boy falls from the sky and the moment is everything and nothing. Extraordinary things happen while people walk past. The last few days with Rhys have been everything, but it's time to crash back down to reality.

"I am no thing."

"Nothing?" Rhys cradles me against him, and I can tell he doesn't know what I'm saying, but maybe he does and it's a big fake. Maybe he thinks I am Harper. Maybe I am Harper and have always been her, and holy shit, now I'm thrashing against his arms. I need him to let me go, because what if he tries to kiss me thinking I'm Harper, not the other one?

The nothing.

# 26

## RHYS

*B*reathe in. Breathe the fuck out. Keep going because it's the only thing that keeps me focused. Auden lies beside me, not moving from the recovery-pose position I set her in an hour ago. Every time she whimpers, my heart rate increases as if I can somehow outrun her pain. It's not working. My limbs are numb and my skull ready to explode. I've never tripped, but Cameron has a few times—spent the whole time laughing. Auden's having a bad one.

She's here, but not really. It's an effort to get her attention. She barely speaks, and when she does, it's garbled.

I rest a steadying hand on her shoulder. "You took psychedelic mushrooms," I repeat for the sixth or seventh time. "This won't last forever."

"I'm broken," she moans. "My mind is broken."

"You aren't brain damaged. Remember, you can't relax before your body does. Take another deep breath."

She obeys, and I rub her back in slow circles, whispering reassurances. At last she dozes off to sleep. I wait for a bit, reassure myself that she's out hard. I don't think she consumed enough that the effects will linger long, but I'm so fucking pissed at Psycho. I nailed him a few times, but it's not enough. He's crossed his last line. We'll have serious words, and I plan on throwing in a few more fists to his gut to punctuate the point.

No doubt he used her to lash out at me, put me off my game before tomorrow's rush to get on the mountain.

Joke's on him. I have bigger plans than La Aguja on the cards.

With a last check on Auden, I creep from the tent to assess the situation. Climbers not climbing can be worse than an old-women sewing circle for stirring up drama.

The gaucho smokes contentedly beside a log, reading a newspaper. His son is behind him, flitting through the trees, waving a stick, battling invisible demons. The games we play as children that never fully cease. The father notices my stare and gives me a nod. *"La chica esta bien?"* he calls.

*"Ella esta durmiendo."* She's sleeping.

*"Que hombre con los hongos."* He spits. *"Hijo de puta."*

*"Sí,"* I respond. The guy with the mushrooms is definitely a son of a bitch, and then some.

The hut is vacated except for Murray. He glances up from his book, giving me a long look.

"I'm no' here to fight more," I say.

He closes the cover and straightens. "How's your girl?"

"Resting. That was a dirty trick."

"It was. You had the right to act as you did. I've known Psycho a long time, but he's a dick."

"Where is he now?"

Murray gives a laconic shrug. "Hiding out somewhere with his tail between his legs. He's jealous of you, you know."

"Don't know why."

Murray gives me an assessing look. "You're better than him."

"Maybe. Depends on the day."

"You really going to solo La Aguja?"

"I'd meant to, but plans have changed."

A look of relief crosses his craggy face. "That's a bloody load off my mind. I didn't look forward to watching you become vulture bait."

I lean against the doorframe. "You have some faith in me, huh?"

"Listen up, Rhys. You mind hearing some old-man advice?"

"You? Old?" I guess he's right, though. Despite his being fit as hell, he's got to be close to fifty. He's got an impressive climbing résumé, and the fact he's lived this long means he gets my respect. No question.

"I've been around awhile."

"Aye, more than most."

"You have something, something special. I'm not just saying you are strong. Anyone can be strong if they work hard enough, but you're mentally fit. One of the strongest mental climbers I've come across."

"Thank you."

"That's why I'm glad you aren't pissing your life away on a bloody stupid stunt."

"I was no' doing it for glory."

"I didn't reckon. Way I figured, you wanted to see if the legend was true."

I shrug. "Maybe."

"That's what has me thrown, because you seem like the kind of bloke who'd know better. They say at the top of that mountain, for the man, or woman, who goes alone, waits the thing they most want, but how bloody stupid. You don't get what you want like that. You get it by going after it."

I can't explain to him that I didn't have any other way. Up until today, all the paths were blocked for me except the one that rose outside that tent. But to know Cameron is coming? My chest is lighter, as if the boulder crushing me has finally rolled away. Everything should be good. And it is, except for the fact that Cameron coming means Auden is leaving. My life is one fucking seesaw, up, down, up, down. What wouldn't I give for balance?

"Cameron arrives tomorrow."

"That a fact?" Murray's eyes widen with surprise. "Well, good. Be like old times."

"Except he doesn't have a hand." We won't do La Aguja, but right now I don't care. Having him come so I can look him in the eye and ask for his forgiveness is all I've dreamed of. I realize that now.

"That was a bloody business in Karakorum, wasn't it?"

That's the good part about Murray. He keeps life understated. Me cutting my brother loose, sending him to his death, causing his hand to be amputated is reduced to "a bloody business."

"Yeah, it was."

"What are your plans?"

"Dunno." I shrug. "Not sure where he's at. I don't want to assume his abilities until he's here."

I glance back out the open door. There is no movement from my tent, but I should head back in case Auden awakens. "Hey, before I go, what about the other journalist?"

"That Dutch wanker?"

"Yeah. Where is he?"

Murray snorts. "Probably halfway to Peru. He rocketed out of here after you kicked Psycho's ass like the devil himself rode on his heels. Don't think he wanted to be the next punching bag."

Good. Guess he's smarter than I gave him credit for.

"Why do you climb with Psycho anyway?" I ask. "I get Goonbag. He's solid. But the other one? He's a liability."

Murray nodded slowly. "This will be my last trip with him. He's gotten too unreliable. He'll need to find himself new partners."

"Yeah." I reach out and bump his knuckles. "Good call."

"Take it easy."

"Will do." So many things have gotten easy. I should be fucking grateful. Maybe the solution for what to do with Auden is forthcoming. I take a deep breath. If I want something, maybe Murray's right; I just need to go after it. If I want her in my life long-term, then the best thing I can do is—

*"Amigo!"* The gaucho comes toward me, waving the newspaper. "Eh?"

*"Muchas gracias."* A fresh bit of reading material is always welcome.

The tent is quiet when I get back inside, but Auden's awake.

"I'm sorry." I freeze in the entrance, catching her stare. "I meant to be here when you woke up."

"It's OK. I still feel a little out of it. What time is it?"

"Close to dinner. Can you eat anything?"

She shakes her head. "My stomach feels gross."

"I have some powdered chicken noodle soup. It's no' gourmet, but it's hot and salty. It might help fix you up, and then I want you to get a good night's sleep."

"Thank you," she says, sitting up.

"What for?"

"Taking care of me again."

"It's a pleasure." And that it is. This girl can manage herself fine, but when things don't go her way, I like to know that I can be the guy who helps makes things easier.

The inclination comes again. I've told her I want her, but how to expand on that, say more? The words are right there, hovering overhead, a different kind of challenge to climb. One I'm not sure I'm ready to face. "I'll step outside and fix that soup."

The weather is shifting. Lenticular clouds stack on top of one another. These clouds are unique, look like flying saucers or hotcakes stacked one on top of the other. They are created when moist air is thrust upward as it travels over mountains. This makes them look like they aren't moving, hovering stationary, but that's an illusion. In reality, the constant flow of moist air comes from the windward side, even as they are losing moisture on the leeward side, like where we are now. Good weather is coming. The cloud is starting to pull back from the flanks of the mountain, like a lady lifting up her skirts inch by inch. The stone is fucking tantalizing. The idea of a climb makes my mouth water, but Cameron won't be in a position to attempt that.

We'll do something different, straightforward. All I want is to reconnect with my brother. My best friend. Then the thought occurs to me.

I can ask Cameron about Auden.

He'll give me solid advice. He's figured all that out, love and shite. Relief settles around me like a mantle. Aye, Cameron will know what to do. I'm no' alone anymore. I'll have backup.

The hot water is boiling in my metal pot, and I fix Auden a mug. I usually keep powdered soup on hand for emergency, but I'm not a fan. I'm too spoiled from all the stew Mum made growing up. Good hearty pots full of mutton or chicken, boiled potatoes and carrots. Things that kept the cold North Atlantic air at bay as you ate them. Warmed you from the inside.

Mum would like Auden. They'd join forces to give me shite. I find myself smiling. Go back in and pass Auden her wee cup, and she takes it with both hands, positioning her face to catch the steam.

"Oh, that's nice. I thought I didn't want anything, but this might settle my stomach."

"Good." I unfold the paper. Ready to kick back and read by the light of the dying day, content to sit in silence as Auden sips her soup.

She opens her mouth and appears to think better of it.

"What is it?" I say, setting the paper down.

"I heard you in the woods," she says, fidgeting. "Talking to Psycho."

"Don't be troubled by him none. He's no' going to bother you again. Once Cameron comes, I'm going to leave this camp. Head somewhere else in the park. There are plenty more quiet places without bullshit."

"And I'll go back to Boulder, start my internship."

"Yes," I say, faltering.

"It will be like nothing ever happened."

The way she says "nothing" is peculiar; she gives it an emphasis.

"You've had a hard day, but if you need to talk about any of it…"

She shakes her head. "Nah, that's cool. Share some paper with me."

"'Course." I fork over the front-page section. It's all in Spanish, and while I speak it fine, reading it will be a bit of an effort, a good distraction.

She settles back, sipping her mug, and begins to skim.

I wish I knew what she was thinking. Thank God Cameron will be here soon.

"Rhys."

The quiet way she whispers my name sends a chill down my spine. The wind picks up, and the dull roar grinds over the tent, rattling the nylon. A few sad drops plop on the ceiling. Not rain, just a grim sprinkling. She stares at me, and it's hard to make out her face exactly, as the daylight is gone, leaving behind a gray gloom.

"Are you unwell?" I reach out, ready to get her outside before she's sick all over herself.

"Oh my God, Rhys. I'm sorry." She's crying now. My heart hammers my chest, striking my ribs like an ice ax. "I'm so sorry."

"Auden." I pull her into my arms to comfort her, but the way she clasps me in return is wrong. All wrong. It's as if she's the one doing the comforting. My stomach turns to water. The time between her next two breaths is endless, and I spin in space, no idea what she's about to say and terrified to know. Whatever it is will have consequences, and I'm not sure what's to be lost. Pressure builds in my skull. I'm doing my best to wait until she's calm enough to speak, but dread tears at me. What's happened to her? What could have changed in the past two minutes?

She stares at me as my organs go into free fall, and then her trembling hands reach up to bracket my face.

"Rhys, I am so sorry."

"Auden, you need to tell—"

"The paper, you haven't read it?"

I give my head a single shake. The gaucho passed it over before he headed back down the mountain.

"There was an accident. A commuter plane crashed during the bad weather a few days ago."

I mentally knock up against the words, like it's a headwall I need to climb. I'm back in the Karakorum. There is ice cutting my eyes. It's hard to see. My sockets burn.

"The paper says there were no survivors. One of the passengers is listed as the climber Cameron MacAskill."

The wind lashes outside with a triumphant howl. It returned for its due, and this time the price was paid.

# 27

## AUDEN

W hy?" He repeats the question in this awful depersonalized voice. "Why did this happen?" I don't even think he's aware that he's spoken.

Silence thickens the air. Sweat pools in my bra. I grip his hand tighter, leaning close to squint at the newspaper in the fast-fading light. The plane from Santiago hit a storm over the mountains. They're waiting for official word from the black box, but primary indications point to bad weather leading to pilot error. The plane stalled and crashed about fifty miles north. Only ten minutes ago, my worst problems were that I'd been given hallucinogenics as a stupid prank and wasn't sure if Rhys had real feelings for me.

Now it's as if everything has been crammed into a blender and turned to liquid.

"Cameron's dead?" He lifts his head, and his thumb circles the grainy photo of Cameron next to an aerial image of a small plane shattered against rock. "He died coming for me."

"Oh, Rhys, I'm so sorry." I hug him hard, try to infuse as much love and warmth as possible into his hard, inflexible body.

It's like trying to warm a slab of marble. "You know this isn't your fault, right? What happened to him is a terrible tragedy, a freak accident."

He doesn't answer. I know this guy in my arms, and the guilt of the accident is going to drag him under. How will he come back from this? How could anyone?

I brush his hair off his forehead. He's not crying, or yelling, or displaying even a modicum of actual human emotion. The guy who'd been with me the last few days has vanished, obliterated by grief.

"When did the crash happen?" He closes his eyes and kneads his brow.

I wet my dry lips. "The day before New Year's Eve. December thirtieth."

"The night you came to my tent," he whispers. "The night the lightning struck twice like an omen..."

"We'll leave at dawn." Screw my story. This takes precedence over any opportunity at *Outsider*. "The park entrance isn't too far. We can take a bus to wherever you need to go. We'll discover the location of...of...his body...help get him home."

He starts gulping air like he'll never get enough. "Amelia is pregnant. I was to be an uncle."

"You still can. Cameron wanted you in his life, remember? That's why he was coming."

He pulls away from me. "He should never have had to. It should have been me going to him, on my knees."

"If he's anything like you, nobody forced him," I say fiercely. "Who is to say he wasn't coming for himself? After surviving an accident like that? Being faced with a life-changing injury like the loss of his hand might have driven him to need this trip for himself as much as to reconnect with you."

His face doesn't change expression. He stares through me as if I'm a ghost, as if I'm in fact nothing. I realize now in some vague truth that he didn't mean the words earlier, that he said them to get Psycho away from sniffing around whatever was happening with us. But now. Now I am nothing. The world is nothing.

To Rhys, everything is ashes.

So I stop talking. There is nothing I can say. I can't tell him he'll be OK, because this is the time to grieve. All I can do is sit beside him and bear witness. Hope my touch acts as a lifeline so that he can find his way back and I'll be there waiting for him. He deserves the first person he sees when he returns to himself to be the face of someone who loves him.

Because that's what I do.

I love him.

I am in love with Rhys MacAskill.

And it might be something people will scoff at, like how can I possibly love this guy I've known for such a short time, but facts are facts. And the fact of the matter is, there's a part of my soul that is no longer my own, but his.

I silently hold him for hours. This isn't an exaggeration. He sits in utter stone silence until my legs cramp and finally fall asleep in slow, prickling tingles. Until the arms that I grasp him with are dull with tired weight and still don't move. He doesn't have to face the long night alone.

I slip into torpor, half dozing, half gripped by the relentless crucible that hasn't released my stomach since Cameron's photo appeared in the paper, when Rhys jerks. At first I think he's fallen asleep, a blessing, because he's going to need to conserve strength. But no. Noiseless violent sobs rack him, soundless pain, even though his cheeks are dry against my own.

"My brother is dead," he says at last, lifting his head, face lost in the night.

"I know." I pull him against me, and he squeezes so hard my next inhalation is almost impossible and still I don't release my grip.

*Any strength inside me, let it pass to him.*

It seems strange to wish for such a thing when he's obviously so much stronger than me, but right now, he's broken. When we first met, I sensed his secret vulnerability, the place inside him held together by a gossamer-thin strand. That's snapped now, and he's blowing adrift, and it's up to me to hold on until he finds a way to tie himself back together.

He buries his face in the top of my head and slides his hands to bracket my shoulders. Then I'm against the ground and he's on top. I kiss first and he responds, shuddering. What happens next isn't pleasurable; it's necessary, a reminder of life in the face of death.

I tear off my shirt as he removes his, and a few more zips and tugs get us naked. There's no foreplay, and I don't want it. That's not what this is. I tear open a condom foil with my teeth and fumble as I try to stretch it over him. He takes charge and sets it in place with one smooth shove of his fist. Then he's taking me and I let him. At first he does nothing but mindlessly thrust. It doesn't hurt, but it's rough and fast, as if he can escape what haunts him. His body hits mine with audible thwacks as his breath grows increasingly ragged. All I can do is keep my arms braced on his shoulders.

Slowly, almost unnoticeably, the tempo changes. He puts his face against me, and there's the first wetness from tears.

"Auden," he gasps.

I don't tell him to shush. I don't tell him everything is going to be OK. This is a time for truth. "I love you."

He stills, buried to the hilt, fingers gripping the small of my back. "I love you, Rhys."

I can't see his eyes, only the hint of his head.

"Jesus, God," he groans, crushing my face to his chest. I kiss the skin over his heart, and the pounding there reverberates against my lips. He cries out, a sob, a note of need, and I add my teeth and tongue, and his thighs begin to tense, a sign of his building climax.

"Auden."

"Rhys." I'm bewildered to find myself here, beside him. There's no good reason I should orgasm, except that the overwhelming intensity between us is enough, and there is no point questioning because fuck it—I'm going over and he falls, too, and we tumble together through sweat, urgent kisses, and tears—his and mine—tying ourselves into something that will hold fast against the coming storm.

———

I wake in the dark. The first hint of pearly dawn aids my eyes in adjusting. For a moment the soreness between my legs focuses me to what passed between Rhys and me in the middle of the night, but just as quickly a sickening soberness sets in.

Cameron is dead and Rhys can't face the next few days alone. We have to get out of the park, contact his family. I rub my eyes. "We should get a start as soon as possible."

"I'm staying."

I study his face until he looks away. "Wait…" It's early, but I'm not computing. "We need—"

"I am staying here."

He isn't going to do what I think he's doing. The next words are a struggle to form. "You can't."

He doesn't look at me. "I said I'm staying."

"No." What he's saying doesn't make sense, because he's had the wits shocked from him. "I can't let you stay and climb La Aguja. You need to come with me. We'll find out where your brother's body is—"

"Stop talking." He holds up a hand. "Stop fucking talking."

"OK, but—OK." I scrub my face with my hands, choking back the overwhelming desire to scream myself hoarse. Damn it. I was close, so close to getting Rhys out of here in one piece. "I need air."

"Good idea."

I grab my light down jacket and zip it to my chin, then crawl past him. He's big, fills most of the tent, and yet moves his body so I don't skim him as we pass. I want to take the used condom that's tied off in the tent pocket waiting for the trash and fling it in his fucking face. He'll make love to me in the night and refuse to speak to me in the morning.

But what happened between us last night wasn't lovemaking. I crawl outside and let the cool morning air shock my lungs before removing my steroid inhaler and taking a puff. I stride blindly past some other earlier riser, ignoring their mumbled greeting as I swipe tears off my cheeks. I told him I loved him for one reason, because it's the truth.

But you don't always have to like the people you love.

I realize I'm heading toward the base of the mountain and increase my speed, until I'm practically jogging. Then I'm there, bracing my hands against the cold granite and staring up. "Fuck you," I yell, to La Aguja for existing so people can risk their lives on it, to Rhys for being stupid and reckless enough to do this rather than face his demons, to me for being unable to fix anything. I pick up a stone and palm it between my hands before heaving it back and throwing it hard. It bounces off the wall like nothing ever happened. I pick up another and throw it harder. Soon I'm raining down rocks on the mountain, and all the while it's only becoming more apparent there is nothing I can do.

I collapse, panting, beneath a tree and rock my head back, seeing the dawn dappled through the canopy. Rhys wanted forgiveness from his brother, and that's never going to happen now. Instead, he is going to hold himself responsible and take part in some sort of a death struggle, as if that will give him absolution. It won't. The realization swells within me. The only person who can forgive Rhys for the accident with his brother is Rhys.

Forgiveness doesn't come from others. It comes from yourself.

He needs to give himself permission to move on with his life.

I close my eyes and listen to the world waking up. I need to forgive myself, too, for not being able to have a functional, healthy relationship with my sister. When I get home, I'm not going to start World War III. I'm not engaging in petty revenge. I'm going to stop trying to make things OK between us. She holds things against me that I can't control. Resentment is her choice, but I have one, too. I can walk away. As much as Rhys needs to retie what's severed inside him, I need to cut Harper loose. Maybe someday she'll want to pursue a kinder relationship, but I'm not going to beat myself up trying to force that.

I forgive myself for walking away and setting clear, protective boundaries. I'm not going to be her doormat ever again.

There are enough amazing people in the world who might want my love and friendship, like the guy back in the tent on his damn suicide mission. He's changed his mind once. Maybe he can change it again. This is just his initial rash impulse. Once he's settled down, he can start grieving, and he'll come to his senses.

I stand up, and morning is here in earnest. The clouds erase and there, far, far overhead, is the summit. There is no way I'll ever stand up there. I'm not someone who is ever going to perch in the aeries of the world. But if that old legend is true, and what I want most in the world is up there, then maybe I can, I don't know, commune with it?

Because what I want most is for this guy I've fallen madly, deeply in love with to love himself even a fraction as much. To realize that he can rise above this darkness and remember that even in the biggest storm, once you pass through the clouds, the sun is shining.

I walk briskly back to the tent with hope in my heart. Hope that's dashed into a hundred little pieces when I find the tent packed and my bag loaded and ready to go. My bag alone.

Rhys crouches beside it. "I've given you my tent," he says. "Has all the proper poles. You know how to put it up now. I don't think you'll get into any more trouble."

"Rhys, please."

He stands and extends a scrap of paper. On it is scratched two phone numbers. "I know you want to do your story, but can you please go call my mum? The other number is Amelia. Tell them... Tell them I'm sorry." His voice cracks.

I wrap my arms around his waist and stare up, wishing my eyes had the power to hypnotize. "Come with me. Call them yourself."

"I will. When I return." He gives me a tight smile. "I don't mean to commit suicide, Auden. I'm not going to throw myself off the mountain. This climb is something I talked about, dreamed about with Cameron. I owe it to his memory to stand on top. What

I want isn't ever going to happen now, but maybe from up there he'll hear me better."

"Oh, Rhys."

"Maybe you'll hear me, too, Auden."

"I can hear you fine here. Please, don't do this."

He sets a hand on top of my head. "Last night you told me you loved me."

"I do. I meant it. I know it's crazy, but, Rhys—"

"I love you, too," he whispers, and the words sound exactly like *good-bye*.

# 28

## RHYS

*W*hy are you doing this?" Tears flow freely down Auden's cheeks.

"You don't understand." I press my lips and offer a silent prayer that the sadness in her eyes won't undo me. "My love hurts people."

She braces her stomach as if I've caused her physical pain and swallows back a sob. "Are you kidding me? How can you say that? How can you actually believe that?"

"My brother is dead because of me, because I let him down, first on the side of that fucking mountain and again by no' having the courage to face him. He had to come track me down and…" That's it. I can't say more. My throat swells shut.

She reaches for my hand and presses it against her heart. Behind her Murray walks to the hut, probably getting ready to cook up breakfast. He starts to wave, but notices our grim posture and averts his face like we're not there.

"Auden."

"Tell me you don't feel this." Her voice is more miserable than angry. "We have a connection, Rhys, and that doesn't occur every day. It's never ever happened to me before, and from everything you told me, it's never been this way for you either."

The truth in her words punches my gut. I can't walk away and leave her crying. As much as I want to go, desperate to escape, retreat into myself, the tears dripping off the end of her chin are some form of cement, rendering me in place.

"We're connected," she repeats, her eyes wide, trusting, so convinced she can make me understand. "It's different from being up on a mountain, but I'm tied to you. We're partners, and whatever happens to you affects me now."

And that's when she does it, gives me the way to escape her. She placed her trust in my hands without realizing it was a knife. Everything she says is true, but it takes me back to the night without hope, the hungry wind, the relentless ice and unceasing dark. "That's your fatal mistake," I say flatly. "Trusting me."

She wipes her eyes. "No! There's no way this is a mis—"

"How can you forget? I'm the last person you want to tie yourself to." I force my face to be utterly emotionless and my insides to settle, just like before, that terrible night. The hardest part is the lead-up; the final severing happens in an instant. "I'm the guy who cuts the rope."

She's falling, and unlike Cameron, I have to bear witness, watch as her features collapse.

"The world is right," she snarls, bending to grab her pack. "You really are an unfeeling, psychopathic monster. I'll go call your family. There is no way I'd stick around here and write a story about a mountain of dreams. It would be a lie. This is a mountain of nightmares."

I give her a sarcastic salute and my hand doesn't even tremble. She's going to walk away, and that will be that. We were never meant to be. I'm fit to be no one's partner. There's no escaping the inevitable. I am a monster, wreaking hurt, pain, and destruction on the few people who are unlucky enough for me to care about them.

Why isn't she gone already?

She closes her eyes and sucks in a shaky breath. When she opens them again, they are red rimmed, and brokenhearted. "For what it's worth, I am truly sorry about your brother."

She sounds like I feel—gutted.

With that she turns and starts to walk away, slower than even her normal pace. *Please don't think I'll stop you, because I won't.*

Halfway to the trail, she pauses and turns. "And for whatever else it's worth, I'm not sorry we met."

My legs are moving before I can stop them. No. Fuck. Letting go needs to be simple, one quick flick of my wrist and then gone. I can't grapple to hang on. But my body isn't listening to my mind, and I'm pulling her against me in a fierce bear hug, breathing in her scent, the memories from the past few days swirling behind my lids: her pale, frightened face peering into my tent, her kitten knickers, the way she breathes in deep sleep, the cheeky glint in her eye when she gives me shit, the way she falls apart when I'm inside her.

"The mountains will always be here, but this chance won't be—don't let me go," she says, muffled against my chest. "As soon as I saw you, I knew my life would never be the same. You are my best adventure. We both came to this place with a goal, but can't we move on, make a new one?"

"I'm sorry. I can't be the guy you need right now or ever. You'll thank me for it."

"Don't condescend and tell me how I should feel," she grinds out. "Say Rhys and Auden aren't happening."

I open my mouth to say the words and they turn traitor, refuse to come.

"You wanted to ask forgiveness from Cameron and that chance is gone, but that was never how things were going to play out. Your brother had already forgiven you. Of that I have no doubt in my mind. But none of that matters in the end. Only you can truly forgive yourself. Only you." She pokes my chest, punctuating the last words. "And if you cut us loose, will you really be able to forgive that?"

I don't have words. I can't even hold her gaze. Instead, I look up, and the mountain, La Aguja, towers overhead in all its glory, not a trace of cloud in the bluebird sky. Will I forgive myself if I don't make this climb for my brother?

"Here's what I can't excuse," Auden says. "Myself if I stay and watch you risk your life due to a misguided attempt at absolution. The only way you are going to begin to deal with your grief is to come now, with me. But I've already asked. So I'm going, and all I can do is believe that once I'm gone, you'll figure it out that I'm right."

"Auden…" I don't know what I even want to say. Every part of me is shutting down.

She takes a long shuddering breath. "If you ever find yourself back in Colorado, look me up."

"I will."

She rises on her toes and brushes her lips against the side of my cheek. "I love you, but you have a hell of a lot to figure out."

Then she's gone. My arms are empty, and when my eyes finally refocus, her shadow is lost in the forest.

I stumble back to my gear. Someone says my name, but I don't turn my head, don't have the energy to do anything more than hold myself together, and I'm doing a piss-poor job of that.

"Rhys! Mate!" Murray comes over, holding out a mug. "Have a drink."

"No coffee." I don't need to be more hyped up than I am.

"No coffee." He thrusts it at me.

I sniff and recognize the bite of alcohol. It's barely morning, not a good time for drinking. I drain the cup in three swallows, the burn in my esophagus doing nothing to dull the burn in my heart.

"Girl problems?" he asks when I hand back his cup.

"Cameron is dead."

His eyes widen. "What?"

I tell him the story in as few sentences as possible. "Auden doesn't think I should do the climb, but she doesn't understand. This is the only way I have to be close to Cameron, to say good-bye."

"Walk with me," Murray says.

He takes off toward the mountain and I follow, unable to summon the strength to resist. Our boots crunch the undergrowth, and half a dozen times I wonder if I'll be sick. My bones seem filled with lead. If I slept now, I might never wake up.

"I've been around a long time," he says at last. "Seen lots of friends go."

I know by "go" that he doesn't mean "lose touch." He means "die."

"Every accident is unique, but many share a common quality."

"What's that?" I say wearily.

"They forget that to successfully make a climb, we have to want it bad, so bad we'll do anything to make it."

"Exactly. That's what I—"

"Not finished with my point here, mate." He halts me with a raised hand. "And at the exact same time, we need to be willing to let that want go. That's the paradox. We have to want it more than anything and yet still be able to walk away."

"I'm afraid I'm not wired that way. Hard-nosed bastard and all."

"I know you are afraid. Remember, though, fear isn't something that just happens. We allow it to come into our lives, give it a place at the table, and feed it."

"When did you get so wise?"

Murray gives a sad smile. "Never said I was wise, mate. I've just been around longer than you. Once I had a girl, and I walked away, afraid of being tied down."

"And what happened?"

Murray stares into the distance, his gaze inward, seeing an invisible face. "I've never stopped regretting it." He gives his head a shake. "So what are you thinking?"

"I don't know, man, and that's the problem. To be on that mountain, I need to be all in. But the same is true about love."

"There's no race to the finish here," Murray responds. "Why don't you walk a bit longer, and I'll see you back at camp. If the weather holds, Psycho and Goon are going to be champing at the bit. Probably start our push tomorrow. You're welcome to join with us. Psycho will whine, but I'll sort him."

"Hey, thanks," I say, extending my hand. "I'll think it over."

"Remember, the mind can be one hell of a convincing liar." Murray gives me a final nod and leaves me on my own. "Let your heart tell you what needs to happen."

I walk through the forest with his words ringing in my ears. This is what I wanted. No one else. If I'm alone, I can hurt no one, except myself. No one else. If I'm alone, I can hurt no one, except myself. Auden told me she loved me, and she meant those words. I saw the truth in her eyes, in every inch of her face. Her love is a gift, one that I couldn't accept, not when I hate myself too much.

I find myself at the base of La Aguja and rest my hand on the stone. How badly I'd hoped forgiveness waited at the top, but what if Auden's right, and the only way to have what I want is to reach within myself and find it?

"Cameron," I whisper, "what should I do?"

There's no reply, only the wind, a light rustle this morning, a faint symphony of branches rubbing against one another.

My brother may be gone, but I know what he'd say if he stood before me. He'd tell me to stop being an arse. Dwelling on what a fucking failure I am won't make me successful. Telling myself that I will hurt the ones I love so I need to stay away won't bring me peace.

"Someday, maybe," I tell La Aguja. "But first I have other things to do."

If I'm going to be the guy who deserves a girl like Auden, then I need to first face down a different kind of mountain, conquer my own self-doubt.

# 29

## *AUDEN*

Dad picks me up at Denver Airport. "How was your little trip?" he asks, taking my backpack.

My little trip. Yeah, right.

"Good," I answer, and that's plenty of information for him. He chats a bit about his work and Mom while we walk to the parking garage and then mostly about Harper. She's being pegged as "the one to beat," by the Olympic press, and I don't doubt it. On the drive home, I close my eyes and pretend to sleep. He turns on some classic-rock station and sings under his breath, oblivious to the fact my lip keeps wobbling.

If I never tell anyone about meeting Rhys MacAskill, maybe it will be like it never happened. When I walked away, I knew that was it, but still, a part of me, a stupid part I wish I could slap like a mosquito, kept hoping he'd appear behind me on the trail. His hair would be mussed. He'd be out of breath.

"Auden," he'd say in the smooth lilt, and that would be enough. That he came for me would be enough.

Instead, I got to the end of the trail the way I began—alone, with no story, with nothing at all. A bus idled, ready to return to Puerto Natales, hikers filing on one by one, all buzzing from their time in the park. A few paused to snap one last picture or do a funny duck-face selfie. I stepped on, and when the driver rolled into first gear, pulling the door closed, the sound of wheels on the gravel had a note of finality.

I wanted Rhys to fight at all costs, fight for me, but more important, for himself.

All I can do is hope he eventually gets the courage.

Right now he could be on La Aguja. Right now he could be—

"Home again, home again, jiggidy jig," Dad calls out four hours later. I never did sleep, but I rub my eyes anyway, feigning a bleary wake-up expression.

My sister's white Tacoma truck is in the driveway. The bumper sticker on the back has two black diamonds and reads I'M DIFFICULT. No shit.

She's already gone, overseas, ensconced at the Olympic Village. Mom and Dad are taking off to join her in a few days. They babble about her all through dinner, with only the most cursory questions about my time in South America. It's like I've never been gone. And to tell you the truth, it's a relief.

When I go upstairs to my room to change into my favorite fuzzy pajama pants, they aren't in the top drawer. Harper must have packed them. That she'd raid my drawers despite everything only shows me that I'm right in my decision to distance myself from her. I sent her an e-mail my last night in South America.

Harper,

For a long time, I believed you made me feel bad about myself. That was wrong. I'm responsible for my own feelings.

You can't "make" me insecure or hurt unless I give you that power.

Those days are over.

I can't maintain a relationship with someone who wants only to take and never give. You aren't willing to accept my limits and have consistently revealed in your actions that you don't value me. Sadly, our relationship does nothing but deplete me.

So for now, I am walking away. I do love you as a family member, but I have to love and respect myself, too. If you ever want to put in the work to repair this relationship, let me know. I'd like that. Until then, please know that I'll be distancing myself from you.

Auden

I didn't get a response, only a notification that the message had been opened. Maybe someday she'll be ready to try to heal what's broken between us, but until then, I've acted in good faith and need to let it go.

I change into a pair of stretchy yoga bottoms instead and head back downstairs with my iPad. My mom fixes me a gigantic bowl of my favorite dessert, apple cobbler with vanilla-bean ice cream, and says for once I can eat in the living room. Dad's got a fire roaring. I came from summer and it's back to winter. The night comes early, so I can't see the Rockies. There's nothing to remind me of Rhys. No reason that my fingers should reach for my iPad and do the one thing I swore I wouldn't do.

Type his name into Google.

What will I do if I read he's had an accident?

But how can I stand never knowing?

I can't.

For once, the Internet takes forever to load, or maybe it's just my own impatience. I shove in ice cream by the spoonful and am in mid brain freeze when the news page finally downloads.

The brain freeze must have spread to my whole body, because I lose control of my hands. My iPad falls to my lap. When I blink my eyes, the headline is still the same:

RHYS MACASKILL RETURNS HOME TO BURY BROTHER AFTER TRAGIC PLANE CRASH

My parents are both washing up in the kitchen, so no one but our two dogs, Gog and Magog, bear witness to my tears.

"He didn't do the climb," I whisper to them. "He went to Cameron instead. He went to his brother."

Magog wags her tail simply because she's friendly like that. Gog perks his ears but clearly is missing the significance.

Rhys flew home with his brother. He can't move forward until he faces his fears, and it looks like he's finally taking a step away from self-destruction and toward peace.

Even though Scotland is thousands of miles away from Colorado, I look out the window and whisper, "I'm proud of you."

———

On my first day at *Outsider* magazine, I submit a new story, not a profile on climbers and La Aguja, but something more autobiographical called "Fear and Loving in Patagonia." To say my editor adored it is an understatement. I jump from internship to paid staff. She fought and got the story into the magazine, and the day it appeared in stores, let's just say not many things could compare with seeing my name in print.

Only the memory of a big Scottish guy pressed against me.

It's been two months, and radio silence from Rhys. Somehow, after reassuring myself that he wasn't engaging in any kind of crazy climbing death wish, I managed to resist the urge to Google stalk him. It hasn't been easy, but I feel like he deserves that from me, that he deserves that from everyone. He's been through so much, and what he needs is time to heal away from prying eyes. Even though I am dying to know what he's up to, I can give him that.

I never told anyone about meeting him. In part because it's so unbelievable—who falls in love in a couple of days? Jesus. I can see my friends rolling their collective eyes or muttering, "Yeah, yeah, you mean you fell in love with his wang."

I don't want to cheapen what happened in Torres del Paine. I know how I feel, and as crazy as it sounds, it's true.

I fell in hard, fast love and still have whiplash. Even though Rhys hasn't contacted me, I haven't wanted to date, even turned down a couple of coworkers who are easy on the eyes. This wasn't lust. It's like our masks got knocked off and I got a good look at his soul and he got one at mine, and how do you come back from that?

It's five o' clock, and while normally I'm not the kind of girl who bolts from her desk right at quitting time, I've got a hot date with myself at the local rock-climbing gym. I've enrolled in a beginners' class, and while I'm not particularly strong or brave, it feels great to try an activity that I never thought I'd do in a million years.

I don't have a jacket. It's a perfect early-spring evening, so it's warm enough to get away with a lightweight knit top. The sky is clearing up after a day of rain, and the air is filled with that delicious fresh smell. I breathe in deep when I hear the thing I've been waiting for since leaving Patagonia.

"Auden."

I don't have to turn around to recognize that voice. All I can do is stand there, on the sidewalk, next to the koi pond, and close my eyes.

"Auden."

This time closer. I turn and he's there, and all I can say is "You shaved."

There's his face, and holy God. I could make a hobby out of studying the lines on his face, the angles in his cheekbones, the edge of his jaw.

"Aye."

A couple of marketing staff walk by us chattering, and slow when they see Rhys.

"Whoa. Friend of yours, Auden?"

I shrug. "Maybe."

One gives me a sly thumbs-up.

"Maybe?" Rhys asks.

I hug myself. "Depends on if you're ready to treat me like one"

"I had to be alone for a few months. Went back to Skye and buried Cameron. After that, I spent time with Mum and Amelia, and it helped. I miss him. I—I won't ever stop, but I'm better now than when you last saw me."

"That's good."

"I am sorry for any hurt I caused you. I know I did wrong in so many ways. And I didn't want to contact you again until I was sure that I had my head screwed on right, or at least better."

"And you do?"

He nods. "You were right. I had a choice, to tear myself apart, or forgive."

My snuffle is audible. "I'm glad."

"But even if I can make peace that what happened to Cameron

wasn't all my fault, I needed to see you, to let you know I've worked hard, and always, when I thought about giving up, there was a little voice in the back of my head, a voice that whispered that I needed to push on, take another breath, keep going. A voice that sounded exactly like you."

"Really?"

"You seem to have left a part of yourself inside me, and I've done my best to look after it. I wonder if you have a part of me inside you, too." He shifts his weight.

"Yes," I whisper, a smile spreading across my face even as the waterworks are turning on. "You've been with me this whole time."

"Tonight, while I waited for you, all I could smell was the rain. That's your scent. When I was home, I'd smell it, and it would be like you were with me. I'd talk to you then, like a mad bastard."

"How long are you here for?"

He runs a hand through his hair. "Long as it takes. I'm half-American, so the country can't go kicking me out."

"Long as it takes for what?"

He finally looks straight in my eyes. "To convince you that I'm the guy to take a chance on."

I throw myself into his arms, and he hikes me up, locking my legs around his hips. "I'll always take a chance on you, Rhys."

"I've got a job at the Mountain School for the summer, not far from here. I'm teaching outdoor ed courses to save up money for university."

"That's only ten minutes from where I live."

"If you'd like, we can see a lot of each other."

"You're going to stick around here and work? What about climbing?"

"You have a job here. I know what it means to you."

"Yes."

"The rest will figure itself out. And that was a bloody good article you wrote, by the way," he says with open pride, his face shining with admiration.

"The 'Fear and Love' one?"

"That and all of them. I've read every word you've written."

"You have?"

He kisses me then, long and slow, and it doesn't take long for the urgency to settle in. His hands are lost in my hair, and I'm done for when his tongue slides over mine, a dance that I haven't forgotten. We sigh into each other, and I know he's feeling the same way as me, that we're home. "I make you this promise: We're a team, partners. I'll never put your interests ahead of my own. Climbing will always be in my life, but it's not the sum total, no' anymore. Any decisions we make about the future, we do so together. I won't cut you loose."

I cover his smooth cheeks with my kisses. "You couldn't if you tried. What ties us together is stronger than anything."

# Epilogue

*I* think I have it," I say, snapping my fingers. Rhys and I are having a picnic in a meadow next to a climb we just finished. Nothing nuts, a straightforward novice route, but it's my first attempt out of the gym and I feel like I've conquered Everest. We're celebrating with chocolate-covered granola bars, bananas, and water, a banquet for champions. "I have a perfect nickname for you."

He glances up from the Edward Abbey book he's reading. "I don't—"

"Loving you is Rhysy Peasy." I clap my hands. "Get it? Like easy peasy?"

His brows raise in mock horror. "Rhysy Peasy?"

"I like it." I arch a brow. "Or we can go with Rhyses Pieces?"

"Absolutely no—"

"Fine. Want to hear the real one?" I lean over to kiss him right on the furrow in his forehead. That's a part of him I'll take as the complete package. I'm well aware this guy can brood, grump, and be gruff. But behind the bark isn't bite. It's a guy who can move mountains when he turns his single-minded focus to something.

There are circles under his eyes. At night he still wakes up, and I roll over to discover our bed empty.

He'll be outside against our balcony, watching the stars, or in the spare room he's turned into a bouldering gym, shirtless and sweaty. That's when he's missing Cameron and going to darker places. But he never ventures so far as to where I can't find him. In those times, I take hold of his hand and say, "You're a good man."

"Why do you tell me that?" he whispers.

"Because it's true."

We repeat this conversation again and again, but I don't mind.

And when he looks at me, like this, he certainly, ahem, moves me.

"My love," I say, and sit back with a smile.

He waits as if I'm going to deliver a punch line.

"That's it." I tousle his thick dark hair, and the lightness of his eyes is a startling contrast. His mouth opens a fraction, but he doesn't say anything.

"My love," I repeat again with a soft but firm insistence. "You don't mind, do you?"

"No." He runs his hand up my calf and squeezes my knee. "Reckon that's a good one."

"You saved me, you know." It's true, and I don't just mean the night he unwillingly rescued me in the Valle del Frances. He saw something in me that I didn't know was there, that I am a girl who can climb mountains, that I am a girl who can do anything I put my mind to.

"That's no' how the story goes. You saved me."

"How about we saved each other?" I murmur.

He brushes his lips tenderly against the corner of my mouth, and before taking our kiss deeper, murmurs, "Aye, that we did."

# ACKNOWLEDGMENTS

Thank you to my fearless editor, Lauren Plude, and agent, Emily Sylvan Kim, for their support and belief in my ability to write this story (even when—no, especially when—I had my doubts). To Elizabeth Turner for my favorite cover to date—you knocked it out of the park. To everyone at Team Forever for being so supportive and dedicated to getting books in the hands of readers. To my family, who dealt with my moodiness while I drafted this over Christmas holidays and was less than holly jolly. To Nick, who hiked Torres del Paine with me and helped give me this plot bunny. To Amy Pine, who always helps me show, not tell, and Jennifer Blackwood, Jules Barnard, and Natalie Blitt for reading snippets and being blunt. To my readers... you are the ketchup to my fries.

If you never get lost, you'll
never be found . . .

See the next page for a preview of

# UPSIDE DOWN

by Lia Riley,
Book 1 in the Off the Map series.

Available now.

# I

# TALIA

*I* breathe on my bedroom window and smear a spy hole in the condensation. Not much going on this morning. A lone crow dips over California bungalow roofs while in the distance Monterey Bay is shrouded in mist. I'm a Santa Cruz girl to the bone, love that fog like it's a childhood blanket.

The downstairs phone rings and Dad turns off NPR. He's a sucker for *Wait Wait...Don't Tell Me!* Once I get on the plane this afternoon, the only noise in the house will be that frigging radio. Guilt grabs me with two cold fists, right in the gut. I should be plopped beside him on the couch, trying to kid around, but I'm not even sure he wants my company.

My sister, Pippa, would know what to do. She was the expert in easy affection. She'd blow through the kitchen on a Friday night, swig a sip of Dad's beer, sling an arm around his neck, and torture him with wet cheek kisses. I've never been a hugger. My role was easy, the joke-cracking sidekick. But there's no work for a side-kick without a hero. These days, if I wander into a room, Dad's gaze automatically slides to the empty space beside me. Somehow, despite everything, I'm the ghost child. I don't want to haunt him, so I keep to my room.

*My room.*

Not ours. No one's slept in the other bed in a year and a half. My sister's one-eyed sock monkey, Seymour, reclines in the middle of her calico pillowcase, wearing an evil expression. *I know your secrets*, he seems to say. *What you keep hidden.* I give the monkey the finger and instantly feel worse.

Seymour and I go way back. To those days after Pippa died and my room was a safe place to shatter. He saw me research phantom medical symptoms until four in the morning, curl beneath my bed wrapped in the comforter so Dad never heard me weep, watched as I knelt in the dormer window seat and counted cars, closing my eyes if I ever spotted a red one because red was bad.

It meant blood.

Death.

Seymour the Sock Monkey knows me for who I am.

The leftover daughter.

"Sorry, Pippa," I mutter. Like my sister gives two shits about my relationship with her fucking stuffed animal. If she can see me from wherever she is, and that's highly suspect, I've given her far greater cause for displeasure.

Seymour's frayed mouth seems to sneer. We're in agreement on that point.

There's a knock on the bedroom door. "Hang on a sec!" I slip on my T-shirt and tighten the bath towel around my waist. My computer is open on the desk. WebMD calls my name, softly seductive, like Maleficent to Princess Aurora. In this case, I'm not offered a spinning wheel spindle but reassurance that I'm not going to die. Dr. Halloway urged me to block access to any health-related sites, but in the shower, the freckle on my right foot looked bigger. Bob Marley died from a melanoma on his toe, so I'm not 100 percent mentally unhinged—more like 85 percent on a bad day.

Despite my best efforts, I can't stop obsessing over what-ifs. What if I have early-stage skin cancer? What if this headache is a tumor? My mind is a bowl of water that I compulsively stir. I want my brain to be still and serene, but for the love of Sweet Baby Jesus, I can't quit agitating it.

There's another knock. More insistent.

"Seriously, I'm changing."

"Your mother's called to say good-bye," Dad says through the door. His voice is tense, pleading, like he holds something unpleasant, an old man's jockstrap, rather than the phone.

I turn the knob and stick my hand out to grab the receiver. "Thanks." I take my time putting it to my ear, humming the soundtrack to *Jaws* under my breath. "Hey, Mom."

"Alooooha." Wow, a perfect extension on the long *o* followed by a short, sharp *ha*. She's been practicing.

I mime a silent gag. "What's up?"

"Your cell went to voice mail." She doesn't like calling the landline. "You know I prefer not to talk to him."

I push up my glasses and roll my eyes. "Such an inconvenience." By *him* she means my dad, Scott Stolfi, the man she was married to for twenty-two years. She can't even say, "May I speak to Talia," without turning it into a thing. He was her high school sweetheart. They had one of those classic love stories, rich girl meets working-class boy. Now, a two-second conversation with the guy yanks her chain.

"You don't understand."

"And you say we never agree on anything." I bend and struggle with the zip to my overstuffed suitcase.

I bet two coconuts that Mom's sprawled by the infinity pool on the cliffside deck overlooking the Pacific. She's been holed up on my grandparents' estate on Kauai's north shore since she bailed last year. After they took Pippa off life support, Mom locked herself in the guest room for two days while Dad tackled an endless series of home repairs. When she finally emerged, he was mending the backyard fence. "You can't fix everything!" she'd screamed. Next thing we knew, she'd bought a one-way ticket to Hawaii. In lieu of a cheesy postcard, she sent Dad divorce papers from the law offices of William C. Kaleolani, Esq.

"Australia is just so far away. You've always talked about doing the Peace Corps one day, but to know you're all grown up..." Her gusty sigh is dramatic. This phone call is her pretending to care, a big show, part of the game she still plays called "Being a Mom." In all fairness, I shouldn't snark, because guess who's bankrolling my trip down under? As much as I hate to ask her for anything, I need this escape.

Mom comes from old Carmel money earned when my great-great-grandfather decimated two-thousand-year-old redwood groves. Environmental pillage made him filthy rich, but the money lost its stink over time, transformed into sustainable energy start-ups and progressive philanthropic causes.

I doubt the stumps rotting in the forest care.

"Has Logan's cookbook arrived?" Mom dials up the rainbow cheer. She's got to be grinding out that forced smile, the one that makes her teeth look like they're breaking. "His tour starts next week, LA and San Francisco. You could have joined us at the Esalen Institute."

The idea of soaking naked in a hippie retreat spa with Logan, Mom's hump buddy/Hawaiian spirit animal, is the stuff of nightmares. To date, I've successfully avoided an encounter with the Wunderchimp. In her photographs, he sports a mean chest 'fro. He's a personal macrobiotic chef to the stars and wannabe guru.

His book, *Eating from Within*, recently released and she mailed me a personal signed copy like I give a one-eyed donkey.

I jam the phone between my ear and shoulder to shimmy into my skinny jeans. "What about the breatharian section? Like, was he serious about gulping air for sustenance?"

"The detoxifying effects are incredible."

Whatever. I'll wager my own enlightenment that she's dying for one of Dad's famous cheeseburgers.

"I've lost five pounds since we got involved." There is a faint noise on the other end of the line, suspiciously like a wine bottle uncorking.

Hawaii is three hours behind.

Please don't let her be drinking before noon.

"Hey, um, are you—"

"Sunny put a new photo of you on Facebook." Mom's a ninja at deflection as well as a social media junkie. She posts daily emo statuses about self-discovery alongside whimsical shots of waterfalls, out-of-focus sunsets, and dolphins. "Are those new shorts? I swear your thighs come straight from your father's side." She makes it sound like my genes sport cankles and triple chins, but she's got a point. I did sprout from Dad's southern Italian roots: Mediterranean curves, brown eyes, and olive skin.

I slip on my shoes, turn sideways in the mirror, and pooch my stomach. "Had a physical last week with Dr. Halloway. Still well within normal range."

"Aren't they stretching those numbers to make big girls feel better?"

Mom is a size 2. To her, everyone is a big girl.

Pippa was Mom's doppelganger. They shared hummingbird-boned bodies and perpetually surprised blue eyes. I shove away the quick-fire anguish, slam my lids shut, and count to ten. The number nine feels wrong, so I do it once more for good measure.

"Talia? I need a little advice." Mom hushes to a "just us girls" level.

"What?" She's going to bash me and then get all buddy-buddy? Who replaced my real mother with this selfish hag?

"Male advice."

"Um, wait, you're joking, right?" This is above my pay grade.

"I just read online how pineapple juice improves semen flavor. Any tips for how to raise the subject with Logan?"

I open my mouth in a silent scream.

"He claims he doesn't enjoy the fruit. But what about me? My needs? He tastes like—"

"Enough." I flop beside my bed, grab a skullcap, shove it on, and yank the brim tight over my eyes in a futile attempt to hide. "You have got to be—"

"I come from a land down under, where women glow and men plunder." Sunny bursts into my room in a whirlwind of sandalwood essential oil and peasant skirts. Beth follows behind wearing the same hand-painted silk sheath gracing the cover of the latest Anthropologie catalogue.

"Hey, I gotta jam. Beth and Sunny arrived to say good-bye." *My mom*, I mouth, pretending to stab the receiver.

They roll their eyes.

"*A hui hou*, Ladybug. Australia waits. Discover your bliss." When Mom gets philosophical, her voice takes on a theatrically British accent for no reason.

"Bye, Mom." I toss the phone on my dresser and fake a seizure.

"Sounds like Mrs. S was in fine form." Sunny tugs off my cap.

Beth's jaw slackens. "OMG, Talia, what did you do to your hair?" She runs her fingers through her own dark flat-ironed locks as if trying to reassure herself of their continued flawlessness.

I skim my hand over the top of my head. "Box dye. Sunflower blond. You hate it, don't you?"

"You'll be easy to find in the dark." Sunny waggles her eyebrows in pervy innuendo. Nothing fazes this girl. I could tattoo a third eye on my forehead and she'd chat about opening root chakras. That's why I love her.

Beth halfway sits before realizing my bed's buried beneath an avalanche of travel guides, bikinis, underwear, power adaptors, and multicolored Australian currency. She never touches Pippa's bed. They were best friends. Beth had been riding shotgun in her Prius when the tweaker ran a stop sign and plowed through the driver's side door. She never talks about that day. Neither of us do. We've been too deeply hurt.

For a long time after the accident we remained optimistic. Pippa's brain showed limited signs of activity, but eventually, hope devoured the heart of my family until nothing remained but ashes and bone. Dad finds solace in warm beer and cold pizza and my mom in baby men. Me? I'm still digging out of the wreckage.

"Earth to Talia." Sunny presses a matcha green tea latte into my hand with a wink. "We picked up your favorite swamp water."

"Hey, thanks." I fake a sip, not having the heart to reveal I cut off caffeine and the accompanying hamster-wheel jitters. It's part of the Talia reboot. Talia 1.0 is outdated and it's time for a new model. Talia 2.0 isn't an anxious freak and is more than Pippa's tragic sister. She didn't lose her virginity to Tanner, her dead sister's long-term boyfriend after the BBQ held to commemorate the one-year anniversary of her passing, and she doesn't count precisely ninety-nine Cheerios into her bowl at breakfast to feel "right." And she certainly isn't going to focus on the fact that she's not graduating in six months—a secret that no one, not her parents or even her best friends, knows.

Old Talia may have royally screwed her GPA. New Talia is focused strictly on the future. A shiny tomorrow. A new-car-smelling do-over.

These girls are everything to me, but they don't have a clue how far I've fallen down the rabbit hole. I'm already one big sad story. Do I really want to be like *Hey, how about my freaky compulsions?*

Pretending to be a normal, functioning member of society is exhausting stuff.

"You're wearing that on the plane?" Beth inventories my jeans, purple Chuck Taylors, and Pippa's favorite tee.

"What?" I glance at the red-stenciled words crossing my chest—HOLDEN CAULFIELD IS MY HOMEBOY.

"There's no way you're getting upgraded," Beth says.

"It's a full flight. Besides, I needed to..." A shrug is my best explanation. The night before Pippa was removed from life support, I pinky-swore my beautiful, brain-dead sister that I'd live enough life for two. This shirt helps remind me of my promise.

Fortunately, Sunny is the resident expert in deciphering vague Talia gestures. "You want to be close to Pippa. I get it." She toys with her feather hair extension and shoots Beth a "let it go" death stare.

"There's an X Games competition in the city next weekend, so Tanner's back in town." Beth's tone is controlled, far too even to be natural. "Did he stop by?" She gazes at me like an implacable jury forewoman, about to pronounce a verdict of guilt.

"Nope."

The ensuing silence makes me want to curl into a catatonic ball and stare as dust motes filter through the air.

I don't mention watching Tanner land heel kicks and pop shuvits while walking past Derby Skate Park last night. Or how he stared right through me. He'd been in love with Pippa since she was twelve. She and I had been walking home from Mission Hill

Middle School when a classmate cornered the two of us on Bay Street with rape threats. Tanner spotted the encounter from the front stoop of his trailer, marched over, and clocked the kid over the head with his skateboard. When Pippa told Mom what happened, she took Tanner out to Marianne's Ice Cream parlor for sundaes. By ninth grade, he and Pippa were going steady and that was that, until the year anniversary of my sister's death.

Tanner will never forgive either of us for the night we got trashed, and then naked, under the Santa Cruz Wharf. I'm sure he guilty-conscience confessed the whole sordid story to Beth, but she never called me on it, a form of punishment in itself.

"What's up, girls?" Dad appears in the hall dressed in well-worn board shorts and a ratty surf competition T-shirt. He looks more like a beach bum than a coastal geologist.

Beth gives him a little wave. "Hey, Mr. S."

His head grazes the top of the door frame. He's huge, my dad, but quiet, more a gentle giant. Mom used to run the show around these parts, a high-strung Chihuahua to his laid-back golden retriever. Now he wanders around like he forgot where he hid his bone. He's not in the right headspace to deal with my crap. All I need to do is fake happy and stay alive.

"You finished yet?" He shifts his weight, eyeing the mess spread over my bed. "We've got to hit the road soon to beat the traffic. Don't want you missing your flight."

Sunny leaps up with a squeal and wraps me in a fierce bear hug. "Safe travels, honeybunch."

She's the only person who occasionally calls me by Pippa's old nickname. I miss hearing it but don't have to look at Dad to know he flinches.

"Remember your promise." Sunny presses her forehead to

mine. "You can't call either Beth or me while you're gone. We'll be fine. This time's just for you. Relax. Get a tan. Ride a platypus. Throw a shrimp on the barbie and whatnot."

"Got it." I nod as she gives me a final squeeze. Sunny's firm in her belief that we can't communicate until I return home. She wants me to escape from my family train wreck, and you can't get much farther than Australia. I'll have five months to screw my head back on straight.

Beth steps forward with a steely look in her gray eyes, but maybe I'm imagining things because in another second it's gone. She rumples my hair. "Don't forget to have fun, Tals."

"Never do," I crack. When's the last time I let go, lived without an invisible boulder crushing my chest? Can't even remember.

"Good times." Dad grabs the suitcase with an easy swing while I cram the rest of my stuff in the bulging duffel. "There's going to be a lot to celebrate when you get home. You three, almost ready to graduate." He casts a hesitant smile in my general direction. He was the first kid in his family to go to college. I know it means the world to him that he can provide me with an opportunity for higher education.

My lungs go on strike. A full breath is impossible.

He'd be so proud to learn his only surviving daughter is a liar and a failure.

I'm letting him down.

Like mother, like daughter.

My core grows cold. The letter from the history undergraduate committee is torn into a hundred pieces in the trash. They denied my petition to extend my senior thesis and the resulting F is a nuclear detonation in my transcript. My GPA is blown and because I didn't pass a mandatory class, I'll have to repeat the semester. Dr. Halloway offered to write a letter requesting medical exemption, but that would mean owning a crazy-ass diagnosis like obsessive-compulsive disorder.

Even before Pippa's accident, there were warning signs. Indicators like being hyperconscious about unplugging electrical devices or rechecking that I locked the front door in a certain way that felt "right." Over the last few years my compulsions intensified. I had to eat my food in pairs, not one M&M, not three M&M's, but two every time. Don't get me started on setting my alarm clock, changing a car radio, or trying to fall asleep. Over the course of last semester, I became convinced I contracted leukemia, thyroid disease, and MS. My nights were spent symptom Googling my way to academic probation.

After breaking down in my childhood doctor's office a few weeks ago, Dr. Halloway wrote me a prescription for a low-dosage antidepressant. He says the medication will increase my serotonin levels and in turn decrease the severity of my symptoms. It's got to work. I can't continue being a closet freak. Dr. Halloway also strongly advised cognitive behavioral therapy, stressing it would be helpful—vital, in fact—in controlling OCD impulses.

Right now, escape is preferable to weekly psychologist meetings. Once Santa Cruz and its ghosts are behind me, I'll feel better.

"Peanut?" Dad's frowning, so are Sunny and Beth. I've zoned out again, lost in my navel-gazing bullshit.

"It's all good." I flick on a megawatt smile because that's what I do best, fake it until I make it. "Australia's going to be great. Just think, tonight I'll be passing the International Date Line. I'm going to Tomorrowland."

Leaving is the only way to move forward.

If I never get lost, I'll never be found.

# About the Author

After studying at the University of Montana, Missoula, **Lia Riley** scoured the world, armed only with a backpack, overconfidence, and a terrible sense of direction. When not torturing heroes (because c'mon, who doesn't love a good tortured hero?), Lia herds unruly chickens, camps, beachcombs, daydreams about as-of-yet-unwritten books, wades through a mile-high TBR pile, and schemes yet another trip. She and her family live mostly in Northern California.